M000104752

Also by Joe Corso

The Revenge of John W
The Old Man and the King
The Time Portal Series
The Starlight Club Series
Lone Jack Kid Series
The Comeback
Lafitte's Treasure
Flames of Fury Series

The Starlight Club II

By Joe Corso

The Starlight Club II

Joe Corso

Published by
Black Horse Publishing

Cover Art by Marina Shipova
Edited by Sherry Thomas
Formatting by BZHercules.com

Black Horse Publishing
www.blackhorsepublishing.com

ISBN: 1483998185
ISBN: 9780578110042

I want to thank Marina Shipova for her wonderful cover, Joe Callarota for his help with selected chapters and characters, Joe D'Albert for his artistic help - and a special thanks to my editor Sherry Thomas of Breathless Video Productions, LLC.

prologue

Present

From the comfortable leather recliner, Bobby Valentine sat relaxing, watching Fox News. He liked here it here in Darien, Connecticut. He was fighting hard to keep from dozing off but midday slumber won the battle until the sound of clanging dishes shook him from his reverie. He lifted his head to see what the fuss was all about and was pleasantly surprised to see his daughter, Lynn, standing over him holding a tray of doughnuts and a cup of steaming espresso.

"I know how much you enjoy your espresso, Dad, so I made a fresh pot for you." She sat down opposite him, was quiet for a moment and said, "Dad?"

"Yes?"

"The other day when you told me the story of the Starlight Club, it was so interesting that I dreamt about it. I keep thinking about it, so then I thought to myself that there must be other stories, more stories that you could share with me. So, tell me some more about the Starlight Club. I want to hear it."

With slightly sad eyes, he looked at her and said, "When I told you about the Starlight Club the other night, it was a bit painful for me. That's why I never mentioned it before. But strangely enough, as I was recalling these memories, my emotions just seem to pour out, more like flood out," he laughed, "and I guess it was cleansing in a way. So the short answer is yes, I feel like I can share a bit more without it bothering me as much as it did before. Telling you about it must have purged all that sadness I had locked up inside. Alright, let me think for a moment." Bobby was silent for a few seconds and then he said, "Well, let's see. It's true there was a lot more that I didn't mention . . . so where do I start? When Jimmy the Hat died, everything seemed to die with him, and for a long time the club really wasn't the same."

"What do you mean dad?"

"Well, I'm not sure I can tell the story in the spirit it deserves, but let's see now. Big Red took an interest in Swifty's career and that by itself is worth tellin' because it's a wonderful story. Then there were Trenchie and Mary. They sure loved each other -kind of a strange relationship if you ask me. I still continued to deliver meat to the club, but one of the things I was disappointed in was that Red's Wednesday horse race operation ended for some reason shortly after Jimmy's death, and I never did find out why. I learned why Trenchie did ten years for a murder he didn't commit and that's another story. Then, there was the problem Bernstein had with some blackmailers in Hollywood and he had no one to turn to for help except Big Red. Had the Queens action so well-organized that it could practically run itself. He always harbored a secret desire to expand his operation to Hollywood and he intended for Jimmy to be his ticket into the film business, but when Jimmy the Hat died, he lost that opportunity. Oh but Red was shrewd and he figured out another way of gettin' into the movie business and that, too is another story. So, where do I start? Okay, let's start with Swifty's story if that's all right with you."

"Okay," his daughter said as her face lit up. "I'm just so happy to have this afternoon free to be with you. So . . . you just start wherever you like." Lynn was delighted. This part of her father's life was still a mystery to her.

"You see, when Red gave me the money that Jimmy had left me in his estate, I invested some of it in the butcher store I worked for. The owner was lookin' to retire and he made it real easy for me to buy him out. So, I became the owner of Four States Meat and Poultry Supply Corp and I hired a driver to deliver the wholesale orders the same as I did, but I kept the account at the Starlight Club for myself. Each day, I stopped by the club on my way home whether it was to deliver meat or just to say hello to the guys. So, it was no coincidence that I was there one particular afternoon when Swifty came to see Red. He was between boxin' fights. Swifty always owed Red money and Red always told him that he had to work it off by doin' odd jobs. But it really wasn't so much the money that Red was concerned with. He cared about Swifty. He didn't want him to end up like other guys who had a lot of potential but just wasted it on fast, hard-livin', so Red took him under his wing. I don't think Swifty knew what Red's true motive was, at least not at first.

chapter one

1962

Swifty sat nervously in front of Red's desk, tapping his fingers, one at a time on the side of his chair, fidgeting uncomfortably while he waited for Red to come talk to him. Red was pissed off about somethin' - that much he was sure of - and the wondering made him nervous. He was probably thinkin' that it was pay up day for all the money he owed Red.

So here he was, back at the club, and Swifty is nervous as hell just waitin'. What Swifty didn't know was that Red had attended his fight on Saturday night. Red didn't *want* Swifty to know he was there. He had bought seats in the *bleachers* - a section of seats they called 'in Sunnyside Gardens.' Besides, Red could see better up there anyway. It was a six round bout and Red admired the tenacity and ferociousness of Swifty, the young neighborhood fighter. When the bout ended, Red shook his head and left before Johnny Addie announced Swifty as the winner. Red came in carrying a spreadsheet.

He sat down at his desk and just kept starin' at that spread sheet. Finally, he put it aside and looked at Swifty.

"Swifty, I'm calling in my marker," he said. "You're gonna pay me the money you owe me, but not for the reasons you think." Swifty looked like somebody dropped a bomb on him. He was scared half to death.

"Look, Red," he said. "I know I owe you money but I ain't never stiffed you yet and you know it, so why do you want it now so bad?"

Big Red's eyebrows went up and he snapped, "Swift, it's not about the money, you knucklehead. It's about you. I'm pissed off and you're sittin' there lookin' at me wonderin' why I'm pissed off . . . right?" Swifty hung his head low, just starin' at his shoelaces.

Red went on. "Well, I'm gonna tell you why." Swifty braced for the worst. He had no clue what was comin'.

"It's because you're nothin' but a lazy, good-for-nothin' bum! You're wastin' your life away and someday you're gonna die in an alley and guess what? Nobody's gonna give two shits about you! *That's* why I'm pissed off. Is that what you want? Do you want to end up like that?" Swifty didn't say a word. He just sat there and then he started makin' excuses. Red cut him off. "Well I'm not gonna let that happen. I've decided that you're fightin' for me from now on. In fact, I scheduled a fight in two weeks. Two weeks! Ya have two weeks to get in shape!" Swifty's face changed from white, to a faint smile, back to 'oh shit - what just hit me?' See, he didn't mind fightin' but until now, he had only fought when he needed money. Now, it sounded like a job, a real job. He could barely manage his words. "Who am I fightin'?" he asked

"A Latin fighter," Red said. "A guy by the name of Henri Valesques." Swifty's eyes got huge. I swear you couldn't see nothin' but white.

"Hey, that guy's good," he said. "We fought on the same card a couple of times and I watched him fight. What? Ya start me out this way? What the hell Red?"

"I know," Red chimed in. "That's why we want you guys to fight. You're both undefeated. You both have similar records. The matchmakers at Sunnyside Gardens want this fight to happen. You have a perfect 20 and 0 record and he has a perfect 19 and 0 record. That should bring the crowds in."

Swifty smiled at Red and said, "Since you're makin' my fight decisions for me, I take it that you've spoken to Ray and discussed my contract."

"Yeah, I talked to Ray," Red stated, waving his hand as if to dismiss such a ridiculous comment. "I made him an offer and he accepted it. He sold me your contract *and* . . . he's agreed to stay on as your cut man. He knows that with him managing you, you'll never get anywhere, but with *me* managing you, you will, and you'll make all of us a pile of dough. You're a good fighter Swifty. You could be a champ someday, but you're lazy, *damn* lazy. You've been wastin' your talent. We're only given talent for so long. Then we grow old and things don't work right anymore. When your talent's gone, you got nothin' because you have no skills, no education. Since all you know how to do is fight, I'm gonna make sure that you get somethin' out of fightin' and more important, I'll see to it that money gets socked away for your retirement one day."

Swifty looked at Red questioningly. "Why do you care Red? You don't owe me nothin', so why are you takin' this interest in me? Why me?"

Red thought a moment. "I told ya. I see a kid like you wastin' your life away and I feel bad about it. You don't have much goin' for you except your good looks and your fightin' skills. I made up my mind that I'm not gonna see that potential go down the drain. If I don't take control of you, then all you'll do is fritter your youth away on bullshit. I'll make sure that doesn't happen. You're fightin' for me from now on where I can keep an eye on 'ya. I care about this community. I want role models for these kids around here. Guess I'm gettin' old and sappy but I just can't stand waste. This community deserves better. Oh, and another thing - when you're not trainin' or fightin', you'll be workin' for me here at the club too, so I expect you here by nine o'clock on weekdays, *every* weekday, capiche?"

Swifty wasn't lazy when it came to his training. He loved to train. He always trained hard and he was always in good shape, but after bein' told that he was fightin' Valesques, he trained especially hard. He knew this guy was the slickest fighter he'd ever go up against. This was goin' to be a real test for him. It could be the toughest fight of his short boxing career.

On the night of the Valesques fight, Trenchie, Tarzan and Moose sat at ringside, while Red stayed in Swifty's corner alongside Ray O'Connell, Swifty's trainer and ex-manager and now cut man. This fight was originally slated as a six rounder, but the matchmakers at Sunnyside Gardens changed that. Even though this was an undercard fight, this was the one folks would come out to see. An eight round fight would please the fans.

Both undefeated fighters breezed through their earlier fights. The fights were all four and six round bouts - fighting chumps that were no contest - easy pocket money. The Swifty Cardinelli-Henri Valesques fight, however, was the big one. It could be a tipping point in both their careers. This could very well be a step up for either of the young men. Valesques was known for his cat-like jab and devastating left hook which he normally followed with a hard right. Swifty was known for his ability to knock a man out with either hand. He knew that in order to win this fight he had to stay away from his opponent's left hook, yet still be close enough to land his punches. Swifty was the harder puncher, but Valesques was the classier, more graceful boxer.

Johnny Addie, the ring announcer, introduced both of the fighters. He stated their records, tellin' the audience that both fighters were unbeaten. Swifty nervously shuffled from foot to foot waitin' for the fight to start. In the other corner, on the opposite side of the ring, Valesques was seated, looking completely relaxed. That didn't go unnoticed by Swifty.

"Will you look at that guy? He looks like he's gonna fall asleep on his stool," he said to Red.

"Don't worry about him," Red told him. "Just go out there and do what you do best. Knock this guy out and let's go home early," he added as he smacked him on the back.

The bell rang for the start of the fight and the boxers shuffled to the center of the ring, cautiously circling one another, tryin' to get a feel for the other guy. For the first two rounds, they jabbed, danced, parried and blocked punches, tryin' to figure out their opponent's style. The fight ebbed and flowed, first to one fighter, then to the other. Suddenly out of nowhere, Swifty emerged with a look on his face that meant business. He savagely landed a series of devastating lefts and rights that momentarily stunned the Latin fighter. Man oh man, the fury of Swifty's punches brought the crowd to their feet. But as soon as Swifty completed his ferocious combinations, Valesques responded in kind, but *not so kind,* with two hard, left hooks of his own and landed his own vicious right. It was a grueling, tough eight rounds of fightin' with neither fighter seemingly gaining a noticeable advantage over the other and when the fight ended, ring announcer Johnny Addie announced the judges' decision . . . *a draw.* This was a first for either man. Remember, they were both completely undefeated but with a draw decision, both fighters *still* remained undefeated. The combatants, uh fighters, congratulated each other before leavin' the ring and goin' their separate ways. I don't think either of them knew what to feel but you can bet that each left with a grudging respect for the other's fightin' ability. The following mornin', Red got on the phone and scheduled two eight round tune-up fights for Swifty so he could get used to fightin' the extra rounds. Red's plan didn't quite work the way it was supposed to 'cuz Swifty won the two fights easily, with knockouts in the fourth and fifth rounds. They never made it to the full eight.

The return match was another eight round bout. It turned out to be a carbon copy of the first fight, up to and including, the decision of the judges. The scorecards were handed to Johnny Addie who paused a moment to read them. Satisfied with what he read, he reached for the microphone and in his distinctive high-pitched voice announced the decision of the judges. *Another draw.* The two fighters were *still* unbeaten. The local papers were eatin' this competition up. It wasn't like this was a Jake LaMotta-Ray Robinson fight. It was a relatively minor, local fight - but it was a fight that everyone in Queens wanted to see. The promoters at Sunnyside Gardens knew that the fans were clamoring for a third, decisive fight. They knew they would have another sellout crowd if they could get the two fighters to agree to just one more fight. The matchmakers decided that if they could make it happen, it would be a ten round bout - a first for both fighters. It was a question of *if.* Both fighters couldn't really see the point of havin' another fight *until* it was pointed out that a ten round, main event fight meant a much larger payday for each of 'em. The money won out and both fighters once again signed on. Swifty's record was now 27 and 0 with two draws.

Swifty used the time leadin' up to the fight to train the way he did when he trained with Rocky Marciano. The Rock used to run in deep snow. He said the snow was good for his legs and it helped give him the endurance he needed to fight fifteen rounds. If you were fortunate enough to ever have seen a Rocky Marciano fight, he was amazin', because at the end of fifteen rounds, he appeared to be as fresh as he was in the first round. Swifty believed that in order to beat Valesques, he had to use the same training methods Marciano used. So Swifty set up his training in the Pocono Mountains where he had access to deep snow and high ground. Slowly this fight was gainin' attention by the national press and a few of the guys from the larger national papers joined Swifty in his training camp. Swifty, after all his fighting, didn't have a scar on his face. He was good looking in a Jack Lemmon sort of way. You couldn't compare him to Jimmy the Hat because he didn't have that sexual magnetism that Jimmy had, but he was just as handsome. Swifty had a great smile and a personality to go along with it, which was very appealing to the women. He attracted them in droves. The writers found the young fighter to be a respectful, amiable guy who didn't look anything like a fighter. They wrote about it in their newspapers. Red liked the attention the press was giving Swifty. He knew that sometime in the future these same reporters could make a difference when Swifty went after a championship belt.

The days of training passed quickly. One day the order to strike was given and the training camp was dismantled. The fight was drawing near. Everyone headed back to Queens to finalize the preparations.

The night of the fight Trenchie, Tarzan and Moose were once again seated at ringside. Big Red sat with Swifty and Ray. When the bell rang for the start of the fight, both fighters spent most of the round feelin' each other out, just like they had done in their two previous fights. Man, these boys were in the best shape of their lives. When the bell for the second round clanged, it signaled war. Both men banged away at the other for three action packed minutes and they kept up this pace for the remaining eight rounds, fighting with a fury. At the end of the tenth round, the popular ring announcer, Johnny Addie, announced the judges' decision. Guess what? It was another stinkin' *draw*. Nobody - the fighters, the managers, nobody ever heard of two fighters fighting three draws. When they were interviewed at ringside, the fighters had nothing but praise for the fighting skill of their opponent and when asked if there would be a fourth fight, both fighters unanimously agreed that three fights were more than enough.

chapter two

Trenchie was quiet. He was always quiet but Red could tell that something was bothering him.

"What's wrong Trenchie? Don't bullshit me, now, 'cuz I can tell when somethin's wrong." Trenchie thought for a moment. You could tell that he really didn't wanna share it.

"Red, you know how I hate to talk about my personal life, but somethin's come up and I don't know if I can handle it." This shocked Red because Trenchie was this real tough guy. Remember when he took on all those guys in The Starlight Club and always just smirked when he beat the tar out of anyone who got in his way? Well, Red starts thinking that maybe there's a contract out on him that the law was after him. Red's mind was racing with all sorts of scenarios. Big Red was becoming exasperated with the way he was procrastinating.

"Come on Trench, are you going to leave me hangin'? Now what the damned hell is it that you can't handle? Talk to me," Red said.

Trenchie looked up at Red and said, "Red you know me. Nothin' bothers me, but this... this is big."

"Damn it! What the fuck is big?" Red said, gettin' more and more annoyed. "You're drivin' me crazy for Christ sake. Just spit it out and tell me what it is and I'll take care of it."

Trenchie hesitated and looked at Red with doubt and a little bit of fear in his eyes and he finally blurted out. "I'm gonna be a father."

Red was speechless. He stood there not makin a sound with his mouth frozen wide open not movin' a muscle.

"Damn you Trenchie," Red said. "Damn you. I'm sittin' here thinkin' that somebody's tryin' to whack you, maybe take *away* a life and you tell me that someone's *bringin'* a life into the world. One's bad, Trench, and one's good - really good! What the hell? Don't you see the difference? I've a good mind to slap you cross-eyed, but now that I know you're gonna be a Dad, I don't think it's such a good idea. The kid deserves better than that - deserves a father in one piece!" And with that, Red walked over to his pal, wrapped his arms around him and gave him a big ole Italian bear hug. "So being a father is what was botherin' you and you don't know how to handle it, eh?"

"Well, not really. I've never been scared of being a father - it's havin' a baby that's got me worried. Look at these mitts of mine. These are big hands. I'm afraid to touch the kid. I keep thinkin' that if I pick it up, I'll break it. I didn't see this one comin'- it was never a part of my plan. I just never thought that I might have to hold a baby one day. I mean, it just never occurred to me. I can hold a gun, Red - that's easy - but a tiny little baby, I just don't know about that. How do ya hold a baby anyways?"

Red's eyes lit up and he laughed. "Trenchie, you'll figure it out. It comes natural, handlin' a baby and all. This is great news. I'm gonna call everybody and I mean *everybody* and we're gonna celebrate! I want you and Mary here next Saturday night because we are *havin' a party*! We are gonna have the biggest damn party this joint has ever seen! So Trench is gonna be a papa," Red smirked as he glanced at Trenchie. Trenchie's face seemed paralyzed in time, as though he hadn't heard a word Red said.

"Oh *marone*!" Red remarked. "Don't look so down in the dumps. You'll be a great father. Don't worry about it. Ya know," Red said, "you had me going there for a minute. I was worried - thought we were about to have a gang war or somethin' and here you go and give me *good* news for a change." Red slapped Trenchie on the back and then gave him a few playful boxing jabs. "My mother always said that babies bring good luck," Red added, "and Mama was never wrong. Get ready Trench. You got good luck comin' your way. This is good luck and Trench, you gotta work on somethin', somethin' besides that lousy attitude of yours," he added.

"What's that?" Trenchie asked. "I know," he then continued, "I have to start thinkin' about drawin' up wills and papers and preparin' for education, and all sorts of responsible stuff."

"Nah, it's more than that," Red said. "It's the way you're talkin', the way you're talkin' about babies. A baby's not an *'it'*. A baby is a *he* or a *she*, so start addressin' him properly."

"Him? How ya know it's gonna be a him?" Trenchie asked.

"Him, she, whatever, but start givin' him respect," Red laughed.

For the first time, Trenchie managed to smile a little and right then, right there in the club, the idea seemed to be growing on him. He adored Mary so having a baby was good and being a dad was probably good too, he mused. He had a lot of dough, was married to a great gal, and life was good. Yeah, what am I worrying about, he thought. A baby is a good thing.

Red sat down at his desk and pulled out his private address book - the one with the names and the telephone numbers of his special customers. He started making calls and inviting everybody to come celebrate Trenchie and Mary's good news. Ralph and Gibby, remember those two - well, they were now with the Genovese family. They had always been fond of Trenchie. Red surprised them with the news and asked them to rearrange their schedules in order to make it to this event. Their answer was instant. They didn't even have to think about it - that's how much respect they had for Trench. Meanwhile, Trenchie just sat there watching Red act like a proud grandpa or somethin'.

When Red finished inviting all of his guests, he smiled and said, "Trench, I'm not gettin' soft on ya or anything, but this baby is gonna bring a whole lot of joy, a spark into The Starlight Club." Just as he finished his sentence, the phone rang.

Moose answered the phone. "Starlight Club. Sure, who's callin'? Okay, hang on a minute. Hey Trench, it's for you." As he walked toward the phone, Trenchie knew that the only two people who would normally call him at the club were Mary or his restaurant manager, Richard. He picked up the phone.

"Trenchie here." He listened silently for a long moment and eventually responded, "What? Okay, I'll be right over. Don't worry about a thing. I'll handle this." Red couldn't help overhearing the conversation. Trenchie's face fell a bit.

"Trouble Trenchie?"

"Yeah, some wise guys are leanin' on my manager. I guess they don't know who the *real* owner of the place is. I'm headin' over there now."

Red looked over at Tarzan. "Come on. We're takin' a little ride. And Frankie," he said, "maybe you should come too."

Moose called from the other side of the bar. "You want me to come boss?"

Red answered, "No, somebody's got to stay and watch the bar. I'll call you if we need ya. Meanwhile, hang tight here."

chapter three

Red and his men walked into the rear of Trenchie's restaurant where they found Richard, Trenchie's longtime restaurant manager, anxiously waiting. They entered his office and sat down on the chairs that Richard had brought in.

"What time are these guys supposed to come in?" Red asked.

"Ten o'clock," answered Richard.

"Okay, it's nine-thirty. We have a half hour before they get here so why don't you tell us what happened?"

Richard began recounting the story. "Nine o'clock Saturday night - there was a knock at my door and I told whoever it was to come in. Two men walked in and sat right down, took seats without even being offered."

Red interrupted him. "Did they tell you that they intended to take over the place?"

"No. They told me that they were organizing business establishments in this part of town and every store had to pay a small 'fee' for their protection."

"What was the amount they asked for?" Trenchie asked.

"They said that they would be back here every Saturday morning to collect fifteen dollars from me. I tried to explain to them who owns this place but they said they didn't care. They just wanted the fifteen bucks."

"Jesus," Tarzan said. "They're charging ten bucks more than us and we provide a *real* service for our customers." See, if any of Red's customers were ever robbed, he always made a concerted effort to find the culprits and when he did, which was usually the case, and if he recovered the stolen items, which he normally did, Red and his men always returned the goods to their rightful owners. So, you see, they *did* provide a service for the money they collected from the storeowners. Strange rationale, but true.

At exactly ten am, two men walked into the restaurant and knocked on the office door. They barged right in without waiting for permission but stopped mid-stride upon seeing four men and the restaurant manager staring back at them. Trenchie looked at Richard and said, "Richie, I think you better go and take care of business up front." Richard didn't say a word, got up, and walked out the door avoiding eye contact with anyone. Richard could sense the danger and the tension. It was as if fireworks were about to explode and he couldn't walk out of that room fast enough. He wasn't used to this kind of drama and was beginning to wonder if maybe a career change might be in order.

Trenchie spoke first. "I'd like to know your names and who you guys are." Then he continued, "And are you the guys that threatened my manager?"

One of the men spoke without fear. "My name is Rocco and my partner here is Mike. We're from Detroit and we've opened a business here in Queens. Do you have a problem with that?"

Red looked at him. "Do you know who I am?

"No."

"And you've never heard the name Big Red?"

"No, I can't say that I have. Is it supposed to mean something to me?"

"Maybe not in Detroit, but in Queens, yes. What organization do you belong to? You say that you're from Detroit so who vouches for you? I want the name and phone number of your boss because I want to speak with him right now."

Rocco smugly smiled and said. "His name is John Magardi."

"Good," Red said. "Give me his telephone number. Let's get John Magardi on the phone right now."

Rocco reached into his pocket and pulled out a card. "He can be reached at this number." Red walked over to the desk, picked up the phone and dialed the number on the card. "Hello, who is this?" a gruff voice asked.

"Hello John. My name is Red Fortunato and I'm callin' from Queens, New York. I'm in a meeting with two men who tell me that they are under your protection and you'll vouch for them. They're tryin' to shake down one of my businesses and I just can't let that happen, John. If they are part of your organization, we need to settle this misunderstanding peacefully. That's why I'm callin' you. Here, I'll put them on."

Rocco spoke to his boss for a few minutes and then handed the phone back to Red. The voice on the other end sounded pissed off. "Look Red, or whatever your name is, I'm gonna check you out before we do any more talkin'. Gimme a number where I can reach you." In the interim, Red and Trenchie showed their true class - they served their 'guests' lots of cocktails. "Geez," Red whispered to Trenchie. "These guys don't know enough to stop slamming back drinks! Makes it easier for us if we have to take 'em out. Elementary rules, though, while on the job - no drinkin' and workin'." About an hour and a half later, the phone rang. Red answered. It was John. His tone was accommodating and contrite.

"Look Red, I checked you out. My boys made a mistake comin' to your joint and it won't happen again."

"John, "Red answered, "I own Queens. Don't make that mistake again. Next time, I won't be so understanding."

"Okay, look, there's no need for threats. Put Rocco back on the phone." Rocco listened without speaking. It appeared to Red that he might be getting a tongue-lashing. Rocco was a bit pale when he hung up the phone. He, too, had adopted a conciliatory tone.

"Look," Rocco said. "I had no idea who you were. I would never have come here if I did. My mistake and it won't happen again."

Red was almost paternal as he spoke. "Look Rocco, I understand that you wanna make a few bucks but attemptin' to do business in Queens *could* have been and *would* have been bad for your health. Do your homework before you go havin' stupid attacks. I own Queens. I'll kill *anybody* who tries to move into my territory, take over one of my businesses, or strong-arm my people. You would be dead already if you weren't connected. Thank your lucky stars for John Magardi answering that phone because he just saved your asses."

Richard watched as the two men exited the building. Trenchie walked over to Richard and patted him on the back. "Relax," Red assured him. "You won't have to worry about those guys again. If it does happen again, you call Trenchie and me just like you did this time." Trenchie chimed in. "Hey Richie, you did good kid. I'm giving you a fifty buck a week raise. Now, can we have some lunch please?"

Richard smiled. He was now back in his element, the restaurant business, right where he belonged. The manager headed straight to the kitchen and started dictating orders to the chef – calamari fra diablo, bruschetta, caprese, a little three cheese tortellini . . . .

chapter four

Red was a loyal friend to the neighborhood. Most everybody loved Big Red. Each year at Thanksgiving, he donated enough turkeys to the Salvation Army to fill the bellies of every hungry soul. When early December rolled around, he bought truckloads of Christmas trees, set them out in the vacant lot across from the club, and sold them for pennies above cost. For the Fourth of July, he secured all the proper permits to put on nothin' short of a mini Grucci - like fireworks display in Flushing Meadows Park. He would help anyone who came to him with a problem. Red was what some in the neighborhood called a 'benevolent dictator.' His neighbors loved him and his *enemies* knew he was the boss of a crime family that numbered a thousand men or more. It was just a given that no crime would take place in this neighborhood, Red's territory. The outcome was well known - a reprisal called 'the wrath of the Red Head' - yeah, that name always made me chuckle - double meanin' and all. Head of the mob, if you didn't get that. Pity the poor guy who attempted something stupid. Red would always handle it. Because of his presence, the neighborhood was safe, safe for everybody, old and young alike.

When Red first purchased The Starlight Club, it quickly became his hobby. He was constantly making changes to the look, the design of the place, but he was never really satisfied with the results. Money wasn't a problem so he called a number of so-called specialists, from architects to interior decorators to carpenters - all who sketched, measured, and presented their ideas. But none were ever really what Red wanted. They just weren't *his* vision. One day Red called Angelo, a carpenter who had learned his trade from a master builder in the old country. When Angelo arrived, Red was quick to mention that a number of carpenters had given him their ideas, none of which he liked.

"I want this room to be somethin' special," Red explained. "When my customers enter this room, I want them to feel like they've been transported. I can't tell you what exactly I want; Angelo, but I can see it. I want this place to be a creative masterpiece, a conversation piece that'll make people wanna come back." Angelo said nothing. He just began to walk around the large room, pad in hand, checkin' out the walls, the ceiling, floors, doors and windows. He studied every inch of the room, never spoke, just scribbled on his pad. After a few minutes of this, Red broke the silence and remarked, "I like this room. It has a lot of personality. I see something great here." Angelo just nodded, indicating that he understood.

Angelo continued to walk and study the room and after this went on for a while, Angelo just stopped, looked intensely at Red's eyes as if he was studying those too, and asked in his thick Italian accent, "Do youuh trusta me?"

Normally, Red would have responded hastily to any other man who might have asked this, giving him a lecture about how trust has to be earned the long and hard way and he only trusted his small group of friends . . . *but* Angelo had a great reputation for his craft and there was something about him that Red liked. "Yeah, I trust ya." Red answered. "Why?"

"I builda you something niceuh, something uh special," Angelo stated confidently. "It mighta takeuh me a little longer because I'mma not the younga boy I used to be," he stated in his deadpan humor, "so if you're notta in a hurry, I take uh it on. If you uh inna hurry, then you need uh looka somebody else uh."

"Angelo, you thinkin' of doin' this yourself?" Red asked. "I thought you retired Angelo, you know, stopped doin' the manual stuff."

"I amma pretty much," Angelo answered. "But you know uh Red, I learnna my trade from the finest in Italy, and we created masterpieces all throughoutta Europe. It's uh been years since I uh had the opportunity to use uh my imagination, to go a little wild uh, to do something truly magnifico. I will uh make uh this room into uh something people willla talka about, something breath uh taking, but I cannotta be uh rushed," he said firmly.

Funny, how this guy stood up to Red. He was a true 'artiste' and Red got a bit of a kick out of him. It was agreed. Angelo would use his creativity to bring this room to life and Red would let him do it without seeing the first sketch. However Red, being the ever astute businessman, did manage to inquire, "How much is this gonna' cost me?"

Angelo answered, "Money in thesa case notta important. You uh pay for materials, and when all issa finito, pay uh me like other estimate by other men uh you uh called." And the men shook hands. That was all it took - old style business - a hand shake and your honor. No need for more.

That ballroom took Angelo a full year to complete. The elder artisan's handiwork filled every inch of the walls and floors. In the rear, near the bandstand, there were four hand-carved columns. The columns showed scenes of Roman Legions marching through the Arc of Triumph in Rome and Knights Templar on their horses, posed for battle in front of a castle fortress. Another depicted Venice and her canals and a fourth column was a carving of Cleopatra, with Caesar beside her, looking out at the pyramids from her palace. There were murals on the ceilings and tiny lights that sparkled as stars against the blue sky that Angelo had painted. The walls were reminiscent of the Sistine Chapel with scenes remarkably similar to The Last Supper. Mosaic tiles that had been imported from Carrera, Italy decorated the walls. Angelo himself had installed the genuine oak floors which had been polished to a glassy sheen, providing the best dance surface a club could imagine.

All throughout the renovations, Angelo had insisted that no one be allowed inside, other than delivery guys unloading materials. Well, the long and short is that when the day came for the big reveal, Red was almost speechless. It was as if Angelo had looked right into his mind and read his thoughts. The room was exactly as Red had envisioned it and he was thrilled. Red walked around the room, touched the walls, gazed at the murals, stared at the ceiling. He was in absolute awe of what he saw. And that solidified his and Angelo's relationship - so much so that he tried to pay Angelo three times the highest quote that he had received, but Angelo would have no part of that. He was old school. He had honor.

"A deal is a deal," Angelo said, and that just endeared him more to Red. He was touched by the elderly man's code of ethics. That ballroom became Red's refuge. Whenever he needed a place to retreat, he would just go into his ballroom and stare at it.

Meanwhile, Angelo became a Sunday morning regular at The Starlight Club. He would sip espresso while sitting in the newly renovated great room. It reminded him of a little place in Italy, near his hometown of Sciacca in Sicily, a place that brought back fond childhood memories. Angelo was the *only person* Red allowed into that room when there wasn't a party or event going on. Strict orders were given to the staff - Angelo could order *whatever* he wanted at the club, *when*ever he came to the club, and *no one* was ever to collect a copper penny from him.

Red's Sunday morning ritual was to sit at his favorite table, opposite the bar by the window, and read the Sunday edition of the newspaper. The morning sun rising in the east always beamed through the glass and highlighted his paper, making it easier for him to read. One particular morning, Angelo approached Red and asked if he could spare a few minutes. Red offered him a seat. The club wasn't officially open for business yet. Moose was busy cleaning the bar while Tarzan played solitaire at nearby table. Swifty the boxer was there as usual, working off some of his past debts to Red.

"Moose, make us a pot of espresso and bring over a bottle of black Sambuca when the coffee's ready," Red instructed.

"What's up Angelo?" Red asked.

In broken English, Angelo began to speak. He told of how some teenagers had been playing street hockey and how a hockey puck had crashed through a large casement window in the front of his house.

"Imma notta unreasonable man Red and I uh know accidents happen," Angelo said, "but I try uh talkin to thesa boys butta thesa kids are wisa guys. They notta listen to me. They laugh uh, throw uh rocksa atta my door. They spray uh paint uh my house. I come uh to see you when they no stoppa."

Moose poured two cups of espresso and carefully counted out three coffee beans (health, happiness, and prosperity) for each of two brandy sniffers. Angelo looked at Red, raised his cup and said in perfect Italian "un centinaio di anni," the affectionate toast meaning "may you live a hundred years." Red smiled, raised his glass and reciprocated. The men enjoyed a few minutes of light chatter and as Angelo rose to leave, Red looked at Swifty and said, "Go with Angelo. He has a little problem that you probably heard us discussin'. Don't use any muscle unless you have to, unless they leave you no choice."

Swifty walked with Angelo the two blocks to his home. He examined the damaged window. It was the large plate glass window in the front of his house that was shattered. Angelo had attempted a makeshift temporary solution, using duct tape and an old blanket. Swifty walked around the outside perimeter of the house. He found shards of glass lying on the lawn and saw the spray painted walls on the sides of Angelo's house. He shook his head and was becoming angry.

"Come on Angelo, let's go see these guys," Swifty said, all irritated. The two of them walked up the block to a house on the corner, at the intersection and Swifty knocked loudly on the door. A big man in a sweat stained tank top, sporting a couple of days of facial growth, opened the door and stood there staring menacingly at the two strangers.

"What do ya want?" he huffed.

Swifty replied pleasantly to the man, "Your son broke my friend's window and now your son and his friends are comin' to his house and botherin' him. They spray painted the sides of his house and it looks like they're enjoyin' harassin' my friend here and that ain't right. It just ain't right."

"So?" the man asked. "What you want me to do about it?"

Once again, Swifty remained calm as he answered the man. "I want you to pay for his window and pay for the cost of gettin' the paint off the sides of his house and . . . I want you to tell your kid and his little buddies to all stay away from Angelo, this man here," he said as he nodded his head Angelo's way, "and his house."

The man just laughed at him. It was obvious why he had such a hellion for a kid. He found all of this amusing. "Get outta here before I call the cops and have you arrested," the man barked.

Swifty tilted his head, made a little 'tsk, tsk' sound with his lips and tongue and said, "It's too bad you feel that way. We tried to do the honorable thing, ya know."

"Hah," the man snarled. "Honorable thing. Kids just havin' fun. Get outta here."

"Come on Angelo I've heard enough," Swifty insisted. "That's right. Go. Run!" the sweaty man yelled. "Pansies. Just a couple of pansies," he seemed to mutter as he just had to get in the last words.

Angelo and Swifty now had their backs to the man and they were headed down the walkway from the house toward the street sidewalk. Swifty stopped in his tracks, calmly turned around and asked in a sarcastic sort of way, "You like your house?"

The man was totally confused by this question. "What are you talkin' about?" he asked. "What do you mean 'do I like my house?'"

Swifty smiled and said, "I'm just askin' if you like your house. Ya see, my friend here likes his house. Most people really wanna take care of their house 'cause it's where they live. It kind'a violates a person when somebody does somethin' to your house. Hmmm . . .," Swifty paused and pondered. "Wonder how this house would look in pink? What do you think, Angelo? Is pink a good color for this house?" Angelo nodded stiffly. He wanted to play along but really wasn't quite sure where all this was headed. "I think he might need a little air conditioning, too - you know, some gentle breezes comin' in through open windows," he smiled.

The man's eyes opened wide, his jowl tightened and he yelled out, "Is that supposed to be a threat, punk?" and he started down the steps toward Swifty and Angelo.

Swifty held up his palm in a non-threatening way and warned, "Don't take another step down those steps or I might have to hurt ya."

The man did not heed Swifty's warning. "Oh really?" he snarled as he continued to walk toward the men. Swifty waited to see just how close the man would get before, in Swifty's mind, his personal space had been completely invaded. The man crossed that limit - that Swifty limit of no more than four feet away from him, his space - not much different from the boxing ring. Swifty didn't even wait for the guy to stop. As quick as a rattlesnake he launched a right uppercut that landed the man on his ass, half on the ground and half on the concrete. He then took a large stone and smashed one window, grabbed another rock, smashed another, and was in the process of tending to a third when he heard, "Okay, okay." "I hear ya," the man grunted from his horizontal position on the front lawn. "No need for this to get out of hand. I'll take care of it. Send me the bill for everything and I'll have a talk with my son."

Swifty nodded and answered, "Great. Angelo here will bring you a bill in a little while. Make sure you're home and make sure you open the door to talk to him and when you *do* open that door, have a check signed ready to just fill in the total. Cash is even better, but either one will do and . . . make sure you keep that kid of yours and his little buddies away from his house. The next trip I make here won't be as pleasant as this one."

"Hey, it's all right. Don't worry. I'll take care of everything," the man replied.

"Good! See that you do. Come on Angelo," Swifty remarked and the two men walked back to Angelo's home. Angelo thanked Swifty many times and Swifty headed back to work.

Red was waiting for Swifty when he returned to the club. "I wanna hear it all, everything from the beginning," he instructed the moment Swifty's feet crossed the doorway. When Swifty had finished his story, Red asked, "So you think you worked it out?"

"Yeah," Swifty answered, "Angelo shouldn't have any more problems with those kids."

"Good! Great job Swifty. You handled it by givin' a warning first and usin' your head. Unfortunately, you had to use your fist; however, I like what you did. It only took one punch to get the message across. Ya know, somebody else mighta' kept hittin' and beatin' the guy even while he was down. I'm proud of you Swifty. You let your head prevail. You got the message across and left him alive," he laughed. "That's good thinkin'. In my business, or any business actually, it's always better to solve problems peaceful-like, if possible. You only use violence if left with no other choice. Understand?"

"Yeah, I understand," Swifty answered. He didn't know that this was gonna be some kind of test. Hell, he had come real close to breaking every rib in the man's body and having him eat a little concrete with his missing teeth. Something was happening to Swifty. He was maturing. Swifty was happy because Red was happy and Red's approval meant something to him, meant everything really.

"I'm not gonna get you involved with the day–to –day of the business, Swifty," Red added, "and none of the wet work, but I may have you handle little problems like these when they come up. My main concern right now is makin' you a champion. *Capiche*?"

chapter five

Larry Bernstein put down the letter for the moment. Remember him? He was the movie guy - the one who made Jimmy the Hat's career. Well, he sighed, picked up this letter again and read it a second time. This was the third one this month. The letter stated that the author had damaging information on the movie studio's number one star, Lana Thomas.

Bernstein thought all had been settled back when Jimmy the Hat and Lana were co-starring in the movie "Mob Enforcer." Jimmy had fought the man who was blackmailing Lana with some video and he forced him to tell him, Jimmy, where he had hidden that film. The man swore that there were no other copies. Bernstein had destroyed that film. Now, he wondered if there were others - other videos that he wasn't aware of. The letter stated that the sender had damaging 'eye witness' affidavits. The letter also insisted that the sender had information on three other Bernstein stars - two females and one male - that would wreak havoc on the stars and the studio. One female, the letter stated, was using heavy drugs. The writer claimed to be in possession of a female star's arrest record for shoplifting and stated that he or she had proof that the studio's leading ladies' man was gay, stating that there were pictures to prove it. The sender ended the letter saying that two million dollars was all it would take to contain this information. A time and place for the monetary exchange would be given in the next letter.

Bernstein was a smart businessman who, like many successful executives, relied on part street smarts, part schooling, and a whole lot of gut instinct. That was his gift and that's why his studio was so successful. As he read the letter for yet another time, he knew that once money had been exchanged, this would not prevent any future demands. It was damnation any way he looked at it if this information was true - ruin the studio by discrediting its stars or bleed the company dry through blackmail. Either way, the press would have a field day over this and Bernstein risked having his image shredded right before the very patrons responsible for what some might consider a fat cat salary.

Larry had a number of competitors in the industry who resented or even hated him, but who would go to such lengths, he thought. The logical move was to take this to the FBI but Bernstein thought of his family and their safety. These people were nuts, he thought and nuts meant dangerous. There was no one in Hollywood he could trust. This was a gossip columnist's dream scoop. As he was about to place the latest letter into the safe with all of the others, it dawned on him. There was someone – someone in New York. Why hadn't he thought of this sooner? He opened his desk drawer and pulled out his private little address book. He scanned it searching for the one name he knew well. Yip, Yip was always his man in New York. They had known each other since childhood, growing up in the same neighborhood. He recalled the time Yip helped him when some schoolyard bullies threatened him, and Yip had helped him again when his father, who owned a jewelry store, was having trouble with a local pack of wise guys. Yip straightened them out. Bernstein and his father never knew *what* Yip did or *how* he did it. They just knew that he *did* it and in both cases, the problems went away. But Yip was dead and Larry hadn't talked to his nephew, Big Red, now in charge, since his biggest star, James Roman, (ne Jimmy the Hat) had been killed. And yes, Bernstein always used the word 'killed' because in essence, that's why he died. He died from an infection from the wounds he received trying to help while Mary's crazy ex-husband was on one of his maniacal binges, hell bent on hurting Trenchie, Mary's new husband, and Jimmy's dear friend. What a shame that was.

Larry had benefited from Roman's death for a while – Jimmy's movies had sold out, his memorabilia commanded premium prices – the theatres were packed anytime the name James Roman was publicized. But it had been hard for Bernstein to find another James Roman. They were few and far between.

Bernstein knew that he could trust Big Red. Red was the man

who had worked, through Yip, to get Jimmy the Hat to California, into the offices of Larry Bernstein and on the road to stardom. Hell, he'd rather give Red the two million than some crazy blackmailer who might never end his demands. Besides, when Red became involved in something, he always got results. Red had interceded and saved one of Larry's stars from being killed during the filming of *To Love A Thief* starring the Hat. That thought brought a smile to Bernstein's face for the first time since he had started receiving the letters. It was time to call in some muscle, some old-fashioned, New York style, street muscle.

Two Years Earlier

Moose drove with Swifty sitting in the front seat. Big Red, Tarzan and Trenchie sat in the back as they drove back from the Swifty-Velasques third and 'final' fight.

"Great fight Swifty," Red said.

"Thanks Red," Swifty responded. "Boy, that kid is a good fighter. I never fought anybody as good as him." Swifty was still pumped up and even though he had said that these three fights with Valesques were enough, he made somewhat of a Freudian slip. "Next time I'll get him," he said. Big Red looked at Tarzan and Trenchie. They just stared back. The car pulled into the parking lot of the club and Tarzan and the other men hesitated and decided to stay in the car.

Red picked up on the awkward silence and said, "Swifty, I have a letter for you - mailman dropped it off at the club. I don't know what it says 'cuz I'm not in the habit of openin' other people's mail, but I think I might recognize the envelope and address. Why don't you open it and then just let us know?"

The men sat motionless as Red took an envelope from his jacket pocket and passed it to Swifty in the front seat. Swifty opened it and read the first word of the first sentence. "Greetings!" it said. As his eyes moved line by line down the letter, Swifty's face changed from uncertainty to confusion to sheer terror.

The letter was an official notice from the United States government informing Swifty that he was to report for an Armed Forces Physical Examination - the first step in the draft process.

He was to be at Thirty-Nine Whitehall Street in Manhattan on June seventeenth at eight am. Swifty was silent for a moment and then, "Jesus - just when my career was starting to take off," as he looked to Red for help.

"Can't you do something about this Red?" he asked.

His eyes were pitiful. It might have been the only time the guys ever saw Swifty as the child boy that he was, only twenty-four, they had to remind themselves. He had always seemed so much older, but here he was, just reaching out for someone to tell him that it was gonna be okay.

"Well, Swiff," Red said, "I can probably get it deferred for a while, but they'd get you in a year or two and you'd be that much older. My best advice is to just go on in and I'll try to pull some strings and get you on the army's boxin' team. You stay in shape and you'll have an easy duty for a couple of years and when you get out, we'll get you right back on track for the goal - a championship belt."

Moose drove Swifty to the city. All the men who reported to Thirty-Nine Whitehall Street that morning had to complete a routine physical examination which Swifty was hoping he'd fail. The line was long and moved slowly. There was some kidding among the men and a few of them were nervous about the injections they would be getting. They had received three shots of heaven knows what when a Sergeant with a booming voice announced that the next shot would be the hardest one in the series. He said that they were about to get the helicopter shot. The men all looked at each other. As the story goes, they were all probably thinking what the hell can a helicopter shot be? It sounded scary. Swifty wasn't worried, but the strapping young man with well - defined muscles standing in front of him in line turned ghost white. He turned to Swifty with a worried look and said, "Look, if I pass out when I get this shot, grab me before I fall. I don't want to embarrass myself and look stupid in front of all these guys." Swifty couldn't help but chuckle a little bit. Here was this big lug who was afraid of a little needle. The guy looked like he could fight five guys in an alley and was asking Swifty to catch him if he fainted.

"Sure, don't worry about a thing," Swifty said. "I got your back."

"Thanks," the big guy said and he put out his hand. "I'm Gonzo."

"I'm Swifty. Nice to meet ya."

"Do you have any idea where you're going?" Gonzo asked.

"No, but I'm pretty sure wherever it is, I'll be on the boxin' team . . . wherever that'll be," Swifty answered confidently.

"Hey, no kiddin'! I'm gonna be on the boxin' team too. What's your weight class?"

"Welterweight. Right now I'm at 165 pounds, but I usually fight at 160."

"I'm a heavyweight," Gonzo said, "as you can probably tell." He laughed and gave Swifty a good-natured slap on the back. Swifty liked the guy and he began thinking that it would be nice if the two of them were assigned to the same company, maybe even the same barrack. The guy was from New York, he was a boxer - it didn't get any better than that to Swifty. Lots in common.

The time had come. A few weeks later, Moose and the rest of the guys drove Swifty to Grand Central Station to begin his journey to Fort Dix in Trenton, New Jersey for basic training. The guys took turns giving Swifty big Italian hugs. Red and Moose started to choke up a little. Swifty tried to remain real cool but when he saw these guys, his idols, getting sappy, his eyes started to get moisten, too. "I gotcha covered," Red said. "Don't you worry, my boy, Big Red's got you covered. Now, you just go and make all of us proud."

Basic training first required a series of five physical training tests. The Lieutenant announced that he'd give the top three men with the highest scores a three-day pass. The first test was pull-ups. Gonzo was feeling a little full of himself and told the Sergeant that he could do them with one hand. "Just name the hand," he bragged. The Sergeant, hands on his hips, eyed him up and down and said, "I never met a man yet who could pull his full body weight up to his chin with one hand." Gonzo first performed the fifteen required, regular, two-handed chin-ups for the test. He then asked the sergeant to watch. Gonzo reached up with his right hand and did three one handed pull–ups. He did the same with the other hand. He looked at the sergeant and remarked, "If I hadn't just done fifteen chin–ups, I could've done a lot more." The Sergeant stood there, eyes wide, and shook his head as if to say yes, he was impressed. The second test was deep knee–bends. Seventy-five in this category was a perfect score. Both Gonzo and Swifty did the seventy-five easily. When they looked around, they saw other recruits falling to the ground and stumbling to get to their next test. Their leg muscles had just given out. The third test was pushups. Twenty-five were needed to pass. Gonzo and Swifty, once again, performed easily. Next were the sit–ups - so easy that the two boxers could have kept going all day. The fifth and final test was the completion of an obstacle course within a three-minute time frame. This included a short run. Both men came in well under the time allotted. Gonzo and Swifty tied for first place. Each of them, as well as the second place winner received three - day passes. Swifty knew exactly where he wanted to go and asked Gonzo if he'd like to accompany him to Queens and spend some time with him at The Starlight Club. The boys were lucky - the Sergeant, who had his own pass was headed their way so they hitched a ride with him to the big apple. During the drive, Swifty and Gonzo talked a lot about boxing.

"Hey Gonzo, ya got any professional fights under your belt?" Swifty asked.

"Yeah," Gonzo answered. "I have fifteen - won thirteen, twelve by knockout, and lost two. I'd like to fight those two guys I lost to again. I'm really more of a bar room brawler and I never took training seriously, so I wasn't in the best of shape when I fought 'em." Swifty liked his honesty. "Next time, I'll make it my business to be in shape and I'll kick their asses. You can be sure of that. How about you? You fight professionally?"

"Yeah, I had thirty fights. Won twenty-seven. Had three draws."

"Wow that's some record. Three draws? That's good. Least you didn't lose."

"Yeah, and all to the same guy."

"What? I never heard of that happenin' before," Gonzo said. "Three draws and to the same guy? Man, you musta been good. He musta have been good, too."

Swifty nodded. "He was the best I ever fought. I hope I meet him again one day. I'd like to tell him what a good fighter I thought he was," Swifty said.

"Who knows?" Gonzo said. "Maybe you'll get a chance to fight him again someday."

"Not on your life man. Three fights with that guy was enough. Un uh - no need to talk about that. Not gonna happen," Swifty said laughing. Sergeant Rodgriguez, turned to the guys and asked. "Do you guys have to go to Queens or can I talk you out of it for something better?" Swifty and Gonzo looked at each other puzzled like. "What did you have in mind Sarge?"

"Well, I was just promoted to Sergeant First Class and my sister is throwing me a party to celebrate my promotion. There'll be home cooked food; plenty of booze and my sister invited her college girlfriends to come to the party. I met her girlfriends and all I can say is they are all knockouts." The two boxers couldn't refuse the offer of a home cooked meal and just hearing that beautiful girls would be coming to the party cinched it for them.

"Ok you convinced us. Do you know of a hotel close by where we can stay?" Gonzo asked. Rodriguez shook his head. "My friends don't stay in hotels. I insist you stay with us. We have an extra room you can use. Come on, say you'll come. You'll have a great time." The two boxers shrugged and looked at each other as smiles spread across their faces. "Sure ... we'd be happy to come. Thanks for inviting us." The three days passed quickly and so did basic training.

Boxing qualified as a critical M.O.S. (Military Occupational Specialty). Because of that, both boys bypassed being sent overseas by ship. Instead, they were flown to Japan by way of a four-engine constellation, a propeller - driven airplane that was used for civilians as well as military air transport. The plane stopped in Hawaii to refuel and on the following day, an overbooked flight, full of officers who had seniority over them, caused the men to be bumped from their flight. Each day for a week, they faithfully reported to their flight, and every morning for a week, they were bumped. The boys loved being bumped. Hawaii was paradise with its temperature in the mid eighties, clear skies and gentle breezes. There was one problem, however. The boxers never really got to enjoy the great state. Instead, they stayed locked in a crap game on the second floor of their temporary barracks near Hickum Air Force Base. Since they carried their payroll records with them. It was easy to go to the paymaster and get an advance on their salary, even before a salary was earned. The crap game was a big one and, one by one, guys were eliminated. Gonzo had to get out because he, like all the others, lost all of his money.

At the end of the three-day-old crap game, it was just Swifty and a Sergeant. The Sergeant suggested that they put all their cash into the pot for a 'winner take all'. Swifty readily agreed. The sergeant picked up the dice. Swifty, who had become suspicious of this guy, kept his eyes on the man, looking for signs of deception. Then, there it was. Swifty spotted the move. It was good, almost unnoticeable, but Swifty had been in crap games like this one all his life growing up on the streets of New York and he knew what to look for. This was a blanket game. Swifty could have insisted that they roll the dice against a wall or something hard, but since the game had been underway long before he joined in, he had kept quiet. It appeared that old serge here was switching the dice - that much he was sure of. Swifty theorized, and logic would state, that when the dice were going well for him, he might not switch the dice because he didn't need to, but when he found his luck changing, that's when he'd make his move.

Now that Swifty had caught him cheating, he waited, waited for him to make that funny move again with the fingers he held the dice with. As soon as the sergeant was about to throw, Swifty put his hand on the man's chest and pushed him away from the blanket that held the money. This caused him to stumble backwards and land on his haunches. Swifty, ignoring the sarge, picked up the dice and felt them. Suspicions validated. The dice were weighted. While the other guys looked on, Swifty said,

"Look. Watch this. I'll throw a seven," and he rolled the dice onto the blanket. Sure enough, he rolled a seven. "These dice are loaded," Swifty said. "This bum's been switchin' the dice the whole time. That's how come he's been winnin'." At least forty pair of eyes trained on the sergeant. "He's good," Swifty continued. "I'll give him that, but he's nothin' but a rat thief." The sergeant, sensing the hostility in the room, lunged slightly toward Swifty. It was more of a 'let me outta here' move than anything, but Swifty had anticipated it. Using the man's forward momentum against him, Swifty stepped back and caught the sergeant with a right hand flush on his jaw. The big guy staggered backwards. Swifty was all over him then, hitting him with lefts, and then rights, until the sergeant just collapsed, in a heap, onto the floor. The sergeant's friends tried moving into position to help him, but Gonzo put out his big hands to stop them.

"The first one who tries to help this guy deals with me," said Gonzo.

The men didn't move a muscle. Gonzo was big. Big and muscular. The men could do nothing but watch as Swifty pummeled their friend mercilessly into unconsciousness. Satisfied that the guy wouldn't be getting up anytime soon, Swifty collected the money on the blanket, bent down, removed the sergeant's wallet from his back pocket, took out all the cash, and threw the empty wallet on top of the unconscious man.

"Come on Gonzo. Let's get outta of this joint. I don't like the smell in here," Swifty said.

"Yeah," Gonzo said. "I think we need to find a new location until we get on that plane. Now's just about as good a time as any to finally see a little of Honolulu." Swifty agreed. Now was a good time. The boys found a cab parked right outside the base.

On the drive to Honolulu, Gonzo looked over at Swifty and said, "You did real good handlin' that guy. I can see why you were undefeated."

"Ah, he was just a bum," Swifty answered modestly. "By the way," Swifty continued, "how much money did you lose?"

"About two forty," Gonzo answered.

Swifty reached into his pocket, pulled out the wad of dough

he has taken, and counted out eighteen hundred dollars. He took out the three hundred dollars that he had started with. There was fifteen hundred remaining. He divided that in half. "Here," he said to Gonzo, "this should cover what you lost plus a few extra bucks." Gonzo laughed as he waved the money in his left hand while slapping Swifty on the shoulder with his right.

"Thanks for that, Swiff," Gonzo said. "Only a good guy would do that. Thanks," he said smiling.

Being bumped every day was getting ridiculous but on the seventh day the boxers found themselves with two seats on the plane. "You know," Gonzo said, "I've been told that with these new jets, you can put a cup of coffee on the table and it won't spill or fall off."

"You're kiddin' me," Swifty said. "If that's the case, then why are we still usin' these old constellations?"

"I don't know. I guess since they have 'em, they have to use 'em. It's probably cheaper that way."

"Yeah I guess you're right. That's probably why we're still using the same jeeps, the same Chevy staff cars, and the same deuces and a half that we used in the Second World War."

The big plane flew high into the blackness of the night as the powerful engines roared and vibrated pulling the plane deeper and higher into darkness. The lights were turned off in the cabin. Swifty looked out the window and thought that he had never seen a sky as black as this one. He turned on one side and then the other and tried to get some sleep, and just as he was about to get comfortable, he was alerted by the Captain's voice informing everyone to prepare for landing at Wake Island - the plane couldn't make it to Japan without refueling. Swifty looked out the window again. He could see lights dancing in the middle of the ocean. The aircraft banked, turned, and touched down, landing smoothly on the black tarmac where it taxied to the waiting buses. The soldiers deplaned, boarded the buses, and drove a short distance to the Quonset huts - those semicircular steel buildings that were so common on military bases.

Wake Island is a small V-shaped island five by two and a half miles. It didn't take long to get there and with this fuel break in the trip, the boys decided now was a good time to get some breakfast. Gonzo and Swifty were among the first. With their bellies full, the boys stepped out of the chow hall to wait for the others to finish eating so that they could all get back onto the bus that would take them back to the plane. While they waited, the fighters walked to the water's edge where the sun was beginning to rise in the east.

"It's weird, ain't it Gonz?" Swifty said. "We're on a volcanic island. Everything's black instead of being green. Those shapes rising out of the darkness are the boats and the planes sunk during World War Two."

"Yeah," Gonzo added, "all the signs of the second world war are plainly in sight."

Swifty wandered over to a pillbox, a concrete trench with openings used to fire artillery, and it struck him - how our brave men had desperately fought for their lives as they were being pushed closer and closer toward the ocean. This must have been where they took their last stand. It was an eerie feeling so he was relieved when the order came to board the bus and soon, with no other air traffic nearby, the powerful engines pulled them along the runway, gaining speed until they lifted the large aircraft high into the morning sky.

On this last leg of their journey, the guys managed to sleep a little. They awoke just as the plane was preparing to land in Tokyo and once again, a bus was there waiting for them. Swifty was glad that Gonzo was with him on the long drive deep into the Japanese countryside. The bus finally reached its destination and the men found themselves at Camp Zama, the Japanese West Point during World War II, now the present site of the Army Forces Far East (AFFE) headquarters.

Swifty and Gonzo were happy to find that they had been assigned to the same barrack. The barracks here were laid out a bit differently than those back in the states. When they entered the front door, there was a hallway on the right with rooms on either side. There were about ten cots in each room on the left. Halfway down the hall, there was the bathroom and showers and in one of them, there was a young man shaving. Swifty walked ahead, thought better of it, took a few steps back and stared at the guy. There was something familiar about him. The guy sensing Swifty's gaze, turned and looked at him. At that moment, something clicked and each man slowly broke into a big grin.

"Henri?" asked Swifty.

"Swifty, didn't we see enough of each other back home?" Henri replied. And with that, Swifty hastily walked over to him and the two men embraced each other in that manly sort of way.

"It's good to see you Henri."

"You too Swifty."

"Gonzo, come on over here. I want you to meet a friend of mine." Gonzo ambled over.

"Gonzo, do you remember me tellin' you about that classy fighter that I fought three draws with?"

"Yeah. Nah, don't tell me this is the guy," he laughed.

"This is him - the only guy I can't beat and the only guy I don't ever wanna fight again." Laughter filled the bathroom and boom - it was instant camaraderie.

Gonzo and Swifty quickly stowed their gear in their new home away from home and hightailed it back to Henri's room. He had a few cold brews stashed in the small cooler next to his cot and he handed one to each of his new friends.

"Gonzo here is our heavyweight fighter," Swifty explained. "He has a decent record for someone who don't like to train much, but we'll change that right, Henri?"

"You got that right," Henri replied. "Do you have any idea how hard I trained when I fought you?"

"Not as hard as I trained to fight you," Swifty retorted. "That's for sure." The three men found themselves laughing and talking for most of the night and from that day on, there was a union - the New York boys unofficial boxer's union. They became fast friends. In the year and a half that they were in Japan, they toured the Far East with the army boxing team, accrued impressive records, and took home the Far East Armed Forces boxing championship.

It was discharge day - that day that every soldier awaits, the day that said 'You've done it. You've done your duty, served your country, and now it's time to go home to family.' Henri,

Gonzo and Swifty were herded onto a one stacker World War II ship, named the *Marine Lynxx*, with a load of other men returning to the states. There was one necessary stop before landing in the states - Korea to pick up other men returning home.

The long ocean voyage home provided the three men the opportunity for long, heartfelt talks. The men spent much of their idle time discussing the future. Henri confided to his two friends the real reason that he had begun boxing. It was to pay for his little brother's education. "Hey guys," Henri said, "My brother is graduating soon from the Hackley School in upstate New York. How about coming to it? I'd like to have you guys there." Good thing he won at boxing because Hackley was expensive. Located in Tarrytown, New York, the prestigious prep school was serious about its academics, academics that weren't cheap.

"Absolutely," Swifty replied. "I'll go with ya."

"I'd love to go too," Gonzo seconded.

"Great," Henri continued, "I count you two as good friends, close friends, and I don't have too many of those. I'd like to really make an effort to stay in touch, if we can."

One evening, while sitting and staring at the stars, Swifty asked, "Do you guys have good managers?"

"I don't," Gonzo said.

"I'm my own manager now," Henri answered.

"Well then, why don't you guys come home with me and stay awhile?" Swifty asked. "The three of us have nothing to do right now and I think it'd be neat for us to hang out for a while. Besides, I'd like you to meet Big Red, my manager. The guy is big time. Man, I used to be this loser - just goin' nowhere in life until Red pulled me aside one day and told me that he had gone and bought out my contract. Seems he didn't want me to end up being a bum," Swifty laughed. "Said I was a lazy bum, which I was. The truth was, I only fought when I needed money but Red gave me the motivation to be better. He made me believe in myself, actually. How many people will do that for you? Make you feel like somebody? I'd love for you guys to meet him. Man, the three of us would make one helluva boxin' team, especially with Red managin' us." The men high fived each other and the mood turned from pensive to cheerful. Maybe it was because

Swifty was giving them some hope now. Kinda' neat how Swifty was gonna try to pay it forward.

The ship passed under the Golden Gate Bridge and docked to the music of a military band playing a Souza march. The boys didn't get a chance to spend any time there in California because they were shepherded aboard a military aircraft that flew them straight to McGuire Air Force base. It was a short bus ride to Fort Dix where they spent the night. With discharge papers in hand, they hopped a cab to the bus stop hoping to find the first bus to New York. No need for that. They never even made it to the ticket booth. As the cab rolled in, Swifty glanced up and there it was – Big Red's Caddy convertible parked in the lot, with the top down, and Moose standing beside it, smiling ear to ear.

"Looks like our ride is waiting for us," Swifty smiled and said. He walked over to Moose, gave him a hug and introduced his two buddies.

Moose looked at Henri and laughed as he pointed to him. "Didn't you get enough of this guy in the ring? You had to spend two years in the army with him, too?" He laughed and slapped Henri on the arm gently. Moose and Gonzo exchanged polite hellos and all four men headed off to the Jersey Turnpike toward the city. The trip to Queens and the Starlight Club took just under two hours. It was a sunny June day and they rode the whole way in that big caddy with the top down. It was the perfect way to return home – wind in their hair, tunes blasting, and stories of the Starlight Club and its cast of characters.

Back at the club, Red paced back and forth in his office waiting for Swifty. He was like the anxious Papa, trying to act cool but the truth was, he had missed Swifty, missed him a lot. Every few seconds, he glanced at his watch, checked the time and then he'd check the screen that monitored the front door just wishing that the minutes would pass faster. He hadn't realized it when Swifty left for the army but he realized it now – Swifty had filled the void that Jimmy the Hat had left when he died. Red thought that could never happen. Red loved the Hat like his own son and now he found himself caring for Swifty in much the same way. The kid had no family, no one to come home to. No one would tell Swifty they missed him. It was sad, you know.

They were good for each other. This kid had lifted Red out of the emptiness and sadness that he felt. Swifty had given him something to get excited about, to care about, but Red would never let on. No one in his organization knew that because he never allowed them to. All they saw was the boss man, always stern, always in charge, and forever leading his men.

The big caddy arrived to find Big Red waiting out front of the Starlight Club. Red grabbed Swifty and gave him a huge welcome home hug. Swifty introduced his two friends. "Red I'm sure you recognize this guy," he said as he put his arm around Henri Valesques. "You remember him. He's the guy who wouldn't let me win a single fight!"

Red laughed and said, "How could I ever forget the man who taught Swifty the fine art of the jab? How you doin' Henri? Has my man been treatin' you all right?"

Henri smiled and said, "If I taught him the fine art of the jab, then I guess he taught me the fine art of the right hand."

"And this is Gonzo. Your new heavyweight fighter," Swifty interjected.

Red smiled. "It's a real pleasure to meet you Gonzo. . . and I would be proud to manage you, that is . . . if you want me to . . . and if you're good enough."

"Oh don't worry, Mr. Red, I'm a pretty good fighter. I never had a good manager before so, hey, why not you?" he teased. "Swifty tells me that you're the best, that you've done wonders with him so I think that maybe I'll take boxin' a little more seriously from now on, and who knows, maybe I'll make a few bucks along the way?"

"Don't worry about making money. If you're a friend of Swifty's, you'll make money, a lot of it. But at the risk of talking shop too soon, I would tend to treat you just like I have Swifty. You win, you invest a part of your earnings so that when you retire, you'll have money." The boys just looked at each other. Red didn't pull any punches. They kinda' liked that.

Red directed the boys to place their gear in the room upstairs that Trenchie and Jimmy the Hat always used and excused himself for a minute, went into the kitchen, and in typical Red fashion, ordered his chef to prepare a meal fit for a King, at least fit for three strapping boxers. He led the young men into his grand ballroom where they sat at a private table and talked for hours about the past two years and what it had meant in their lives.

A couple of days passed. The men had had time to relax, sleep late, and just take in their newfound "freedom", if you will. Swifty decided that it was now time for a little fun.

"Come on guys. Get dressed," Swifty announced one morning. "We're going to the Aquacade". The Aquacade was located on Horace Harding Boulevard and was a famous aquatic entertainment arena where the locals could swim during the day for .75 cents and the famous aquacade show spectacle was presented in the evenings. The boys spent the day there, celebrating their homecoming and just being silly boys. Wine, women, and song was the credo - a little too much wine, well beer, to be exact. Just around midday while sitting outside around the pool, a beautiful young lady in a flaming red bikini strolled by. She was working that bikini, swinging her hips in a tantalizing way. Swifty, in his less than sober state, decided to show off a little.

"Hey, are you a working girl?" he asked.

"Could be," she answered.

"How much?" Swifty asked.

"You tell me," she replied.

"How about seventy-five dollars for a BJ?" Swifty continued. And just like three young soldiers returning from the isolation of war zones, the boys laughed like schoolboys.

"*How* much?" the girl asked.

"Seventy-five," Swifty repeated.

The girl smiled and calmly reached into her little purse. The boys were all smiles until they got a clear shot of what she was holding in her hand. The bikini clad girl flashed her badge and announced, "The three of you are under arrest for soliciting." The boys, drunken stupor and all, continued to laugh as they were herded into the police wagon, seemingly not caring at all about what had just transpired. "You'll have to wait here in the van for the others, until the van's full," one officer announced and it wasn't long before they were joined by another group of kids, also in a convertible. They had made the same mistake - they had whistled at a pretty girl, made some remarks, and had found themselves in the same paddy wagon as Swifty and his friends. I guess the van, or the police, whoever it was, had made quota now, so off they went to the police station. Between the drive there and the wait in the lobby, the boxers seemed to sober up a little. Reality began to settle in a little and they decided that this situation and the idea of spending the night in a dirty jail cell was no longer funny. Swifty informed the desk sergeant that he wanted to make the one phone call which he knew he was allowed. Of course he called Big Red.

"Red, this is Swifty. I'm at the Queens County Courthouse. They got me for soliciting a prostitute. It was a case of entrapment, it really was. No lie, but I want you to come down here because I'm gonna have a little fun with the judge."

"Swifty, don't do anything foolish," Red ordered. "I'll get Doc and we'll be down there as soon as I can."

Swifty's two buddies were released because they didn't actually proposition the cop, but they remained in the courtroom, had to, because they were visiting Swifty. Hours passed and finally Swifty's name was called to appear before the judge. The judge asked for his plea - innocent or guilty.

"Guilty with an explanation Your Honor," Swifty said with a smile.

The judge looked at him, saw the smile, and replied with another question. "What's your explanation?"

Swifty smiled and said, "Your Honor, me and my two friends just returned from spending two years in the army and a year and a half of it in the Far East and we were just havin' a little fun celebratin' our discharge. We were at the Aquacade enjoyin' ourselves when this beautiful girl, with a dynamite figure I might add, passes us in a bikini, so as a joke I asked her if she was a working girl and she told me maybe. So I asked her, 'How much?' And she said how much would I give her, so I told her about seventy-five dollars for a little head. Now Your Honor, you and everybody in this courtroom know that I had to be joking because every guy knows that you can get a blow job, anywhere in the city, for five bucks so . . . I had to be one of two things - jokin', or just plain stupid. I haven't seen a girl yet that deserves seventy-five dollars for a BJ, maybe for other things, Your Honor, but not for a BJ. Nope. No way. " And with that the whole courtroom erupted into laughter, including the judge, who then tried hard to contain himself but still managed to let a smile creep across his face as he shook his head. The district attorney was just about to bust a gut and break through the seams of his nicely tailored suit. The personable cockiness of Swifty was apparent and his likeability factor soared off the charts. It worked. The judge brought down his gavel and declared, "That was one helluva story son but you told it well. Case dismissed."

Red managed a little smile too, but all the way home, Swifty had to listen to him lecture about his career and staying out of trouble. Secretly, Red had been just as entertained as everyone else. He told the story to each of his buddies at the club and some of his favored patrons, but ordered them all not to glorify Swifty's behavior, *at least to his face*.

chapter six

When the Gallo crew became part of the Genovese family, Tarzan didn't join with them. Instead, he joined Red's organization, but before leaving the Gallo's, he told Kid Blast that he'd like to purchase the Gallo vending machine route. Since Joey was now dead, Kid Blast agreed to sell. Once Tarzan officially joined Red's team, he moved Margaret and their son to Queens to be closer to the central workings, the headquarters, if you will. Tarzan could have joined any of the crime families but he preferred Red. He liked it there - Red's generosity, and the way he took care of his men. Red was the polar opposite of Profaci. His men loathed Profaci, because of his greed. When the Gallo - Profaci war began, Crazy Joey Gallo split his mob up into small groups so they wouldn't be in the same place at the same time. This was a precaution so that harm wouldn't come to all of them at the same time and wipe out the whole family. Gallo sent his men to various clubs throughout the five boroughs for extended stays. Tarzan, Gibby and Ralph were sent to The Starlight Club. While there, Red began to depend on Tarzan and likewise, Tarzan became accustomed to working with Red and his crew. Tarzan was a lot like Red. He was tough, reliable, yet fair in his dealings. Joey had made Tarzan a capo in the Gallo mob and he put him in charge of all of his vending machines. Tarzan handled the route for The Starlight Club, so as the Gallo's were inducted into the Genovese family, Tarzan mentioned to Red that he'd like to join him and his family. Red welcomed him with open arms.

Moose knocked on Red's door. "Come on in," Red bellowed.

"Red, Angelo is back and his son is with him. Do you want to see them or should I tell him to come back later?"

"No send them in. It must be important for him to come here with his son."

Angelo and his son took a seat and Angelo began the conversation. "Red, this is my son Roberto and he has a problem that I can't help him with. We came to you. Go on Roberto. Tell Mr. Red what happened."

Red looked at the young man. The kid was one big purple bruise. His eye was almost completely shut and his lips were swollen so badly he could hardly speak. "Who did this to you … and why?" Red asked, clearly annoyed by what he saw.

Roberto spoke slowly though his pain. "I think the men who did this were from Staten Island but I'm not sure. The trouble started when my three friends opened a small brokerage house in the financial district in lower Manhattan. They're only in their early twenties but they're sharp kids, nonetheless. They're pretty ambitious and hard-working and they were excited about opening a little business for themselves. They started at first with their own money and then added some money they received from a small group of people who wanted their money invested. The boys invested carefully and pretty conservatively and even in a slow economy, they managed to give their clients a twenty-two percent return. Well, news like that travels fast and these clients told other friends and so on until the firm began to grow into a sizable company. Soon, the kids, the owners, were driving expensive cars and doing what young boys, who never had money and who suddenly find themselves rolling in it, do - they spent it. All that flashiness was getting them attention and they loved it but apparently, some wise guys with their own agenda were watching them. They wanted to know how these kids could afford the fancy cars they drove and the fancy suits they wore. So one day they stopped into their office and they gave my friend Tommy fifty thousand dollars to invest. Tommy invested the money and the man was surprised when he received a twenty-five percent return on his investment. That man, who calls himself Reilly, returned the following week with two of his friends and told Tommy and his partners that they were taking over the brokerage business and informed them that they, my friends, would now be considered their employees. Well that didn't settle too well with Tommy so he came to me with a proposition. He knew that I wanted to open a smoke shop slash coffee house and needed investors, so he gave me the one hundred fifty thousand dollars I needed. Tommy didn't want the money in his account because he was afraid that these guys would discover it and claim it was theirs. Well, somehow they found out about Tommy giving me the money and they worked him over. They even showed up at Tommy's wedding. They did it just to intimidate him. To make a long story short, these men came to see me and told me that Tommy had no right to give me *their* money and they wanted it back. I told them I didn't have it. The following day they returned and asked me *again* for *their* money. I told them again that I didn't have it so they roughed me up and told me to find it. They left with, 'We don't care if you borrow it or if you steal it, but the money better be here waiting for us when we return in one week. One week - that's all you get.' So my father took out a loan on his house and I borrowed as much as I could but all I could come up with is a hundred thirty-five thousand and I'm still short fifteen grand."

All throughout the story, Red could feel his body getting hotter and hotter, swelling with anger. Tarzan, too, was steaming. It was obvious 'cause he kept opening and closing his fists like he was ready to lay someone out.

It was Red's turn now. "Do these guys think that they can lean on my friend's son and get away with it?" he said to Tarzan. He looked back at Roberto. "When is this guy supposed to be comin' back? Where? The office?"

"He's going over to the brokerage house, the one they took over, on Wall Street at nine-thirty tomorrow morning. Told me I'd better be there waiting for them."

"What does he look like?"

"Well, red faced, you know, like a lot of Irish guys. Big nose, bulbous nose, typical Irish drinker look, with light skin and a red face with a big nose."

"Got it. Okay, don't worry about nothin'," Red said. "Just be here tomorrow morning at eight and we'll drive down to their office together."

At exactly eight am the following morning, Roberto walked into The Starlight Club. Red, Tarzan, Trenchie, and Frankie the cop were all waiting for him. With Frankie behind the wheel, they all piled into Red's Caddy and made their way through downtown Manhattan to the brokerage house. Reilly and his men were on time. They were expecting to find the three kids there working at their desks and Roberto, but they were surprised to see Roberto with four strangers.

Big Red looked at Roberto and pointed at Reilly. "Is this the bum that beat you up?"

"Yeah, he's the one." Red walked right over to Reilly and without warning, hit him with a right hand that knocked him off his feet. Red didn't give him a chance to get up. Instead, he kicked him hard in the stomach and again in the face. He reached down and grabbed a hand full of his hair and slammed his face on the hard floor. A tooth flew across the floor. The man grabbed his nose. It was broken and bloody. He then felt his mouth. Four front teeth were loose and just hanging. Red rolled the man over on his back. "You wanted my friend's son to give you a hundred fifty thousand dollars this morning? Now I'm tellin' *you* - you owe *me* a hundred fifty thou. We're takin' a little trip to the bank and you're gonna withdraw *my money*."

Reilly tried to speak. He wanted to say something but Tarzan interrupted. "I never liked you Irish bastards to begin with. You better get your ass off the floor, shithead, because we're goin' for our money right now. So go get your ugly ass into the bathroom and clean yourself up and make it fast." Reilly's two friends tried to make a move but Trenchie glared right into their eyes and then slowly pulled his jacket back to reveal his gun tucked under his belt.

Reilly, a little unsteady on his feet, did a double take of Tarzan and mumbled through a swollen mouth, "Hey, didn't I see you on television? Weren't you on trial in Mineola?"

"Yeah, that was me. What about it?"

"Nothing. Nothing. Look, you guys can have this place. We don't want any more trouble and we won't bother the kids."

"That's fine," Red said, "but we still want the one hundred fifty grand."

Reilly knew he was in dangerous waters. He had to think quickly. "Look, there's a big deal comin' down and I need this money to invest in it. I could include you in it if you'll agree to let me keep the money."

Red was curious. "What kind of deal?"

Reilly began explaining. "A friend of mine has a connection with a major movie studio. He's got the goods on a few of their top stars and he's shakin' down the president of the company for two million. And that's just the beginning. Once he starts payin', he'll be payin' us for the rest of his life, only he don't know it yet."

"What's your friend's name? What studio and who's the mark?"

"My buddy's name is Bob Gray. The company is Columbia Pictures and the guy they're shakin' down is Larry Bernstein. Bob's got the goods on his fag male star and Bernstein's three female stars will be finished in movies if we release what we have on them. Neat huh? So do you want in?" he asked while holding a damp towel to his face.

"Bob Gray's your friend?" Red questioned.

"Yeah, he's the guy I need the money for. He's got the Detroit mob backin' him on this deal."

"So why are you givin' your money to Gray instead of the Detroit mob?"

He smiled through his swollen face. "They're not interested in runnin' Columbia Pictures. That's where Bob comes in. They want him to run it for them. We'll make money on both ends. So, are you in?"

Red shook his head. "I'm not interested. Now let's go get my money."

But Reilly wasn't through quite yet. He had trouble speaking but he managed to say, "There's some bad people involved in this deal and they're takin' over the company with or without you. If you want my advice, I wouldn't mess with 'em."

"Well, I don't want your advice," Red said, almost offended that the bruised man offered it, "and as for these tough guys, they don't know who they're messin' with. Now let's go get my money." As he was about to leave Red turned to Roberto and said, "Roberto, you and your friends stay right here, in the office, until I return." The four young men nodded, still a little shaken over what they had just heard and witnessed. The viciousness that Red was capable of was a part of Red that most people never saw.

Reilly was in no position to argue. He was hoping that this money would buy his life, at least for the moment. Revenge could come later, but right now, he had to survive this day.

Tarzan covered his gun with his hand as Red ordered Reilly and gang into Reilly's car. There was a method to his madness. If any blood was to be spilled, it would ruin Reilly's interior, not Red's Caddy. Red accompanied Reilly into the bank while the other men waited in the car. Reilly, when questioned by the teller about wanting that much cash withdrawn, simply stated that it was needed for a new business that required capital. The teller dutifully drew up a cashier's check for half and the rest she gave in cash for a total of one hundred fifty thousand dollars. Once outside, Reilly handed the check and the cash to Red and both walked back to the car. Inside the car Red had Tarzan count the money. Red then placed both the cash and the check into his attaché case.

When the men arrived back at the brokerage house, Red tossed Frankie the keys to his convertible and told him to follow them. That was a clear signal to Red's men as to what was about to take place. If he let Reilly go, he would always be looking over his shoulder. Sooner or later, Reilly, like a lot of other wise guys, would make an attempt at revenge. And there was the problem with his men. Would they want revenge too? These were always the tough questions in a situation like this and they were on Red's mind as they headed toward Red's junkyard near Flushing. Red studied Reilly's men. The only conclusion he could draw was that these guys were dangerous, but he didn't want to kill them if he didn't have to. He didn't murder people without good reason. Red told Moose to stop the car. He didn't want them to see the junkyard just ahead.

"You two get out of the car," Red ordered. The two men stepped out of the car, their eyes darting everywhere, looking for a chance to run. Red knew what they were thinking. "Don't even think about it," Red said.

The younger of the two began pleading. "Please, don't do this. I have a wife and two kids. Let me go and you'll never see me again."

Red looked at the other guy. "What about you? Do you have

any kids?"

"I got a wife but no kids yet."

Red had to make a quick tough decision. If he let these guys go, they would be witnesses to a murder and he'd always worry about them either ratting on him or coming after him. He pointed to the younger man. "Give me your wallet." The man was only too eager to comply and handed Red his wallet. Red removed his driver's license, put it into his shirt pocket, and handed him back his wallet. "You two get back in the car." He motioned to Moose to continue driving into the yard. At the entrance, Red stepped out and nodded to Trenchie and Tarzan. The car moved slowly ahead until it reached a huge yellow machine that held remnants of cars. It was the car crusher. Reilly and his men instantly knew their fate. There were whimpers from inside the car, grown men pleading, pleading for their lives, begging for mercy.

Red couldn't hear the gunshots due to the noise in the junkyard, but the muzzle flashes lit up the interior of the Caddy like small bolts of lightning on a dark night. Reilly's car was then placed into the yellow machine where soon human parts and sheets of steel meshed into oblivion. Frankie drove Red and the guys back to the brokerage house where Red informed the four young men that Reilly and his men would never bother them again. The three young brokers were elated and relieved, but none dared to ask questions. There was an understood, unspoken silence.

Red turned to Roberto. "Your father's a good man, Roberto. I've known him a long time now. He did me a big favor once." As Red turned to leave, Tommy, one of the kids, asked him if they owed him anything. Red wasn't that kind of a mobster. He had his own set of standards and taking money from some kids who were struggling to keep their business above water wasn't one of them. "Nah. You don't owe me anything. Glad I was able to help you. Now go put the money that you were giving to Reilly back into the bank and start workin' again. But I will give you a little piece of advice. Don't go callin' too much attention to yourselves. Have fun, enjoy life, but tone it down a bit. Flashy people have a target on their backs. Got that?" The boys nodded, and each echoed their understanding.

Heading back to The Starlight Club, Red took the seventy-five grand cashiers check out of the envelope that Reilly had given him. He handed it to Tarzan along with the dead man's license. "Cash this check at one of our banks and take this to his widow. See that she gets it. I really hated to whack those two guys but they were witnesses to a murder. I had no choice. Make sure she gets the money - she's gonna need it." He took the remaining seventy–five thousand and parceled out fifteen thousand dollars to each of his four men. He kept the remaining fifteen for himself.

Big Red walked to a storage room in the rear of the building and opened the door. He switched on the light and looked for the box that contained Jimmy the Hat's belongings. It was still there right on the top shelf right where he had placed it after Jimmy died. He pulled it down and put the box on the table. He paused a moment before cutting the tape and opening it. There wasn't much inside the box considering how famous Jimmy was, but Red wasn't looking for much. He found Jimmy's wallet sitting on top of his meager possessions. Red opened the wallet and looked through it hoping to find that slip of paper with the name of Lana Thomas's blackmailer on it. Bingo! It was the first slip of paper he pulled out. If you remember, this guy was blackmailing Lana Thomas, the studio's biggest female star. Jimmy had stopped the guy when Jimmy's camera operator friend had videotaped an entire scene of the blackmail-taking place. Jimmy then told Larry Bernstein, the studio head, where to find the film, the proof. Bernstein had sent his studio head of security to retrieve the film and he then personally destroyed the tape. Well, when Reilly mentioned Bob Gray's name, an alarm went off in Red's head. He remembered Jimmy mentioning this name, too. Red was hoping that this would be the name on this slip of paper. Not only was his name there, but so was Gray's address, if he still lived there, that is. He could have probably located the address by way of the phonebook, but it would have taken longer because the name Gray was such a common one.

Red picked up his little black book and thumbed through it for Larry Bernstein's private number. Bernstein's secretary pressed the intercom and informed her boss that a man who called himself 'Big Red' was holding for him. Bernstein was only too happy to hear from him. "Red, I'm so glad to hear from you. Thought you might have forgotten me now that James is no longer with us."

"Not at all, Larry. I've been thinkin' about your problem."

Bernstein was hanging onto Red's every word and he asked, "You think you can help?"

"I think so Larry. I think I can make this little problem go away," Red said confidently. Larry sucked in his breath. "Really Red? That would be huge. Really huge."

"Yeah, I'll fly out there next week to see ya. This calls for a personal visit."

"Send me all the info," Bernstein replied. "There'll be a studio limo waiting for ya."

"Will do Larry."

Bernstein hung up his office phone and let out an audible sigh. He was incredibly relieved to know that Red was on his way, but the fact remained that he was on his own until Red's arrival and that was seven days away. If the blackmailers did contact him again, he'd have to come up with some excuse to put them off at least until next week.

chapter seven

Red, Trenchie, Tarzan, and Frankie the cop were all sitting at a table in the ballroom, far away from anyone who could hear their conversation. Red wanted to recap what happened earlier. "What happened today, in my opinion, isn't going to stop. I don't trust these guys. I want one of our guys to follow them day and night to find out what they're up to. Who do we have that's good at tailin' them?" The men looked at one another and appeared to be at a loss. Trenchie had been away for ten years, Tarzan had just become a member of the crew, and Frankie the cop was kept out of Big Red's business for his own good. It was Moose who offered a suggestion. He had overheard the question while bringing drinks to the table.

"How about Shooter? He's available." Red thought about it for a moment.

"I didn't think of him but you're right. He'd be perfect for this job."

Shooter, whose real name was Joey Shuterelli, was an enforcer in Red's family. He worked with the crew from the Ridgewood section of Queens. He became known as Joey Six-Gun Shooter, a derivative of his last name, but eventually the Six-Gun part was dropped. Shooter stuck. Joey was thirty-seven years old - slim, wirey, loyal, intelligent and totally ruthless. Shooter fit him because he always carried a Colt single action gun, which was the gun, almost everyone owned a hundred and forty years ago. It was known as the gun that won the west. Joey believed in reincarnation. He believed that he had lived in the Wild, Wild West. He read all about the legendary gunslingers of that era - Wyatt Earp, Doc Holliday, Wild Bill Hickock, the James Boys, the Dalton Brothers and many others. He had a 1851 Navy Colt just like the one Wild Bill owned, but since it was a black powder gun, he kept it more as a keepsake than a weapon. The gun that fascinated him most was the gun that Colt manufactured from 1873 up to the present. The single action Colt was the most popular gun the Colt Firearms company made even though Sam Colt had died in 1862 before it was introduced. This gun became synonymous with the company. It was known throughout the west as the Colt Single Action gun. It was a six gun repeater, a breakthrough gun that allowed the user to fire six rounds and use the same caliber bullet, in both his rifle and his pistol, thus avoiding the cumbersome burden of having to carry two different types of ammunition. It came in a variety of cartridge sizes.

While on vacation in Florida, Joey had attended a gun show at the Fort Lauderdale War Memorial. As he walked down one of the aisles filled with gun vendors, he spotted a single action Colt being sold by a private seller and bought it. It was a first generation Colt in perfect condition, chambered for the forty-five-caliber cartridge, and manufactured in 1903. First generation Colts generally used black powder but this gun didn't. It was manufactured after smokeless cartridges had replaced black powder. Because Shooter bought the gun from a private party, he didn't need a background check or a three-day waiting period and because it was a first generation SAA, he paid a premium price for it. Its grips were made of rare, hand-carved ivory. He had read somewhere that Wild Bill thought sissies only carried pearl handled guns but real men used ivory gripped guns. Wild Bill wore his two ivory gripped six guns when he demonstrated his shooting skills and when he dressed up in his finest, but he used the regular 1851 Navy Colts for everyday use.

Joey bought the gun along with twenty boxes of forty-five caliber cartridges. Now that he owned the gun of his dreams, he was determined to practice until he became as good a shot as any of the men he had read about in the old west. Every free moment he had, Joey practiced shooting in a warehouse that Red owned. He fired thousands of rounds for months until his efforts payed off. He mastered the quick draw and at the same time could expertly fire his six-gun. The day he put six shots into the center of the bull's eye target at twenty-five yards, he ordered a quick draw holster, custom-made, which fit under his belt. The holster pivoted on an angle and allowed Joey to not only carry his gun inside his jacket, undetected, but it also allowed him to use his quick draw with freedom of movement. He practiced different scenarios where he would spin and as he turned his body, his hand would slide along the handle of the gun where it would stick to his palm as if it were magnetized. In seconds, he could fire six bullets in a perfect grouping, spanning no more than the size of a silver dollar in the center of that bull's eye.

Red told Moose, "Get him down here. In fact, do me a favor and go get him now. It'll be faster that way."

Moose left to get Shooter and the boys settled into a discussion of what happened earlier, what the guys from Detroit might do in the future, and what the plan would be should that happen.

Red was summoned to a phone call. Tarzan used this time to talk to Trenchie. Something had been on his mind for quite some time. He pulled Trenchie aside.

"Do you mind if I ask you something Trenchie?"

Trenchie seemed a little puzzled but nodded and answered, "No, not at all."

Tarzan continued, "Before I joined with Red, I was told that you did ten years for something you didn't do. I did ten years, too, but I was guilty of what they accused me of. But you did ten years for something and didn't deserve it. Now that's something else. Could you tell me what happened if you don't mind?" Trenchie thought for a moment. He didn't like discussing his personal business but Tarzan wasn't just anyone - Trenchie liked him. He was one of the few guys he felt comfortable with.

"It happened a long time ago. After bein' in Yip's gang for about twelve years, I was initiated. I'm not gonna go into what I was into because we're all into the same thing even now. Back then Yip had just become head of the family. He was picked over Emilio Big Head Strunzi who was underboss to Johnny "Tangerine" Tangerello, our boss at the time. Tangerine died of a sudden heart attack while golfin' and Big Head assumed that he would be the boss. Big Head wasn't really liked by too many people including the guys in his crew and while he was out of town vacationing in Florida, Yip was elected by the captains to head the family. Yip was a reasonable man while Big Head ran his crew like a dictatorship. Another consideration was that Yip was a bigger earner then Big Head. He brought in a lot more. When Big Head found out that Yip was the new boss, he lost it, blew a fuse. To his face, he showed Yip respect, but behind his back, he constantly complained about how he should have been chosen to head the family. He was really bitter about it. So, with a few loyal men from his old crew, he conspired to have Yip whacked. Yip thought that all his men were loyal to him but I never trusted Big Head. I had nothin' to go on but a gut feelin' so I told Yip that from then on, he wasn't goin' nowhere without me. I told him I'd watch his back."

"That was something Trenchie." Tarzan interjected.

"Well, Yip was surprised with how passionate I was about the danger," Trenchie continued. "I know he caught my drift. I told him he had to be very careful. Sure enough, behind the scenes, Big Head was preparin' to make his move. Word got back to me - one of the men loyal to me - so I convinced Yip to carry a weapon just until things sorted themselves out. I carried one too. Big Head knew that every Saturday night, after Yip closed the Corona Gentleman's Club, that he walked to The Starlight Club to have a few drinks with his nephew Red. This one particular Saturday evenin', I felt somethin', call it intuition, but I felt somethin' in the air, had an uneasy feeling, so I stepped out the back door and walked along the alley beside the club. I was hidden by the shadows. I glanced out at the street and that's when I saw it, a car parked by a streetlight across the street about two stores down. There were four men in it. The streetlight gave off enough light for me to recognize 'em all includin' Big Head himself. I ran down the alley, back into the store, and told Yip what I saw. We took out our guns and made sure they were hot. Then we went out the back door and snuck up the alley, keeping in the shadows. We stepped out of the shadows, careful not to be seen, and walked away from the car in the opposite direction. When we were far enough from the club, we crossed the street and walked back toward the car, intendin' to kill all of 'em. Yip told me to watch his back while he took care of the 'four traitors' as he called 'em. I didn't like it, but I did as he wanted and watched him while he walked to their car. The men were so busy concentratin' on the club that they didn't see Yip raise up his gun and fire. Shots shattered the passenger window and Yip opened the door to make sure that all of 'em were dead, especially Big Head. He found him in the back seat, but there were only *three* men total, dead in the car. I had counted four, was positive that there were four, but the fourth guy wasn't there. Yip was busy checkin' out the car when I spotted him, spotted another guy runnin' towards Yip with a gun in his hand. I hollered to Yip to watch out but he couldn't hear me with his head in the car. I fired at the guy, hittin' him in the shoulder and spinnin' him in a semicircle, but on the turn, he fired back - hit me with two lucky shots - knocked the wind out of me. Felt like I was hit with a sledgehammer. I collapsed to the floor, unable to move. Yip saw the whole thing, but before he could help me, he had to finish off the fourth man. The guy saw Yip walkin' toward him. He tried to lift his gun but Yip got him with a shot to the head before he could get off a round. Yip started runnin' toward me to help me, but I heard sirens comin' closer - told him to beat it before the cops got there. 'I'll be all right.' I told him; 'There's no sense in both of us gettin' caught, so get out of here now!' I insisted. Yip knew I was right, so he took off. When the cops got there, they found three dead men in a car and me and this other guy, shot up, layin' dead in the street. I was taken to the hospital and treated for two gunshot wounds. When I recovered, I was taken into custody and questioned by the police. An autopsy had already been done and the bullets taken from the bodies didn't match the bullets from my gun, so they knew there was a second shooter. They tried to get me to talk. They offered me a deal. If I would tell 'em who the other shooter was, I would get a much lighter sentence and maybe a pass, but I wouldn't do it, wouldn't give up Yip. When I went to trial, they found me guilty and gave me ten years in the Q - San Quentin. That's it. That's my story."

Tarzan shook his head. "Wow, you could have walked if you gave Yip up. You did the right thing though and I'm sure Yip appreciated that. I would have done the same thing in your place - because there's nothing more I hate than a bum who'd rat on his friends."

"I know . . . but I didn't. He's my friend. I don't rat on

friends."

chapter eight

Swifty picked up the phone on the first ring. "Yeah Henri . . . sure. Come on over. We're all set to go. Just honk the horn when you get here and we'll come out." It was Henri's little brother's special day.

Swifty and Gonzo were out the door as soon as they heard the horn beep. Henri was driving a late model Chrysler that was a few years old, but Henri kept it looking brand new. The day was clear and the drive upstate was pleasant. They arrived at the Hackley School in less than two hours. The parking lots were full. School monitors handled the logistics of parking by guiding drivers with hand signals, showing them where to park on the crowded streets. And since the school buildings were situated on a series of hills, their cars were parked with the front pointing down a steep hill. They all walked uphill a short distance and followed signs that lead to a large tent where graduation ceremonies were about to take place. Most of the seats were taken by elderly men and women, representing old money, handed down from generation to generation. The graduates entered the tent and were led single file to their seats with girls sitting on the left and boys on the right, filling the first eight rows of seats in front of the stage. They sat through a series of boring speeches, given by both staff and students that took what seemed an interminable amount of time. The exception was the keynote speaker, given by a John A Morgenstein, an old alumnus, who had become a successful lawyer and later had gone on to become Vice-President and Chief Council to Columbia Pictures. He was impressive, very relaxed with his audience. His speech, even though long, was interesting - laced with humor. He seemed down-to-earth and approachable. Swifty decided to let him know how much he enjoyed his address and told Gonzo that he was going to try to speak with the man outside.

"Hey, I'll come with you," Gonzo said. "It'll give Henri and his brother some time to be alone. They probably have a lot of things they want to talk about privately."

Henri pointed to a gangly young man sitting in the second row who was busy scanning the crowds, looking for his big brother. He spotted Henri. "There," Henri said as he pointed," there's Jorge, my brother." A broad smile crossed Jorge's face. He was excited that his brother was there to see him graduate from high school with honors no less. Henri looked at Swifty and said, "Red better get us some big money fights, fast, because I have to have enough money to send my little bro to college, to Harvard." At that moment, Swifty spotted Morgenstein leaving with his family. His youngest daughter was in cap and gown, indicating that she had been in the graduating class. Now that it was over, the speaker appeared anxious to leave. Swifty tapped Gonzo on the arm and pointed to Mr. Morgenstein. "Come on, let's go," he said.

The boys looked around and searched for the man in the crowded reception room. They spotted him by an exit, saying a brief goodbye to some friends on his way out. The boxers were catching up fast when without warning two men stepped in front of Mr. Morgenstein as he approached his car. One of them put his hands on him in a menacing manner while the other said something to his wife. She looked frightened and raised her hand to her face as if to hide from him. She instinctively reached out to pull her daughters close as if to protect them. The boys ran over to get a closer look. One of the men had Mr. Morgenstein by his jacket collar. They weren't close enough to hear what he was saying but what he was doing to him was enough. Swifty stepped in between them.

"Are these men bothering you?" Swifty asked. Morgenstein nodded yes.

Swifty turned to the big guy and told him to back off. The guy just looked at Swifty and laughed.

"If I don't, now whatta you gonna do?" the man said sarcastically.

"I don't have to tell anyone what I'm gonna do," Swifty smarted back.

The thug turned to Morgenstein and said, "This won't take

long, then we'll finish our little talk." Swifty saw it coming - a sucker right hand amateurishly thrown out of left field. Swifty ducked it easily. Gonzo was watching, ready at any time to jump in, but he knew Swifty could handle it. This guy had no idea who he was up against - two boxers, two good friends with a bond of having served their country together - a bond that no one could understand - brother to brother, like flesh and blood.

Swifty slammed his right fist hard and deep into the guy's abdomen. The guy doubled over trying to catch his breath and when he did, Swifty hit him again with a combination of fast and furious punches. The guy folded like an accordion. It was obvious that the guy wasn't in shape at all. It was all a little too easy until his partner came at Swifty from behind. That's when Gonzo stepped in, clipping him with a hard right to the temple. He caved. And it was over that fast.

"Are you all right?" Swifty asked Morgenstein.

"Yeah, yeah," he said. "I'm fine but what about you? Where'd you boys come from?"

Swifty smiled sheepishly. "I heard your speech and I wanted to catch up to you to tell you how much I enjoyed it," Swifty answered.

Morgenstein was at a loss for words but then added, "You men must be trained in some sort of martial arts discipline the way you handled yourselves."

Swifty laughed and said, "No, me and Gonzo are professional prize fighters and we came here with a buddy of ours, another fighter, for his brother's graduation. We left them alone so they could have some time together and we came over here to speak with you."

"I'm sure glad you did. Those men have been stalking my family and me, but I didn't think they would bother me here. I guess I was wrong about that. Let me introduce you to my wife, Lydia, and my daughters, June and Gloria. Gloria just graduated and we're having a party at our home later this afternoon. We'd be honored to have you join us. Mr.? I'm sorry, what did you say your names were?

"This big lug here is Gonzo, Henri you'll meet later, and I'm Swifty. I'd like to bring my buddy Henri and his brother with us if that's all right with you."

"Absolutely. All of you can come. To be honest, I'd feel much better having you boys with us at the party. Is your friend a prize fighter too?" he asked. Swifty laughed.

"Yeah, he sure is."

Morgenstein noticed a slight smile and asked, "Did I miss something here?"

Swifty laughed again and added, "Well, Henri is not only a prize fighter but him and I fought each other. The man is tough." As Swifty was talking, Morgenstein noticed his daughter June listening intently to Swifty, her eyes glistening. She seemed captivated by the boxer who braved standing up to those guys.

At that moment, the guy on the ground stirred. Swifty bent down, reached into the man's jacket and removed his wallet just as he was trying to stand back up. He nodded toward the other guy and told Gonzo, "Get his wallet, too, and gimme his license. Let's see who these guys are. And don't take any chances. Check to see if they're wearing ankle guns." Gonzo searched both men. He found nothing on them but their wallets. Swifty asked them where their car was parked and one man pointed down the street.

"Do you have a minute Mr. Morgenstein?" Swifty asked.

"Yes. Why?"

"I want to check their car before you leave. It wouldn't do if they had more weapons hidden somewhere in there. This'll only take a minute. I'll be right back."

Swifty took the first guy by his arm while Gonzo escorted the second man. When they arrived at the car, Swifty gave it a thorough search while Gonzo watched the still aching, groaning men.

"I found two automatics in the trunk but the car's clean now so let 'em go."

When the men got into their car, one turned to Swifty and said, "This ain't over. We'll find you . . . and when we do, you'll pay for this."

Swifty laughed and said, "Be careful what you wish for 'cause you're liable to get it. Take my advice – don't come back. Could be bad for your health."

The boys watched the car speed away and waited until they lost sight of it as it made a turn at the bottom of the hill. Swifty put the guns under his belt, in the nape of his back, with his jacket hiding them. They walked back to the Morgenstein's. They were glad to see that Henri and his brother had made their way to the front of the room. The Velasquez' brothers had been looking for Gonzo and Swifty. Swifty reached under his jacket and pulled the two guns out to show Morgenstein. He put them back, making sure to cover them with his jacket.

"It's a good thing you thought to check their car," Morgenstein said while writing his address on the back of his business card, which he then handed to Swifty. "Come over whenever you like. We're hosting an after-graduation party." The boys liked that idea and decided to leave for the party as soon as Jorge returned from storing his cap and gown and diploma in his dorm room.

Henri had told Gonzo and Swifty that Hackley was a prestigious boarding school and that they'd need to be dressed nicely. They were glad they had worn their suits. Everyone there was dressed to the nines and at the party, the boys felt right at ease. Morgenstein spotted them, broke away to greet them, and insisted that the three not leave the event before he could free up some time to spend with them. Meanwhile, the boxers ate a little, drank a little, and mostly talked among themselves. Swifty, at one point, walked over to the bar to refresh his drink. As he did, he heard, "Just Pepsi?" and turned to see a smiling June, Morrgenstein's daughter. "Will you be seeing my father anytime soon?"

"Yeah," Swifty replied. "He wants to talk to us in a little while."

"No, I don't mean that," June added. "I mean, like tomorrow or during the week."

"Well, I don't think so," Swifty answered rather puzzled. "There's no reason for me to." Swifty hadn't noticed that June had been watching him from the other side of the room. She had patiently waited for her opportunity. And then he saw it. Swifty noticed the look, that feline predatory look all over her face and quickly added . . . "Or is there?" She was beautiful - long auburn hair, green eyes, these great curves, but he found himself in a convincing argument with his head saying 'don't get involved – this babe is way out of your league.'

"I couldn't believe how you confronted that brute," June said. "You didn't seem the least bit afraid."

"Well . . . I wasn't really that scared of him but you know who really scares me?" he asked conspiratorially. Her eyes lit up.

"Tell me. Who scares you?"

"You see that guy I was talking to?"

"Henri?"

"Yep. He scares me to death." And he laughed a sweet laugh. His words charmed her.

"Oh really? Why am I not buying that?"

"Well, he does," Swifty, responded.

"Well, now," June continued, "I can't say that I've ever met anyone quite like you. You knock out a guy like without batting an eye and then point to a smiling face and tell me he scares you? So, besides being afraid of Henri, tell me about yourself," she teased.

"Nope. Nothin' to tell," he said as he smiled, all the while taking note of her face, her lips, her hair.

She tilted her head and smiled. "Let me rephrase that. I never met guys like the *three* of you. Are you serious? Henri scares you to death?"

"Hell yeah, I'm serious. I fought him three times and I couldn't beat him."

"Oooh. So *that's* why you're afraid of him? Because he beat you three times."

"No, no. He didn't beat me. We fought three times . . . to a *draw*. Henri is the best fighter I ever fought." He had her then. She couldn't get enough of him.

"How many fights have you had?"

"Twenty-eight fights, no losses. My manager expects the three of us to win championship belts someday.

June smiled and said, "Pretty high goal, don't ya think?"

"Not really," Swifty replied. June's mind was swimming. Talking with him exhilarated her.

"How old are you?" she asked.

"Twenty-five."

"When did you have your last fight?"

"My last fight? That was two years ago and it was with Henri." She was a little confused.

"Two years? Why so long between fights?" She was unabashedly firing questions, one after another.

"Because I spent the last two years boxin' for the army in the Far East. Let me back up a little 'cause I'm not makin' myself clear. When I say I didn't fight for two years, I mean professionally. The three of us fought in the army as amateurs and together we won the Far East Army Boxin' Championship, but my last professional fight was two years ago."

"Can I come and watch your next fight?" June asked.

"Sure, if your father lets you."

"Wait a minute. Wait just one minute. I'm twenty-two years old. I adore my Dad but I'm a little too old for that now. If I want to come to see you fight, I'll come see you fight." She changed the subject and shot off another question.

"How'd you get the name Swifty? That's not your given name is it?" Swifty laughed. He enjoyed her questions.

"Slow down a minute," he laughed. "Where are all these questions coming from? Okay - I'm called Swifty because I knock people out - *swiftly*, that's why."

"Well that's interesting, but what's your real name?" June pursued.

"That, my dear June, I will not tell you," Swifty said as he lowered his chin a bit and looked up at her. "You can call me 'Swifty' or 'Hey You' but my real name is private, okay?" It was love right there, at that moment. He was physically strong, assertive - just the right amount of confidence that makes women swoon. June was smitten.

At that moment, Swifty felt a tap on his shoulder. It was June's father.

"Can I have a word with you Swifty?"

"Sure." And the two of them walked out to the veranda to join the other two fighters, leaving June to ponder the many questions that she hadn't gotten around to ask him yet.

Outside at a table, Mr. Morgenstein instructed all the boys to have a seat.

"I'm indebted to you boys," he began. "I don't know what I would have done if you hadn't shown up when you did. I'd like to give you something, a little reward, to show my gratitude for helping me out."

"We're not looking for any reward Mr. Morgenstein," Swifty stated. "We helped you because you were in trouble. It's not necessary, but I do have a question. It's none of my business, Mr. Morgenstein, but what did those guys want from you?"

Morgenstein took a deep breath, let it out slowly and said, "They want my studio. They want to steal Columbia Pictures from us and they're putting a lot of pressure on me. Besides being Vice–President of Columbia Pictures, I'm also their Chief Legal Counsel. I think they intended to intimidate me just to show their muscle. Who knows? They might have really harmed me but I think that this time was more about the message - letting me know that they're stalking me, know my whereabouts."

"Where are they from?" Swifty asked.

"They're out of Detroit but some of them are staying in California."

"California?" Swifty asked.

"Yes. Hollywood to be exact."

"Can I use your phone?" Swifty asked.

"Sure, it's to your right as you walk into the room." Swifty exited and returned a few minutes later. "Mr. Morgenstein, when you mentioned Columbia Pictures was being threatened with a take–over, something sounded familiar. I remembered hearing something about that so I called someone, my manager, and told him the short version of what happened today. He said he'd like to see you tomorrow."

"Who's your boss Swifty?" Morgenstein asked.

"Did you ever hear of The Starlight Club?" Swifty replied.

chapter nine

Moose parked his car in front of the Ridgewood Sporting Bar and Grill. He walked over to Charlie tending bar and asked if he'd seen Shooter.

"Yeah, he was here a moment ago. Hey Sammy did you see where Shooter went?" Charlie called out.

"He went to the head." Just then the door to the bathroom opened and Shooter walked out adjusting his jacket. Moose waved to get his attention and motioned for him to come over. Shooter ambled over.

"What's up Moose?"

"Big Red wants to see you right now. He said for you to drop everything and come with me."

"Where to?"

"The Starlight Club. We're leavin' right now."

"Okay partner. Let's vamoose. Sounds serious."

Moose took his time driving, staying within the speed limit and Shooter was getting antsy. "Come on Moose, step on it. If he wants us there right away, it must be important. Step on the gas." Moose shook his head.

"I can't go any faster Shooter."

"Yeah, why not?"

"Red lights, that's why not." Shooter leaned out the window and fired two shots knocking out the light in the center of the road and the one by the curb.

"Well now, there's no lights here to worry about. You just keep driving and I'll make sure the lights don't slow you up." Moose shook his head and just looked at him.

"You know . . . you are one crazy sonnuva bitch shootin' out red lights like that. You're gonna get us both arrested. Then what? I'll tell you what. We'll never get you to Red's, that's what." Shooter smiled and leaned back in his seat.

"You worry too much Moose. That's what's wrong with you."

The truth was that Moose rarely worried about anything.

Moose pulled his car into the parking lot across from The Starlight Club and the two men entered the bar. Moose was about to ask Tarzan, who was behind the bar where Red was, but he spotted him in the corner by the window sitting at his favorite table, reading the paper. When Red eyed them, he put his paper aside and motioned for the men to come over and take a seat. Shooter, who stood about five nine, was thin and wiry. He had a hawk-like face that rarely showed emotion. He wasn't a bad looking man but you wouldn't consider him handsome. There was a rough attractiveness to him and a devil-may-care attitude but his primary strong suit was his fierce loyalty . . . to Red. He was as dependable as they came.

"What's up Red? Must be pretty important for you to send Moose to get me when a phone call would have done the trick." Red smiled. He was pleased with how quickly Shooter could size up a situation.

"Yeah, it is important. We have some hustlers lookin' to move in on our action. They tried takin' over Trenchie's place which I don't think was a coincidence. They had to know who owned the joint. When we confronted 'em, they said they wouldn't pull that shit again in Queens, but I don't believe it. I think somethin's going on that I don't know about, so I want you to tail those guys. I want to know where they go and what they do. While I was waitin' for you two to get here, I got a call from Jake over at the Zebra club and he said two guys walked in to his place and they began askin' a lot of questions. When I asked what sort of questions, he said they wanted to know if this was one of Big Red's joints. While the two of 'em were havin' a drink, Jake who was tendin' bar, overheard them say they had to call Detroit, and then they'd be back tomorrow. I want you to hang around the Zebra club and when those guys come back, Zeke will tip you off. When Zeke does that, gimme a call right away. I'm sending Jackie Piss Clam to back you up." Shooter opened his jacket and patted his gun.

"This is the only backup I'll need if they're gonna try any rough stuff." Red's face reddened. He didn't like being interrupted when he gave an order.

"Look." he said. "Just do what I tell you to do alright! You call me if they show up and let me do the thinkin' around here. Understand?"

"Yeah boss. I didn't mean anything by it," Shooter answered, realizing that he had crossed a line with Red. "I just wanted you to know that as long as I have this," and he patted his jacket where his gun was, "I could handle anything that happens, but don't worry, I'll call you before I do anything."

"Good," Red said. "Crazy shit is happenin' pretty fast around here and it all seems to be related. I just haven't figured it all out yet." Red reached into his pocket and took out his car keys and handed them to Shooter. "Take my convertible- the blue caddy in the lot across the street. Tell Jake why you're there so he won't wonder and worry." Shooter smiled and threw the car keys a few inches in the air and like a juggler he caught them in the palm of his hand.

"Don't worry boss. I'll take care of everything." Red didn't tell Shooter about the secrets the car hid. He didn't know that the car was armor plated and had bulletproof glass. Red had the satisfaction of knowing this car would protect not only him but anyone in it. As soon as Shooter had left, Red yelled for Moose to come into his office.

"What's up boss?"

"Get on the phone and call Jackie Piss Clam. Tell him Shooter is at the Zebra Club and to get his ass over there pronto. Let him know he's Shooter's back-up and wherever Shooter goes, he goes. Got it?"

"Got it boss."

As Moose turned to leave Red added, "And one more thing. Tell Piss Clam to go there heeled. And tell him to not hesitate to use it if he has to."

chapter ten

The following morning around ten am, John A. Morgenstein walked into The Starlight Club. The club didn't open until noon so Red typically reserved mornings to discuss family business. Morgenstein waited a moment for his eyes to adjust to the dim light and then he spotted a man he assumed was Red rising from a table by the window. He walked toward him. "Hi," Red greeted. "You must be Mr. Morgenstein?"

"That's right. Who do I have the pleasure of speaking with?"

"I'm Red, Red Fortunato. I own the place. Please . . . have a seat. It's private. I can assure you that no one will hear us unless they're invited. Red instructed Moose to bring the usual guest gifts – two cups of espresso and a bottle of Sambuca. Red wasted no time. He turned to Morgenstein and said, "Swifty told me what happened yesterday. I'm glad he was there to help out. But before we begin, do you mind if I have my two associates sit in? I'd like for them to hear what you have to say." Morgenstein nodded in approval. Red lifted a phone from his table, buzzed the intercom, and asked Trenchie and Tarzan to join him.

"John, this is Trenchie." Trenchie nodded and shook his hand. "And this here's Tarzan." Tarzan smiled and shook also. Morgenstein tensed up a bit. These two men seemed a bit rough around the edges and hard. He looked at the door and thought that maybe meeting Red was a mistake. He had a momentary urge to politely excuse himself. Red, sensing his uneasiness smiled and got right to it.

"Why don't you tell us why those men are harassin' you?" he stated rather than asked. Morgenstein was quiet for a moment, trying to figure out if any of this was a good idea. There were three men sitting at the table with him, just waiting for him to speak. It was a bit intimidating. Red couldn't blame him. He knew how to read people so he took a different approach. "Look, John, I'll ask a few questions and if you feel that the question is too personal, then just don't answer it. But I think I should tell you a few things before we get started. Ya see, a few days ago Larry Bernstein contacted me. He told me a little about what's going on. Did you know that?" Morgenstein's face and eyes changed instantly from fear to both shock *and* fear. Red studied Morgenstein's face. "No? I didn't think so. A few years ago I sent one of my men, Jimmy the Hat to Larry and he made it big in Hollywood under the name of James Roman? Maybe you heard of him."

"Of course. Everyone's heard of James Roman," Morgenstein answered. Red continued.

"Did you know that Jimmy saved the studio from a major scandal when he got hold of some damaging film of Lana Thomas at a party when she was a kid? She did some, let's say, inappropriate things, things that might hurt the studio and her reputation and those things were captured on film. Lana was being blackmailed. Larry destroyed the film and he thought that was the end of it. Did you know that Larry had a problem with the union and it got so bad that one of his leadin' men was about to be killed in an 'accident'? I took care of things like this Mr. Morgenstein - took care of Larry. So, when he called me the other day, I snooped around a bit and found out that some pretty powerful wise guys are plannin' to take over Columbia Pictures by getting rid of you and Larry. Now, how they do it is another story - either by intimidation or by knockin' you off. The word I got was that it doesn't matter to them which it is as long as the goal of gaining control of the company is achieved. Well, I know who's behind the planned coup. Now, knowin' what I just told you, will you now answer my questions? If you don't, then we'll shake hands, call it a day, and part as acquaintances." Morgenstein could tell by the way he talked that Red was a man used to getting his way and used to getting results, but other than that, he didn't know anything about him.

"Okay, what is it you want to know?" Morgenstein offered. Red smiled.

"Tell me the first time you were approached by these people."

"A month ago. I began receiving some disturbing letters similar to the ones Larry received. No return address and the stamp on the envelope was never stamped from the same location. Most of the letters were stamped from out of state. I was pretty concerned over the threats so I hired a bodyguard. He was with me for three straight days, but on the fourth day, he didn't show up for work. When I finally reached him, he told me that he resigned, that he didn't want to work for me any longer and asked me to find someone else. He wouldn't state a reason."

"Was there anything besides the letters?" Red asked.

"Yes, I was confronted by two men, in front of my home, when I got out of my car one evening and I was told that if I didn't give them what they wanted, that the next time we met, there would be casualties. I never, ever, thought they would come to my daughter's school during her graduation, much less be so brazen as to threaten me in front of my family . . . but they did. And if it wasn't for Swifty, who knows what they would have done to my family or me?" Red shook his head.

"I hate hearing things like this. A man's family should be kept out of business no matter what kind of business it is. Did they ask you for money?"

"No, not directly but they did by innuendo. They told me they wanted to retain me as the company's Chief Counsel and I was instructed to convince Larry to turn over control of the company to them and when he did, they promised that would be the end of it - nobody would get hurt."

"Well, now," Red said to both Trenchie and Tarzan, "does this sound a little familiar? Sounds a lot like what happened to our stock broker friends."

"When do you intend to return to California?" Red asked.

"I'm leaving Monday morning," Morgenstein answered.

"Okay," Red continued. "All five of us are goin' with you to California. And from now on, Shooter and Piss Clam will be your bodyguards. We'll work out the logistics of your family. Don't worry; they'll be watched twenty-four seven. Just know that the guys I'm assigning are the best, so put your mind at ease and let us handle this from now on. Now seein' as how you're here through the week-end, you and your family will join us here on Saturday. We're havin' a party for Trenchie here. He's gonna be a father." Trenchie's face turned crimson. He didn't like talking about his personal affairs.

"C'mon Red. Don't go there," Trenchie said as he shook his head.

Red smiled and said to Morgenstein, "Trenchie and I go way back, all the way back to childhood. We grew up together. He's like a brother to me. Couldn't ask for a better friend."

Red quickly returned to the subject of Saturday night's party. "Try to come. You seem like a man who appreciates some of the finer things in life. Our food here is the best you'll find anywhere around these parts. I'm sure your wife and daughters will enjoy it. You're all safe here."

"Sure. Okay. We'll be here Saturday night," Morgenstein answered reluctantly. He really was not enthused about any of this but asked, "What time?"

"Dinner starts at six. I serve the best of foods," Red continued to brag. It was one of the few times that Red really kept on about something. He was proud of the meticulous selection of ingredients that it took to turn out such extraordinary gastronomical delights. He was right. His food was the finest around.

"My beef is all prime meat," Red continued. "My vegetables are straight off the farm, well pretty close," he chuckled, "and the fish here, well, it still has the hook in its mouth." Morgenstein and the other men all laughed a little. It was the first time John had loosened up a bit. "I promise you that you and the family will have a good time. Don't worry about the men who gave you trouble today. They won't bother you again while you're here in New York. They might try somethin' in California, but you'll be protected. Do you have room to put the five of us up at your home?"

"Well . . . I . . . I . . . I mean . . . sure," Morgenstein stammered. He was clearly caught off guard by this question. Up until now, he thought the guys would just be hangin' around outside the house. Come to think of it, logic dictated that they had to stay somewhere and right at the house seemed even more comforting.

"Five of us will be with you for a day or two," Red continued, "but when we leave, Shooter and Piss Clam will be with you at all times." Morgenstein nodded his head.

"We live in a decent sized house," Morgenstein added hastily.

The idea was really growing on him. "There'll be no problem finding you fellas a place to sleep. As a matter of fact, I would feel a lot better with you staying in the house with us."

"I can only think of one big problem you could have with those guys," Red smirked. That got Morgenstein's attention.

"And what would that be?" he asked with a worried look on his face.

"Those two eat like horses. They're liable to bankrupt you with their appetites."

"You had me worried there for a moment," Morgenstein responded as he let out a sigh and laughed a little. "Don't worry about that. I'll *gladly* cover their eating expenses. My wife likes to cook and so do I and there are plenty of take-out places in the area."

About an hour of discussing and planning followed. The men worked out details of the house, studied the roads in the area, and got a handle on the Morgenstein daily family schedule. Morgenstein looked at his watch and said, "I better be on my way. I promised my wife I'd be back by two and with all that's been going on, I don't want to worry her. I want to thank you. I don't know how to thank you actually, but I'll see you on Saturday night and we'll talk more."

"Good," Red said as he gently patted the table with his hand. "I look forward to seein' you and your family. Swifty tells me you have a lovely wife and two beautiful daughters. A word of caution - keep your eyes on Swifty. He's young, just returned from the army, and he's liable to steal one of 'em away."

Morgenstein laughed and said, "Don't worry - when it comes to my daughters, I have eyes all over my body." Morgenstein said his goodbyes to Trenchie and Tarzan and just as he was about to leave, he walked over to Red and thanked him once again for his help. Red waited a few moments for him to leave and then asked, "Whadda you think?" He always solicited input from his men. This was no different.

"He seems like a helluva guy. He don't deserve what those rats are doin' to him and his family," Tarzan replied.

"Yeah, I agree." Trenchie chimed in. But Trenchie being the eternal pragmatist asked, "After we help 'em out, what's in it for us?" Red thought a moment.

"I made up my mind a long time ago," Red began, "that one way or another, I'm goin' into the movie business. Maybe by takin' care of their problem, a door will open and that just might be the door I've been waitin' for." The men were about to leave the table when Moose came over.

"Boss, you know what I just heard? Bam Bam and Peanuts were in the city last night having dinner at Cine 9 – that posh new eatery everybody's talking about in Manhattan – and because they're part of us, our family, they were given a pass on the meals."

Big Red was not happy. His nostrils flared and his face turned cherry red. Red always had this way of his nostrils flaring open like a clean shot highway when he got mad and he was mad now. "Who told you this?"

"One of the waiters from the neighborhood. He lives in Corona Heights and stops in for a drink once in a while before headin' for work." Everyone in Red's mob knew how he felt about taking advantage of someone because of who they were. Red, as did Yip his uncle who was the boss before he was killed, always made it a point to never to take a free meal from anyone. If a waiter brought over the check and told them there was no charge for the meal, they would each say the same thing – 'Look, when I come in here, I'm just another customer looking to enjoy a good meal. I always pay.' Then each man was to generously over tip the waiter. Everyone respected Red and Yip because they didn't take advantage of their power. That's what really pissed Red off about these two knuckleheads. "Get word to 'em. Tell 'em I wanna see 'em right away. I don't care what they're doin' or where they are. Tell 'em to get over here right away. Capiche?"

It wasn't long before the two men were standin' before Red receiving' a tongue lashing while Trenchie and Tarzan looked on. Red looked at Bam Bam and said. "Do I treat you guys good?"

"Yeah boss. Why?"

"Do you make enough money with me?" The two men looked at each other not knowing where this conversation was going.

"Yeah boss, you treat us real good."

"So if I'm treatin' you good and you're makin' a lot of money tell me, why the hell is it you can't pay for a meal? You have to get it on the arm." The two men looked at each other sheepishly.

"What meal are you talking about Red?" one man asked as he quizzically looked at the other.

"You know God damned well what meal I'm talking about! You two morons went to dinner at Cine 9 and walked out without payin'. Everyone in that place works hard for their money and because you work for me, you think you have the right to walk in a joint, eat a meal, and walk out without payin' for it, knowin' that you represent me and especially knowin' that I always pay for my own meals wherever I go? Now if I can pay for my own meals, it stands to reason that you should pay for yours, am I right? Or am I missin' somethin' here?" Red *always* paid his own way. That was one of the reasons people respected him so much. The other being that he was so approachable - he'd listen to anybody with a problem. Every one of his men knew his policy . . . you pay your way. That was a slogan of his 'You Pay Your Way.' Other crime family members liked to usurp their power by taking advantage of their positions in life. They liked the power that intimidation gave them. They loved entering a place and wining and dining, watching people buzz around like bees, falling all over themselves, and hearing that it was 'all on the house,' but not Red. No, not Red.

"I want you to guys to go back to Cine 9 and have dinner again. I want you to order one of everything on the menu - everything. Only this time you pay for your meal and you will leave a very generous tip for the waiter. You will also find the waiter who served you before and you will leave him a generous gift, too. Do you understand?"

"Yes boss," the men hastily answered.

"Good. Let me know when you're plannin' your next outing there and don't let me hear of you pullin' this shit again - makes me look bad. Now get out of here." After the two men had exited, Red turned to his two men.

"I never want to be like that cheap bastard Profaci who doesn't share a thing with his men. I want my guys to make money. Hell, there's enough dough comin' in for everyone to live well. I pay my men good - no shakin' down some poor chump who works minimum wage and scrapes and scrimps just to put enough money away to feed his family. Not happenin' on my watch."

chapter eleven

The Starlight Club was always crowded on Saturday nights. It was an honor for anyone to receive a personal invitation from Big Red for something on any night, but especially a Saturday night - a special invitation meant a special event. Red always did it up right - the finest money could buy. That reminds me. Let me tell you the story of his meats.

One day Bobby, who at the time worked for Four States Meat and Poultry Supply, visited The Starlight Club an account he always wanted, and pleaded with Red to give his meats a try. Bobby was a guy who had a wife and kids to feed. He worked hard and new meat orders were a big deal to his pocket. He wanted to prove to Red what quality meat should taste like. Bobby challenged Red to a blind steak test – use the same seasonings on two steaks, one from the supplier that Red currently used and one from Bobby's 'prime cuts', and cook them exactly the same way to the same temperature. The chef, the staff, and Red would all judge the steaks. If Bobby's steak won, then Red would be a new steady customer. Red liked the kid and appreciated anyone who would go out on a limb like that. That was the sort of confidence that he respected in somebody. He relented. Steak tasting day came and sure enough, Bobby's steak won hands down. Red had unknowingly been buying meat that was substandard and was really not thrilled that his chef had not brought this to his attention. From that day on, he gave Bobby all of his orders - both meat and poultry and became Bobby's biggest account. That one client provided Bobby with a comfortable living but Bobby didn't take Red for granted. He personally selected the best ribs and hinds of beef he could find. Many a time his hands froze over as he picked through barrels of beef liver until he found the few that were the right size and the right color. He would sort through hundreds of prime ribs and shell strips of beef. With Bobby's efforts, The Starlight Club soon acquired the reputation of being one of the top restaurants in New York City.

Karen and Marco were seated at the table with Trenchie, and

a very pregnant Mary, when the grand ballroom doors opened and in walked Red escorting the Morgenstein family. The Morgensteins were struck by the beauty of the room, each commenting on its exquisite beauty. Red led the family to a ten top in the back, joining the already seated guests. Lydia Morgenstein was seated next to Karen. The two ladies chatted amiably as Mary strained to hear. Mary, defying the assigned seat protocol, asked Trenchie to switch seats with her so she could join the girls' conversation. Before long, the three women were chatting away like old friends. But June, who was sitting next to her father, had no interest in talking. Her eyes were fixated on the doors of the ballroom, hoping Swifty would walk in at any moment. Her heart fluttered when she finally saw the three boxers saunter into the ballroom. There he was - Swifty and friends. It was hard to hide June's glow. Swifty was different, she said later to everybody. Seemed she had always dated guys from prestigious colleges, the preppy type, but Swifty was a bit scrappy and she liked that. She had always thought that prizefighters were just ignorant ole ogres with cauliflower ears and broken noses. Swifty was different. He had no marks on him, and he, along with his friends, were all pretty nice looking in a rough sort of way. He had a small town boyish look and if you didn't know he was a fighter, you would never have guessed it.

Swifty had no idea that June was coming to Red's event. June approached his table quietly from behind, covered his eyes with her hands, and said. "Guess who?"

"Ann Margaret," he replied. "No I'm wrong, it's Elizabeth Taylor." She put a make believe frown on her face and said. "No silly. It's someone faaaar more interesting. Take another guess."

"Wait a minute. The voice is familiar. Could this be the gal that I met at the graduation ceremony?"

"Well, it could be but how many did you meet at the graduation?" she shot back.

"Well, let's see - there was Lisa and Tina, oh, and that pretty blonde - Linda, yeah Linda."

"Really?" she said. "And that's it?"

"Yep, that's it. There was another little girl but I cannot remember her name for the life of me."

"Well," she said as she smacked him on the head. "Does this help you remember?" and she smacked him again. Swifty broke into laughter. Gonzo and Henri just sat there smiling at the banter-taking place between the two of them.

"Got ya, didn't I?" Swifty asked as he turned to her and smiled.

"Yes, you did," June giggled. "Now how about a dance before they serve dinner?"

Swifty was full of confidence most everywhere, everywhere but the dance floor. He had never learned the finer points of becoming a good dancer and for someone who had to dance a lot inside a boxing ring, well, on the dance floor, he felt a bit inadequate, but in the spirit of the evening, he followed June right onto the dance floor. Good thing he did. He found himself dancing to the rhythm of a slow foxtrot. It was a great excuse to get to hold her. June moved her hands up and down his muscled arms pretending to be trying to find a comfortable position for her hands. She could feel the tightness of the muscles in his back as they danced - she knew that she had to see more of him. Just then Ralph and Gibby walked in and June asked Swifty who the two scary looking men were.

"They're friends of Big Red's."

"Big Red? Is that the man my father came to see?"

"Yeah, that's the guy. He's also my manager."

"Do you trust him?" she asked. Swifty stopped dancing, looked at her for a moment and in a serious tone stated, "I trust him with my life." It was as though she had touched a nerve and a dark side had manifested itself. "So don't go there," he said, and then as quickly as his anger had reared its head, it left, and he placed his hand on her waist, pulled her close to him once again, and off they went . . . dancing. Swifty began to walk her to her table but she stopped him.

"I'd rather sit with you and your friends if you don't mind."

"Are you always so pushy?" he asked. June's face fell. She didn't know how to take that. Swifty saw that he had hurt her feelings. "Just kidding," he added. "Come on. We have a few empty seats at our table." She chose the empty seat right next to him. June gazed around the room once again taking in the beauty of the ballroom.

"How long have you known Red?" she asked.

"Red was in the money lendin' business and whenever I needed money, I would borrow from him. He never bothered me about the money even long after it was due. But if I wanted to fight, I had to fight for him and no one else. My life was goin' nowhere and I only fought to pay Red the money I owed him. Then I'd borrow some more and blow that on good times and one day Red decided that I should have a life, so he bought my contract and became my manager. He's investin' some of my money so when I get older, I'll have somethin' to fall back on."

"And you believe him?"

"There you go again. Of course I believe him. Red is one of the richest men I know. He has businesses and he inherited millions from his uncle. Do you think he needs to steal the few dollars he's investin' for me?" he answered clearly annoyed. He didn't like where this conversation was going and he wasn't used to a woman questioning him about his personal business. "Now drop it. I don't wanna talk about him anymore and you need to learn not to stick your nose in people's personal affairs, especially mine. Understand?" June blanched. She wasn't used to being spoken to like this, especially by a man. It was just another reason that Swifty was different. But June knew that she had made a mistake by talking to him like she did and she needed to think fast to salvage the situation. She put her hand on his arm.

"I'm sorry. I didn't mean to pry. It's just that I never met a guy like you before so please forgive me if I ask too many questions." That seemed to mollify him. Swifty relaxed.

"It's alright," he said. He glanced at her then felt kind of bad for coming down on her so hard. "You know . . . me and the boys are fightin' at Sunnyside Gardens next month. Why don't you come and see us? If you tell me you'll come, I'll have tickets waitin' at the box office, that is ... if you wanna come." Her face brightened.

"I'd love to come. Could I bring my two girlfriends? Would that be alright? I mean I don't want you to think I'm being pushy." Swifty laughed. June loved hearing him laugh.

"That'd be great. Bring two of your pretty girl friends for my two buddies."

"Deal," June responded.

Henri was a striking Latino man with jet-black hair and a set of pearly white teeth that you could see a mile away. He was a catch for any girl. Gonzo was another story. He was six feet four, well built, with dark hair, cut military style short, but he was the only one of the three that had noticeable scars. His nose had been broken a few times and his face had been cut with a knife when he was nineteen years old. However, his rugged looks, devil-may-care personality, and happy-go-lucky disposition was appealing to women.

Morgenstein complimented Red on the food and then remarked, "This place is beautiful, so different. What a wonderful surprise. And thank you - I'm glad my wife and kids are enjoying themselves after what happened. While I have the opportunity, I'd like to ask you something."

"What is it?" Red asked.

"I was so grateful for Swifty and Gonzo helping me that I wanted to do something for them, but they wouldn't accept anything from me."

"Yeah that's the way those boys are," Red said proudly.

"Well, I thought of something else. That young man - Henri Valesques, You manage him right?"

"Yes I do. He's Swifty's friend. The three of 'em just returned from spendin' two years in the Far East and now that they're back, they asked me to manage 'em."

"My point is," Morgenstein continued. "I know that the young man had to fight in order to earn money to send to his brother to the Hackley School and now he's going to continue fighting in order to earn more money to send him to college. Am I right?"

"Yes you are."

"Well, my point is - I want to pay for his brother Jorge to go to the college of his choice." Red looked at Morgenstein with a completely surprised look.

"You'd do that for the boy?"

"Yes I would and since I'm a lawyer, I can set up an educational trust fund for him."

"Well let's get him over here right now and you can give him the good news." Red motioned for Moose to come to the table. "Get Henri and ask him to come here."

"Sure boss." Morgenstein noticed the respect Moose gave Red and how his words were never questioned. They were just obeyed without question. This was a simple request but Morgenstein had the feeling that no matter what the request from Red, Moose would oblige. A few minutes later Henri came to the table.

"Did you want to see me Red?"

"Yes. Mr. Morgenstein here has something to tell you. Henri looked at Morgenstein questioningly.

"Red told me that you fought to earn money to put your brother through school. He said that you intend to use the money you earn fighting to pay for your brother's college tuition, am I correct?"

"Yes. That's true. I want my little brother to get a good education, have a decent chance in life."

"I want to cover your brother's college expenses," Morgenstein said matter-of-factly. "Tell him to choose any college and I'll pay for it. I'll just have to ask you a few questions in order to set up a trust fund for him. Is that agreeable to you?" Henri was speechless. He tried not to tear up and he fought hard against it, but the tear won and the big ole strapping military tough guy fighter managed to let a lonely teardrop stream down the right side of his face. This was the question that had been nagging him since his brother's graduation. Where the hell would he get the money to send Jorge to college? Even if he had fought every day, he knew that he couldn't make that much money. Now this man was sitting in front of him, a man he had just met and hardly knew, and was offering to pay for his brother's education. Henri struggled for words.

"But why? I mean, I will be eternally in your debt and don't worry I'll pay you back as soon as I can. All I have to give you right now is my word but it's as good as gold."

"I don't want your money Henri. I'm a financially blessed man. I want to do this in return for what your friends did for me." Henri was so taken by this turn of events that his eyes now filled completely with water. Henri sat patiently and answered Morgenstein's many questions necessary for the legal documentation.

This all seemed like a dream until Henri heard, "Okay, I have everything I need. The only thing you have to do is let me know what college your brother wants to attend. His tuition will be paid in full for four years. He'll have a credit card for his books, clothes, rent, typewriters, food, and whatever else he needs. I'll be doing a lot of business with Red so if you have any questions, pass them to him and he'll see to it that I get them." Henri walked back to his table in a daze. He couldn't believe what had just happened. He had simply agreed to accompany Swifty to The Starlight Club and meet Big Red – all this from just saying yes to a friend. Maybe Swifty was right. Maybe there was something magical about The Starlight Club. Whatever it was, he liked it. God bless Morgenstein, he thought.

When dinner ended, Red excused himself from the table, went to the podium and took the microphone. "Excuse me ladies and gentlemen," he began. "The last time I was at this podium, two things happened. One was when my friend Trenchie proposed to his beautiful wife Mary. The second was when I introduced a young man from the neighborhood by the name of James Roman. Do you remember him?" Applause and whistles filled the room. "Well, tonight it has to do with Trenchie and Mary again. Tonight we're celebratin' an addition to The Starlight Club - a little Trenchie Jr," he laughed. "Okay, maybe a little Mary Jr., but I say it's a boy, but. . . I did not invite you here to The Starlight Club to listen to me talk about my friends and their babies. So, let's just all toast to Trenchie and Mary and get back to havin' a good time. And just to make sure of that, I have a little treat for you." Red turned and looked behind him at the curtains. "You boys can come out now." A ten-piece band emerged from behind the stage and began filling the stage with their instruments. "Ladies and Gentlemen, please welcome . . . Mr. Jerry Vale." The crowd went crazy. Vale, one of the most popular male vocalists in America walked out to thunderous applause. Seems Red had called his buddies at the famous Copa Cabana in Manhattan and asked him if they could arrange to get Jerry Vale, Vic Damone, or even the impossibly hard to get Frank Sinatra, for a one night affair at The Starlight Club. Money was no object. Red received a call from the Copa a short time later - Vale was available.

Red was at his table, fully engaged in conversation and enjoying the big band sounds, when Ralph and Gibby walked over. They apologized for interrupting and asked him for a private moment. Red led them to a quiet table far from the other guests. Ralph did the talking while Gibby scanned the room, as was his habit, making sure there was nothing unusual that might require some attention.

"We heard that you have a problem," Ralph said. "I want you to know that me and Gibby are available if you need us." Red embraced Ralph.

"Thanks guys. I didn't call you because you don't work for me - you work for the Genovese's."

Ralph nodded and said, "Understood, but we can still help our friends on our own time so don't worry about that. Call us if you need us." Red smiled at Ralph's offer.

"I hope it doesn't come to that, but it's nice to know that I can still count on you guys."

The two men turned to leave then Ralph looked back at Red and said, "Thanks for invitin' us Red. It was a great party."

chapter twelve

Jacky Piss Clam was on the phone bringing Red up to speed on what was happening at the Zebra Club.

"Boss, you were right. Those two guys came back last night and threatened Jake. They said that unless he pays them protection money, they'd hurt him first and then wreck his bar." Red frowned. He was not a happy camper.

"You guys didn't do anything to them, did ya?" Red asked.

"Nope. We figured we'd call you first and fill you in."

"Good. Come on back to the club. I don't want to talk on the phone. We'll discuss it when you get here." When Shooter and Piss Clam arrived at The Starlight Club, Red was waiting for them by the front door. Instead of going into his soundproof office to discuss the situation, he motioned for the guys to follow him into the lot across the street. Once there, they walked into the mechanic's office, out a side door to a mechanics bay, and through another door in the rear that opened into a small area just large enough for a picnic table. Red swept The Starlight Club every three days for bugs to weed out inquiring minds. Even though it was probably safe to talk there, he was never one for taking chances. He didn't want some snooping feds eavesdropping, using one of their remote devices. He motioned for the men to come closer. "I want you guys to camp out at the Zebra Club and keep a sharp eye out for those guys. The next time those two morons come into the club, I want you to nab 'em and take 'em to the new baseball stadium under construction at Flushing Meadows. Take 'em right to the area where the cement trucks pour concrete into the forms, the forms that make the up walls of the stadium and then . . . plug both of 'em. I wanna make a statement with these two guys. Don't make 'em part of the architecture. Just leave 'em there. I want 'em found. I want 'em seen. I wanna send a message to Detroit that you can't just waltz into Queens and take over our territories. Not gonna happen."

When morning arrived, Piss Clam and Shooter met Jake at his home and followed him to work. They parked their car in the Zebra Club's small employee parking lot at the rear of the club. Satisfied that everything inside checked out, they would seat themselves at a table in the corner with a bird's eye view of the front door. With two fingers, they motioned for Jake to bring two coffees to the table and that was the routine for two days. Red's men became constant fixtures at the Zebra Club all throughout the day. They were there when the club opened and left when Jake locked the front door. They followed Jake home, keeping a discreet distance. They waited outside for the living room light to blink twice – Jake's message that no one but his family was in the house. Once the signal was given, they drove slowly past the cars parked near Jake's house, checking for anything suspicious.

On the third day, a Thursday, the bar wouldn't open until noon. Two men walked into the Zebra Club shortly after it opened and headed straight to the bar. They didn't notice Shooter and Piss Clam sitting at their table hidden in the shadows – the one that gave them a view of both entrances. Jake was busy cleaning the bar when the two men grabbed the damp cloth from his hand. Satisfied that they had his attention, one man said, "You got money for us?"

Jake answered, "Look guys. I'm already paying Big Red Fortunato for protection. I can't be giving money to the two of you. It's just not right

"This has nothing to do with fair," the man who appeared to be the leader sneered. "Where's Big Red's protection when you need it Jake? Why isn't Big Red protecting you now?"

At that moment, Shooter shot out of his chair and said, "His protection is right behind you . . . shithead," he said. The men were startled. Shooter continued, "Put your hands on the bar where I can see 'em and don't make any funny moves or I'll drill ya . . . right where you stand." Shooter was standing there unarmed, barking orders. Both men, as fast as a snake, went for their guns but Shooter's gun was out and aimed at them before they could clear their holsters. Shooter nodded to Piss Clam. "Get their guns and do a search. Check the ankles, guys." Piss Clam patted down both men. He found one ankle gun and placed it with the others onto the bar. Shooter picked up one gun, put it in his coat pocket, and told Jake to put the others somewhere safe. Piss Clam began going through their wallets until he found their Detroit licenses. Shooter reached into the side pocket of his jacket and pulled out the two sets of handcuffs that Red had given him and handed them to Jake. Jake cuffed both men's wrists and Shooter and Piss Clam headed out the door, one gun to one man each, and right in the small of their backs. Shooter sat in the back of the rental car with one of the men and trained his gun on the nape of the neck of the other as he ordered him to drive, handcuffed, toward the construction site of the new baseball stadium. Piss Clam followed in Red's car. The driver, all the way there, kept warning Shooter that they worked for a powerful Detroit family, that there would be severe retaliations if anything happened to them. He kept shooting his off his mouth about a second Valentine's Day massacre. Shooter just kept answering, "Yeah, yeah. You're scarin' me. Now shut up and drive."

They parked both cars near the future site of the home team dugout. Shooter ordered the two men to stay in the car. He got out, walked around to the driver's side, opened the door, and without so much as a word, shot them both, point blank, using the gun that had been removed from one of the now dead men. Gunshots reverberated throughout the empty stadium. Piss Clam sat patiently, seemingly unfazed at the shots. He watched as the flashes lit up like little fireworks. Shooter removed the handcuffs from each man and placed them into his pocket. And as a final parting message to Detroit, he put the barrel of the gun close to the face of each man and methodically shot him again, rendering each man virtually unrecognizable. Then Shooter meticulously wiped the gun clean and threw it into the back seat.

chapter thirteen

Red was on the phone tying up some loose ends so he could leave for the West Coast on Monday with some sort of peace of mind. One loose end was his three fighters. Red phoned Benny Spinoza, the fight card manager for Sunnyside Gardens, and apologized for calling him at home on a Sunday morning. He expressed to him that he was leaving town and wanted a match scheduled for all three boxers before he left. Spinoza was only too happy to accommodate Red's request. All three were amazing fighters - a good draw for boxing fans. Swifty and Henri were popular fighters in Queens and Benny's customers remembered the three tough fights they had with each other. Now Red was offering him a third fighter, a heavyweight. A good heavyweight on the card always filled the house. Benny knew that Red wouldn't send him a stiff. He quickly agreed to line up a fight for the guys. He placed Red on hold for on a moment and returned to say, "Okay Red. I have an opening on Saturday night August the third, three weeks from now. Does that work for you?" Red settled back into his chair.

"That sounds great Benny, thanks."

"Okay it's confirmed." Benny said. "Send me some mug shots and stats and have your boys at the arena by seven pm. They'll be the three final bouts of the evening. Your heavyweight will fight the main event. Fans love watching a heavyweight bout." Red was pleased.

"I'll have the boys there by seven. Thanks again Benny." When he hung up Red leaned back, once again, into the plush leather chair, pleased that business was moving along, including that issue that Shooter and Piss Clam had resolved.

Gonzo was the only unknown in these fights and Red wondered how he would do. He knew that the other two fighters would put on a good show, but Gonzo was a question mark. His record wasn't bad. Fifteen wins, thirteen by knockout, two losses

– not bad he thought. Red smiled, knowing that Gonzo had been training with Swifty and Henri. He knew those boys would motivate him and get him into shape.

Moose placed three large chairs around the large desk in Red's office. When the Henri, Gonzo, and Swifty arrived, Red told the three boys that he was leaving town on unexpected business. "But I have some good news for you. I've scheduled fights for all three of you for Saturday, three weeks from now, at Sunnyside Gardens. I'll be back in time, but until then I hired Gil Clancy, the best in the business, to train you, and if for some reason I *can't* get back, you listen to him. He's waitin' right now for the three of you at Stillman's gym. So scram. Train hard and listen to him."

"How do you know Gil Clancy?" Swifty asked.

"His father was a commercial artist."

"What's that?" Swifty sort of mumbled.

"He's a guy who designs and paints signs for a store. He lives in Rockaway Beach. I did him a few favors. That's where I met his son Gil Clancy Jr. Satisfied?"

"Yeah. Thanks Red. I was curious that's all." Red nodded in acknowledgment and then pointed to Gonzo.

"I checked your record. It's a good one and you won those fights without really trainin' for them. Put your heart into what Clancy tells you and you'll all be champions. Now, I don't know if you know it or not but I never really intended on gettin' in the fight game. I just got into this racket because Swifty was nothing but a lazy sonnuva bitch going nowhere – aggravated the hell out of me whenever I thought about him. He would have just kept partyin' if I hadn't stepped in and bought his contract. Now, I don't want any bullshit from any of you. I wanna be proud of you so train hard, fight hard, do your best and leave the rest to me. Listen to Gil Clancy and learn what he has to teach you. It just might secure your future. Your fight is three weeks from now so get in shape and be at the arena by seven pm on fight night. Oh and Gonzo . . . you're fightin' the main event so make sure you're in shape for it because I wasn't told who you guys will be fightin'." Red turned to Swifty and Henri, tilted his chin downward and sternly said, "But that won't matter if you're in shape." He was sending them a message, one that wasn't lost on the boys. Red didn't like laziness. "Now get out of here. I want you at Stillman's gym in an hour. Got that?"

Swifty looked at Red and said, "Red, Stillman's is on Eighth Avenue in Manhattan. That's four blocks from Madison Square Garden and that's all the way over on the West side. We'll never make it in an hour." Red nodded.

"Then get there as soon as you can and don't make any stops on your way there, understand?" The boxers unanimously nodded. "Now go train hard and make me proud. I don't like being embarrassed."

Next on the agenda was Moose. He didn't know it yet, but he and Frankie the cop, were going to be in charge of the club while Red was gone. He wanted and needed Trenchie and Tarzan in California with him. Red thought for a moment and decided that more was better. He'd take Shooter and Jackie Piss Clam, too. Red called Shooter and told him to pack a bag. Then he called Piss Clam and gave him the same instructions. Next, he called John Morgenstein and told him to book five seats on whatever flight he was taking to the west coast and gave him the names. Morgenstein was eager to do so and assured Red that it was no problem, that everything was considered a company expense, a major company expense for that matter. There was still one dangling little thread that needed attention before he could tie the final knot and leave in peace. Charlie "Tag" Tagorelli picked up on the second ring.

"Tag here."

"Tag, it's Red."

"Red, is that really you? Christ, it's been a while. How can I help you?"

"I got a little business to take care of in California. I'm flyin' into LAX with four business associates and I need some office products. If you could meet me there, I'll give you a complete list, but for now, here are some of them. I'll need some regular staple guns and one or two automatic staplers, the ones that hold the large staples. Do you have any in stock?"

"Yeah, I have a few left."

"Good. I'll need a few lighters too. Some of the guys still

smoke. Nasty habit. Do you have any in stock?"

"Yeah, as a matter of fact I have a few Zippos, the custom Zippos, so they're gonna cost you a little more than the regular ones. Not many people smoke any more but I have what you're lookin' for in stock."

"Perfect. How fast can I get 'em?"

"Well, I'll meet you at the airport, get your full order and go back to the warehouse. I should have them for you later in the evening."

"That's great Tag. I'll call you back when I confirm the flight info."

"Good. I'll be waiting for your call," Red said and hung up the phone. Red had just told Tagorelli that he needed two assault weapons, a few hand grenades and some other guns.

chapter fourteen

The plane took off from LaGuardia at two twenty-five in the afternoon and arrived at LAX at four twenty five-pm west coast time. Charlie Tags was waiting by the luggage carousel. Red spotted him right away and waved to get his attention. He mouthed, "I'll be right there."

Red instructed his men to wait for the baggage and he walked toward Charlie. In typical Italian fashion, the two men embraced - two old friends exchanging fond hellos. They hadn't seen each other in person for a while. Red tilted his head toward the door and the two men headed outside, through the automatic doors, away from the crowds, where they could have a more private conversation. They stepped out into the hot Southern California sun. Nearby, they found a shady spot, in an alcove near the doors leading in and out of the airport.

"It's great to see you Red. It's been too long," Tag said.

"Yes it has. It's good to see you too, Tag." Red waited a moment before speaking while Tag lit up a smoke. "You still smokin'? Didn't your mother tell you smokin's not good for you?"

"I know. I know. One of these days I'll stop, but for now it calms me, ya know? I cut down a lot and now I smoke half of what I used to, but even cutting down like I did, I still smoke too much." Red tried not to be obvious as he looked around making sure that there were no ears listening. He reached into his jacket pocket and palmed a slip of paper, which he handed to Tag.

"These are the other items."

Tag glanced at it and said, "A single action Colt? You gotta be kidding me . . . a six shooter? Who uses that gun in this day and age?" Red smiled.

"Yeah I hear you, but one of my men specializes in this weapon. He's as deadly a shooter and as fast a draw artist as any of the old time gunfighters so I'd appreciate it if you could locate one for him. You'll be paid for the guns when they're delivered and when I go back east, I'll either give them back to you or tell you where to pick 'em up. If I decide to get into the movie business, then I'm gonna need the guns, so I'll just store them in a locker somewhere. But for the time being, I just need to rent 'em, borrow 'em. I'll call you as soon as I know where I'll be stayin' and we'll get together later."

"Don't worry about the weapons. I'll hold them until you make up your mind what you're gonna do. If you decide to open a business here, then I'll just deliver them to you here to whatever address. It'll give us another chance to get together again." Red smiled and nodded in agreement.

Red and Tag had been part of Yip's mob until Tag flew west to visit his ex-wife and three kids in Anaheim. Once there, he really liked it and decided to stay. When his ex-wife realized he was serious about staying in California, she invited him to stay with her and the kids and yes, you guessed it, they got along well and eventually remarried. His wife Susan said that she did it for the kids but truth be told, they still loved each other. She knew that even though Tag had changed his ways in regards to family relationships, he still had the same roguish profession. She just chose to turn a blind eye this time. Lots of people needed weapons in southern California - the Latino gangs, the Mexicans, the wise guys, the drug runners from Latin America. Everybody needed guns and Tag had them and what he didn't have, he knew where to get them. He had a prosperous business running guns and he was careful to cover himself by making some pretty generous donations to the local judges and politicians.

Tag left his warehouse in Anaheim and headed to the Hollywood Hills address that Red had given him. Red wasn't impressed easily but John Morgenstein's sixty-five hundred square foot house, nestled on approximately two acres of land, was stunning. It boasted seven bedrooms, two kitchens, a large covered patio and a screening room the size of a small theatre.

Red had already prepped Morgenstein and had insisted on privacy in order to protect John's position within the movie company as well as his livelihood as an attorney. Morgenstein's butler greeted Tag when he arrived and escorted him straight to

Red's bedroom - a large suite complete with a bar and outdoor deck that looked out over the heated Olympic sized swimming pool. With all its amenities, it appeared to Red and the boys that the bed was added to the room as an afterthought.

Tag opened up a large duffle bag. It was identical to the ones the soldiers in Korea carried, only this one was designed to carry guns, all sizes of guns. The first package Tag removed from the duffle bag was a set of handguns wrapped in a large, chamois type cloth. This protected the guns from scratches. He laid the bundle on the bed and unfolded the cloth. The first gun he revealed was a forty-five caliber S.A.A. Colt, single action. Shooter's eyes lit up.

"Red, you remembered. Thanks a million."

"Don't thank me. Thank Tag here. He's the one who found it for you."

Shooter looked at Tag. "Thanks man. That's pretty cool."

Tag smiled and said, "I only got it for you because Red tells me you're good with it. So when this is over, you're gonna give me a little demonstration, right?"

"You got a deal. I'll show you how this gun should *really* be used." After all the handguns were unwrapped, Red's eyes locked on a forty caliber Sig. He reached down and took that one for himself and he told his men to each choose one of the remaining guns for themselves. When the guns were divvied up, Tag reached into the bag and pulled out four of the new heavy bulletproof vests. He then pulled out another long package and unwrapped two AK forty-sevens. Tag was like a drill sergeant, a drill sergeant who was doing a television commercial, explaining the automatic weapons.

"The AK-47 is a selective-fire, gas-operated, 7.62×39mm assault rifle," he explained, "and absolutely perfect for what Red has in mind.". Tag then lifted the duffle bag, which looked to be empty, turned it upside down, shook it a little, and out rolled two hand grenades right onto the soft folds of the bed. The men's eyes all widened and Shooter shouted as he jumped back, "Shit, man. Are you crazy? Those are hand grenades." Tag picked up the grenades and casually lobbed them about a foot into the air, just to make a point and caught them with ease as they came back down. Then he tossed the grenades to Red. Red caught them easily and smiled.

"You even managed to get two of these," Red commented as if not at all surprised.

"Yep, I sure did, but you might not be laughing when I tell you the price of these big boy toys," Tag added.

With all the weapons hidden safely out of sight, Red used the fancy little intercom that rang right through to Morgenstein's study and asked him to join them upstairs in Red's room.

"I need to go over a few things on the agenda for tomorrow," Red stated. A few moments later Morgenstein was upstairs, his full attention directed toward Red.

"John, I want you to call Larry Bernstein and set up a meeting for us early tomorrow morning."

"I'll set it up right now," Morgenstein replied and he picked up the phone, placed it on speakerphone, and dialed Bernstein. "Larry, it's John. I just arrived and I'm with Red and a few of his associates. I have you on speakerphone. Red would like to meet with you at your office. What's a good time for you early tomorrow morning? "

"Red, I know you can hear me," Bernstein replied. "Get here whenever you can. Anything you want is a priority. I'll clear my calendar. Everything else gets put on hold."

"Thanks Larry," Morgenstein answered.

"We'll see you tomorrow morning," Red ended.

Red then began to explain the plan to everyone in the room. "Tomorrow morning, you, me, Trenchie and Tarzan will attend the meeting," Red answered. "Shooter and Piss Clam will stay with your family, John, until this is over. They will go wherever your family goes. If your wife goes to the store or to the hairdresser, one of 'em will go with her and the other will stay with your daughter. Now as for your other daughter in New York, our guy Frankie will be there for her protection. Tell your family that if any suspicious calls come in, just hand me the phone or Frankie in New York and we'll talk to them. If I'm not here, get a phone number and tell 'em I'll call 'em back. Are we good?"

"Yes. We're all good. Everyone will cooperate with you and

your guys fully," Morgenstein responded.

Red continued, "We'll just take this as it comes. Tomorrow mornin' I'll speak with Larry then I want to pay a visit to Bob Gray and hear what he has to say."

chapter fifteen

Swifty and his two comrades were busy working up a sweat at Stillman's Gym. It was a seedy, rat hole of a gymnasium, but it was the gym of the champs. They all came here to endure weeks of endless kick-ass training. When Gil Clancy got his hands on you, word was you were gonna be a champion whether you wanted to be or not. He didn't give up. You could spot a guy in the ring and tell if he had that Clancy mark stamped on him. It was a signature style of training and fighting that led to winners.

Swifty was in the ring sparring with a young prospect. He had been away far too long and was working on getting back his timing. He had on his protective face piece and wore a sweat stained jersey with the sleeves cut off and was banging away with his usual in-your-face power punches, all under the watchful eyes of Gil.

"Okay Swifty. Take a break. I've seen enough," Clancy called out. He looked around for Gonzo but didn't see him. "Gonzo," he yelled. "Where are you Gonzo? This is a working gym. I need you ready at all times."

"I'm coming Gil," Gonzo replied. "Had to get my head gear from the locker."

"Get in the ring and let's see what you got." The bell rang and Clancy nodded to Gonzo's opponent. Okay, Gonzo, Clancy thought to himself - let's see what you're made of. Gonzo's sparring partner had a peek-a-boo style of fighting. He hid his face behind his hands while his shoulders hunched over a bit. He was a good looking, well-conditioned black fighter who was right at home in the ring. Gonzo's sparring partner wasted no time and came at him with a strong combination of lefts and rights, just hitting him non-stop seemingly not even working up a sweat. Gonzo was getting frustrated at his inability to stop the guy. He was being pummeled relentlessly. Geez. Try as he may, Gonzo just couldn't escape the guy and Gonzo was getting madder and testier by the second. Finally, he had had enough. Gonzo waited, accepted a few more punches, and waited for the opening he was looking for. His opponent missed a left hook and then it came unexpectedly - Gonzo timed his right hand perfectly and hit the guy flush on the chin, scoring a flash knockdown but lo and behold. . . the guy jumped right back up and was ready for more.

"That's enough," Clancy yelled out. "Floyd," he called the guy, "I've seen enough," and Floyd walked over to Clancy. "Thanks Floyd," he continued,

"I appreciate it."

"Your man is rough," Floyd said, still rubbing his chin. "Real rough, but also tough. Yep - rough and tough - got a lot of heart for the sport too. Gil, this kid hits like a mule. He's hardly a pro for Chrissake and he knocked me off of my feet. This kid'll do good with you trainin' him." And with that he leaned over and shook Gonzo's hand and headed back to the locker room.

"I appreciate that Floyd. Good luck on your upcoming fight."

"See you at ringside," Floyd said still walking.

"Who was that guy?" Gonzo asked the moment he was out of sight.

Gil smiled and said, "Oh, he's nobody special, only Floyd Patterson the heavyweight champion of the world."

"What the hell? What? You had me sparring with the heavyweight champion of the world?"

"I sure did and guess what?"

"What?" Gonzo asked.

"You just knocked him down, in the ring, right here at Clancy's gym. Put that in your memory book and store it for a while," Gil said smiling.

It didn't all quite sink in with Gonzo. He just walked away, headed toward the showers, all the while just shaking his head, saying, "I just decked the heavyweight champion of the world."

"Valesques, where are you?" Clancy hollered. "Henri dashed out of the locker room.

"Oh man, Gil. What you got in store for me now? I just heard what you did with Gonzo. Hey Gil, I don't like surprises," he said as he smirked a bit.

"Just get your headgear on and show me what you have," Gil ordered. Henri took to the ring and sparred just as Gil had anticipated. Clancy already knew about Henri - knew he was a natural. All he had to do was refine the fighter's technique. The kid had a picture perfect left hook - the best Clancy had seen in years.

Next there was Swifty. He was just the opposite. He was a smaller version of Marciano - rough but powerful, but he too showed promise. Red had told Clancy that all these boys needed was to believe in themselves and after Gil observed them, he believed that to be especially true. Gonzo was going to be his challenge. Gil would have to convert a bar room brawler into a professional prizefighter - something he excelled in.

Swifty walked to the water cooler, took off his drenched sweatshirt, revealing his finely toned musculature. He splashed water over his chest and face in an effort to cool down before taking a shower. June and two of her girlfriends had been watching from behind a beam in the upper area. All were a little speechless at the sight of these three men engaging in such a brutal sport. There was something intriguing about a sport that most women could not understand - a sport where grown men get paid to beat the crap out of each other and claim victory when they'd rendered their opponents unconscious. It was barbaric, it was rough and it was . . . manly. Swifty was a combination of all of the above but he was a sweet and thoughtful man, June thought, who could turn on a dime into this tough guy. She wanted him all for herself.

Swifty threw his towel around his shoulders and turned to walk to the showers when June called out to him. He looked around and spotted her in the gallery with two of her friends.

"Hey, what are you doing here? This isn't a fight."

"Well, I heard you were training at Stillman's and well, there's only one Stillman's, so I asked my girlfriends if they would like to see how fighters train. So here we are. Would you like to join us for lunch?" she asked.

"It would have to be a late lunch," Swifty said. "I have to wait for my buddies to finish their workouts. If you're in not in a hurry, we can do a late lunch." June squealed with delight.

"Oh that's no problem at all. We'll drop back by, what in a couple of hours?"

"Sounds good," he answered.

June was ecstatic. The men who usually asked her out to lunch were, more often than not, the nerdy types - not that she didn't like intellectuals, it was just that they didn't ignite that same spark in her as the tough boys did. That spark had been ignited the moment Swifty burst onto the scene by coming to the rescue of her father. Waiting for two hours would be one of longest waits of her life.

chapter sixteen

The five men enjoyed a good night's rest at the Morgenstein home. The following morning, Red instructed Shooter and Piss Clam to stay with the women and cautioned them. "Do not leave them alone for a minute. If one of them has to leave the house, then one of you guys goes along. Go everywhere with the women except into the ladies room and if they happen to go there, then you stand right by the door until they come out. Never let 'em out of your sight. You and you alone are responsible for their safety. If something happens to 'em, it means that someone had to kill you in order to get to them. Understand? I don't want anything to happen to any of you but you get the message."

Red told Tarzan, "Put the four bullet proof vests in the trunk. We just might need 'em." He, Tarzan, and Trenchie then left for the meeting with Larry Bernstein.

Red and his guys arrived at Larry Bernstein's office at exactly six-thirty in the morning. They buzzed from downstairs. A voice asked them to identify themselves. Inside, they found Larry behind his desk, tending to paperwork. When Bernstein saw Red, he got up from his desk and rushed to greet him. "Thank God you're here. I've been concerned as to when I might get a visit from those goons." Red looked around.

"Larry, how could they get in here?" Red asked. "It's pretty fortified around here. You have the studio security team, you have outside security on the payroll, a buzz-in system for the office, so what are you worried about?"

"I'm on edge Red. I'm jumping at shadows. Not like me but I admit it - I've been on edge." Red could see it. He was visibly nervous.

"Take it easy. Let me do the worryin' from now on. Your problems are now my problems. Look, Trenchie's gonna stay with you around the clock. They'd have to get past Trenchie first and I'd personally pin a medal on the guy that does that, to be honest, and then of course I'd whack him," he chuckled.

"Hey," Trenchie spoke up. "Having a little fun at my expense, are we?"

Red just smiled. "He'll stay with you until we find the guys behind all this. Feel better now?"

Bernstein looked up at the giant, rough-looking hulk of a man towering above him - the man who would be his companion for the next few days and muttered slightly under his breath, "I'm glad he's on our side." He then said aloud, "Yes. He looks like he can do the job. And yes, I feel a whole lot better now."

Red asked, "Have you received any more letters?"

"No, but I got a phone call telling me that I'm being summoned to a meeting today. Also told me to be prepared to sign a contract stating that I am turning my company over to these men. They insisted that I would be kept on as President and given a salary, but made it clear that I would have no say in the company. Seems to me that there is someone behind the throne and that these guys are just the front men. They warned me. They stated it twice. "If you don't show up for this meeting, you will never have an opportunity to attend anything, anywhere, *ever again*."

"I see," Red mused. "Sounds like a threat to me. Did they say when this meeting would happen, what time?"

"I'm expecting a call this morning telling me where to meet them."

"When they call, tell 'em you'll send someone in your place with the power to speak for you. If they insist you come yourself, then tell 'em 'no deal.' Tell 'em that you have a studio to run and you're in the middle of a big production - you don't have the time to go, so you're sendin' someone in your place with the authority, as your representative, to sign papers on your behalf. Tell 'em something along those lines."

Larry instructed his secretary to hold all of his calls and cancel all of his appointments while he waited with Red for the phone call that he knew was to come. At eleven ten his private phone rang - the one, which bypassed his secretary and came directly to his office. Before picking up the phone, he pressed the speakerphone button so that everyone in the room could hear what was being discussed. Then he hit the talk.

"Yes. Yes. I understand, but I can't meet you now."

"You better make time to see us. We have documents, information that can destroy your company. We're prepared to use them. "

"Look," Bernstein insisted. "I'm in the middle of a very costly production and I can't just leave, but I can send someone who has the authority to act on my behalf."

"Are you talking about the lawyer? There won't be any productions to worry about if you don't drop whatever you're doing and make it to this meeting."

"No, he doesn't have the authority to speak for me, but the person I'm sending does."

The caller said, "I don't like it. Let me make something very clear. No funny stuff, you hear. Don't get any ideas. Hold on." The caller was back in a few short seconds. "Okay, we're gonna let your *substitute* meet with us only because we have a contract that needs to be signed today. Here's the address, write it down. Tell him to be there in an hour." The phone went silent. Bernstein searched Red's face for any sign of hope.

"What do you think?"

Red just shrugged and said, "I think we need transportation, that's what I think. Do you have a limo we can borrow?"

"Yes, of course," Bernstein replied.

"Have it brought to the front of this building. Trenchie, you'll drive. I'll sit in the back." Trenchie looked concerned. This was unusual for him as he never showed any emotion.

"Red," Trenchie said, "you're the boss of a large organization. You can't put yourself in the line of fire like this. Let me and Tarzan handle it." Red put out his hand and asked Morgenstein for the keys to his car. He tossed them to Tarzan and told him to go down to the car and take the vests out of the trunk to bring back upstairs. Upon his return, Red instructed the men to don the vests under their shirts. As the men started unbuttoning their shirts, Trenchie tried to reason with Red.

"Let us handle it, Red," Trenchie insisted. It's not like we ain't done this sort of thing before. Stay out of it Red. You owe it to the family. Don't let stubborn pride get in the way of clear thinkin'.

We got this." Trenchie had a point and Red realized he was right. He had a responsibility to over a thousand men and he owed them his leadership.

"Okay," Red said, finally relenting. "Tarzan, you drive. Trenchie, you sit in the back and be me. Tarzan, when he gets out of the car, you get out with him but stay about ten feet behind him. I want you to watch his back. And don't either of you guys go into the place alone. I want whatever has to be said to be said outside, where you both can see what's happenin'. If you walk inside, you could both get ambushed, so stay out of an inside meeting. Is that clear?" Both men nodded yes. "I wish Shooter was here. If he was, I'd put him on the roof with an AK47, but he's not, so we just have to make the best of it."

The stretch limo pulled into the parking lot opposite the address Bernstein had written down. The men sat in the car waiting for the door to open. Tarzan beeped the horn to alert the men that they had arrived, even though both he and Trenchie knew that the men were already fully aware of their presence. After about ten minutes, a door opened and two men walked over to the car.

"There was only supposed to be one of you, not two," one of the men said.

"Tell your boss that I'm here," Trenchie said. "Tell him to bring the contract with him. I need to read it first and then I'll sign it. Go ahead. Go tell him that." Trenchie words were calm and firm.

Another set of minutes passed until the door once again opened and this time, three men emerged from the building. One of them held a stack of papers in his hand. As they approached the car, Tarzan reached for the gun he had placed onto the passenger seat. He pulled back the slide and checked the chamber once again as a precaution. Tarzan whispered to Trenchie. "Maybe we should just shoot all three of 'em now and be done with it."

Trenchie said stoically, "If we did that we wouldn't know who's behind this little caper."

"I hear you," Tarzan continued, "but it would make me feel a whole lot better knowin' these guys were done with."

"Let's hear what they have to say before we make a move," Trenchie stated.

One of the men approached and tapped on the car window. Trenchie lowered his back window just enough so they could speak.

"Look, we can't talk with you sittin' in the car," the guy said. "Step out so we can talk." Trenchie was busy sizing up the guys. These weren't the small Hispanic guys that he fought when he first got out of the joint. These were big, strapping, muscular guys who looked like mercenaries or ex-military. He wasn't particularly worried but nevertheless, one needed to know his enemies.

"Sure, we can talk better outside the car," Trenchie said but Tarzan was worried. He, too, stepped out of the car but he kept his distance, standing by the front fender. Tarzan had a clear shot of Trenchie and the three men who talked near the rear of the car. Tarzan's eyes moved among the three men looking for any movements out of the ordinary. Suddenly, from behind, Tarzan felt something hard crash against his head and everything went black. Trenchie had his back to Tarzan so he couldn't see but when he heard a clunk against the car he turned to see Tarzan, and his gun, on the ground. Trenchie whipped back around right into the face of a fourth man standing there with his gun trained on Trenchie's forehead.

The men bound Trenchie's hands behind his back and shoved him inside a car. They drove for a few minutes to another warehouse on the other side of this large complex. One of the men got out of the car and raised a large bay door that allowed the car to continue into the empty, cavernous warehouse floor. The men ordered Trenchie to walk, at gunpoint, across the concrete floor and to a steel pole, near a workbench, close to the wall. There, two of the men tied Trenchie to the pole. Satisfied that Trenchie was a no risk prisoner, one man introduced himself as Sal and promptly slammed a roundhouse right hand hard into Trenchie's face, cutting the area around his eye with his large diamond ring. Blood spewed down the left side of Trenchie's face, drenching his shirt. Trenchie smirked, looked at him, and smarted off, "Is that the best you have? You hit like a girl for

Chrissake."

"How about this wise guy?" and Sal, putting all of his weight behind his fist, hit him again in the face. He followed with a punch to the gut. This time the attacker recoiled as his hand struck hard against Trenchie's protective vest. "What's this?' he taunted. "You're wearing a bulletproof vest? You son of a bitch. I almost broke my hand on it."

Trenchie laughed and countered with, "I hope you did break it. Might toughen you up a bit. You hit like a pussy!" That was all it took. All four men began taking turns, punching and kicking Trenchie senseless until he faded into unconsciousness.

chapter seventeen

Trenchie had never really lost consciousness. The men were all high on themselves, pumped up over having gotten the best of the big guy. There was no question that the pounding had weakened him. He was tied to a pole, his legs hurt, his face throbbed, and he had a massive headache but he still had his senses about him. Trenchie was careful to appear lifeless and remained slumped over the plastic ties that bound his wrists, feigning unconsciousness while he devised his plan. The men lifted Trenchie upright and the rope that bound him dug into his wrists. One of the men looked at his three buddies and sneered, "He's not so tough now is he?" Trenchie's thoughts were not pleasant. He could feel the anger welling up inside of him - that old prison anger, the same anger he felt when a bunch of jerks decided to trash the club.

The leader turned to his buddies. "He's unconscious so we might as well grab some coffee from the kitchen while we're waiting for him to wake up," Sal said.

"Good idea Sal," one man concurred. "Looks like our tough guy's gonna be out for a while."

Trenchie waited for the men to leave and gradually began working his fingers toward the innocent looking adhesive bandage just above his wrist. He stretched his fingers a bit and inched them closer and closer until he felt its edge. He gently dug his nail underneath the cotton square in the middle of the adhesive, raised it up a bit, and grabbed hold of the razor blade. It was a trick he had learned in prison and one that he used when faced with situations like these. Those fools never even bothered to check under his sleeve. All he could hope for now was that he wouldn't drop it. He slowly worked the blade into a tight grasp of three fingers. It seemed secure. There was no time to waste as he began to cut through the ropes, thanking God that they hadn't used wire or handcuffs. It didn't take long until he had safely freed one hand, then the other. It was decision time. He could try to make it out of there, but it was quite a distance to the exit, and the men could walk through the door at any moment. He needed a weapon but all he could see was a large empty warehouse. Behind him, he spotted a workbench which had some tools stored underneath it. He walked over to the bench and quietly sorted through them until he found a large adjustable plumber's wrench. It was the only semblance of a weapon he could find. He picked it up and swung it back and forth to get the feel of it, all the while making a plan. He could storm into the kitchen and take the men by surprise or . . . he could return to the pole, play dead, and make his move when they came to get him. If he waited at the steel pole, he risked someone spotting the wrench. Quickly, he gathered the loose plastic ties and threw them into the garbage bin sitting next to the workbench. He returned to the pole and put his hands behind his back, all the while firmly gripping the wrench. Trenchie let his head droop, pretending to still be unconscious. Just as he had repositioned himself, the door flew open and the four men emerged from the kitchen. The men were laughing and making snide remarks about Trenchie, calling him a pussy because he was still unconscious. Careful to keep his head down, he waited for them to move closer. Sal picked up Trenchie's chin and taunted, "Are you awake buttercup? Can you hear me?" Trenchie nodded and raised his head a little so that he could look into his eyes. "Good you're awake. I didn't want to kill you until you were awake and you understood what was about to happen to ya. I'm gonna kill you like you guys killed my friends, like your movie star friend hurt my pal. Ya know my pal Bob Gray? I didn't really care for what your guy did to my buddy." Trenchie's eyes widened with the mentioned of Gray's name. "Oh so you recognize the name. You didn't know that Bob was a friend of mine? Oh well, too bad. Now I'm gonna take this nice and slow. It'll be a little painful, but in the end it won't hurt anymore 'cause you'll be dead," he laughed. "So if you don't mind, me and the guys here are just gonna sit here and watch you die slowly, you punk. You may be big, but you're not really so big right now, are ya?" he said.

Trenchie raised his head and heaved a big wad of spit right

into the guy's face. It landed square in his eye. As Sal brought his hand up to wipe it away, Trenchie seized the moment. His arm swung around hard and Trenchie slammed the wrench into the top of Sal's head in a downward motion, splitting his skull like a coconut. And as he was falling, Trenchie, at the speed of a pickpocket, managed to grab his gun from his waist. The wrench rested deep inside Sal's brain. He was dead before he hit the floor. Without hesitation, Trenchie fired a shot into the second guy's kneecap, shattering it. He fell to the ground, holding his knee and writhing in pain. The man served as a bit of a barrier between Trenchie and the remaining guys. Trenchie grabbed that man's gun and then armed with a weapon in each hand, started firing like an old western hero. Shooter would be proud. Bam–bam–bam–he fired shots into each of the other two men, killing them instantly. Trenchie struggled to get up but ambled over to the guy with the broken knee. He looked right into his eyes and saw pure fear. Trenchie smiled and said, "This won't hurt a bit," pressed the gun against the man's forehead, and pulled the trigger. The bullet took part of his head with it. Bone fragments, brain matter and blood filled the air and painted the walls. Trenchie reached over and collected the other guns. He rifled through the men's wallets, grabbed their car keys from their pockets, and placed them all onto the bench. He remembered Sal mentioning that there was coffee in the kitchen so that's where he headed – to the kitchen. The sink reminded him that he should probably take a moment to clean up. He turned on the cold water and with a paper towel, carefully washed his bloody face. He cut a dish towel into strips and dressed his wounded wrists as best as he could and then did what every killer does right after knocking off four guys – he poured himself a cup of coffee. To his surprise, it was fresh and robust – just the way he liked it. Must be some sort of omen, he thought. Very considerate of them to make him coffee the way he took it, he mused. Trenchie finished one cup and poured himself a second. By this time, he was beginning to feel a bit better, even though he knew that caffeine was probably not the best medicine for a headache. With the hot cup of coffee in his hand, he walked back to the bench, as refreshed as a man could be who had just taken a savage beating and had left four men lying dead, on a cold concrete floor. His strength was slowly returning and for some crazy reason, he thought of how Samson must have felt after Delilah gave him that famous haircut. There was no question about it - the beating had taken a lot out of him. He glanced at the dead men on the floor and said out loud, "There's a silver lining in everything. I'll take tired over dead any day." Trenchie walked back over to bench, set his cup on top of it and began searching the wallets. When he finished sorting, he found they each had slips of paper with the same phone number on it. He placed them into a bag with the guns they had. He wiped down everything in the area including the wrench, washed the cup he used, picked up his bullet proof vest and took all four sets of car keys, not sure which one would start the black late model Mercedes that was sitting there in the middle of the empty warehouse. With the bag in hand, he walked toward the car. The first two keys failed but the third set opened the lock. Trenchie tossed the bag into the back seat and followed the red exit sign at the other end of the warehouse. There, as he looked around cautiously, he waited for the gated doors to open and drove off into the cool night air. All in a day's work.

chapter eighteen

Just like Trenchie, Tarzan had a pounding headache when he regained consciousness. He looked up and saw the limousine but no one else. Trenchie, he thought, he must be in trouble and all he could think was how in the hell had he let that happen? What was he going to tell Red? He was a bit shaky as he pulled himself to his feet and he stood still for a few moments. Shaking the cobwebs from his head, he got into the car and started driving along Santa Monica Boulevard. He stopped when he spotted a gas station with a pay phone. He knew he had to get it over with. Red had to be called. Tarzan explained briefly what happened to them as best he could recall the events. Surprisingly, Red was calm and simply ordered him back to the studio.

"We can't do anything else until either Trenchie or those punks call us," Red stated. "Only then can we make a move. We'll be waitin' for you here."

Tarzan left the car parked in front of the building and walked up toward Bernstein's office. Crusted blood coated his head. Red and the studio head were sitting in Bernstein's office. Bernstein wasted no time. He immediately called for the studio nurse, telling her that he had a man in his office with a head wound who needed medical attention now. Red paced the floor willing the nurse to complete her work on Tarzan's head. They needed to be ready, ready for the phone call. After almost two hours, the phone did ring. It was Trenchie calling to give them the good news that he was downstairs. Red was relieved and he made no secret about it. His buddy was safe. Now he had to find out what had happened to him.

As Trenchie walked past the secretaries' desks, he could see the ladies cringe. Judging from the rearview mirror inside the car, he knew he looked a bit scary. Trenchie looked like he'd fought sixteen rounds and had never gotten off a punch. He opened the door to the office and stood there for a moment filling the doorway like a wounded behemoth. His head was matted with blood, his eye badly cut and almost completely closed; his face was bruised and swollen. He looked like a cross between the elephant man and that famous purple dinosaur. Everyone in the room just stared until he broke the silence. "It looks worse than it is," he said as he waved off Red who was walking toward him to get a closer look. Trenchie settled into the plush leather chair at the side of Bernstein's desk.

"What happened?" Red asked. Trenchie began his story. He explained how he had heard Tarzan's gun hit the fender, heard him fall to the ground, and explained what happened after that.

"When I was no longer a threat to them and when I couldn't defend myself, the bastards beat the shit out of me," Trenchie said in a controlled anger type fashion. Red's eyebrows shot up at these words.

"How'd you get out of there?" Red asked.

Trenchie looked around the room at Morgenstein, then at Bernstein. He wondered if he should say anything further. "Let's just say that I left the place and those four bastards didn't." Morgenstein was in awe. He could not understand how a man with his hands tied behind his back; unable to defend himself, could walk away from four killers.

Trenchie looked at Bernstein and said, "Larry send someone down to the car. I have a bag in the trunk. Tell them to bring it up here and warn 'em not to look inside it."

Bernstein sent his secretary to get the bag from the limo and Trenchie waited until a nurse finished tending to his wounds and left before speaking again. "Red," Trenchie said, "I forgot to mention somethin'. While they were working me over, the guy called Sal said the beating was for what Jimmy the Hat did to his friend Bob Gray."

"Ok," Red said. "Well, now we know for sure that Gray was part of the Detroit mob when Jimmy broke his knees. The question is – is he still part of that mob?"

Trenchie spread out the items on Larry's desk. Tarzan took the cards, cash, and notes of any kind, and placed them into a pile so they could look through them hoping to find a clue. "Red, check the business cards and slips of papers I found in their wallets," Trenchie suggested. "One number keeps popping up." Red turned to Larry and said, "We have to find out who that number belongs to. Do you have any contacts in the police department?"

"Are you kidding? I donate a substantial amount of money to the Police Benevolent Society. The department loves me." Larry pressed his intercom. "Lucille, please get Sergeant Withers on the phone for me." A few minutes later Lucille buzzed back with Withers on hold. "Sarge, I need a favor," Bernstein stated rather than asked.

"Sure, Mr. Bernstein, what's that?"

"I need a name and address for a phone number I have." Bernstein recited the number to him. "That's no problem," and the sergeant placed him on hold. It was no more than five minutes later when Sergeant Withers returned to the phone. Larry carefully wrote down the address and double-checked it by reciting it back to the police man. "I appreciate this Serge," Larry said. "I'll make it up to you when Christmas time rolls around." Bernstein handed Red the name and address he was given. Red's eyes showed rage when he read the name.

"Robert Gray again . . . that son of a bitch. He has some balls after what Jimmy told him what he'd do to him." Red looked at Tarzan. "Do you feel up to visitin' this guy?" Trenchie, too, was pissed.

"I'll do it," Trenchie said. "Nothing would make me happier," he said while clinching his teeth.

"Trenchie you stay put," Red ordered. "You're in no shape to go anywhere, much less try to kick someone's ass right now. Me and Tarzan can handle this guy."

"Bullshit," Trenchie insisted. "I'm comin' with you. You actually think that I'm gonna sit here while that SOB runs roughshod over us?" Red knew his friend well. He knew there was no arguing with him. He was like a mule so it didn't take long for Red to recant. Red turned to Larry. "Do me a favor and send one of your secretaries to your prop room. Tell her to find Trenchie the largest shirt she can find and bring it here – the shirt he's wearing is full of blood." A little while later wearing his new shirt Trenchie and the men said their good-byes and headed off to take care of business. The door closed and Bernstein looked at Morgenstein.

"What are your thoughts on what's happening?" Bernstein asked.

"My thoughts? I'm glad these guys are on our side," Morgenstein responded.

Larry added, "Trenchie killed four kidnappers all by himself. I would never have believed that one man could do that if I hadn't heard it with my own ears. I should know better than to ever underestimate Red or his people." Morgenstein nodded in agreement even though Red and this world were all new to him.

"What do you think Red will want from you when this is all over, Larry?" Morgenstein asked. He was no dummy. It didn't take a Rhodes Scholar to figure that out. Bernstein didn't hesitate.

"I dealt with Big Red when James Roman was alive," Larry answered. "He took care of a union problem for me and never asked for anything. He had every right to ask me for a favor in return, yet he didn't. This business that they're helping us with now is huge so yes, they'll probably ask for something, but Red is typically not real greedy, so whatever he asks for, it'll most likely be reasonable."

"I hope you're right," Morgenstein replied. "I hope you're right. You just don't find people sticking their necks out like this without a heavyweight IOU somewhere."

"Red is head of a mafia family that has over a thousand soldiers in it," Bernstein said, "and yet he's handling this for me personally. Another thing you may not be aware of and that is Red is worth hundreds of millions of dollars so I don't think money is what he'll ask for." The attorney shook his head almost in disbelief.

"Well now. I had a feeling he was powerful, in the street sense, but I had no idea he controlled that many men and I would certainly never have guessed his net worth. He's not showy and he seems to care about his men. He's managing those three kids, you know, the fighters. He confided in me that he worries about their future, that he wants them to have something when their fighting days are over. Said that was what motivated him to manage them."

"What a movie that would make," Bernstein said. "Hey, let me ask you a question. The fighter, the one you call Swifty, does his face look busted up or does he have some looks?" Morgenstein smiled.

"He looks a lot like Jack Lemmon. He's a damn good looking boy for a fighter."

Larry thought for a moment then said, "Don't say anything to Red, but maybe we'll give this kid a screen test when all this business is done with. I did all right with the first guy Red sent me, that James Roman kid. Who knows - maybe this kid has it in him also. You know, women love a rough edge on a man. We'll just have to see if the camera loves him the same way."

chapter nineteen

June and her friends had remained in their seats where they waited for the boys while they showered and got dressed. The three fighters walked to where they sat. June smiled and said, "I would like to introduce you gentlemen to my two girlfriends. This is Sarah," and she pointed to the shorter of her two friends, a pretty blonde, blue-eyed girl with curves in all the right places, "and this is Loretta." Loretta was about five eleven with auburn hair, dark sexy eyes, and long well-defined legs that seemed to go on forever. Loretta was known to be choosy about the men she went out with because when she wore heels, she usually towered over them. It made her uncomfortable. As she walked alongside Gonzo's six feet four inch frame, she was enjoying the fact that she could look up to him.

The group decided to have lunch at the Empire Diner located on Tenth Avenue, at the corner of West Twenty-Second Street. June suggested that the easiest way to get there was to take the C or E train to the Twenty-Third Street Station and walk a block from there. It was a good decision as noontime traffic made it difficult to secure a cab. The two-stop train ride only took about five minutes. The guys and gals left the dimly lit station and stepped out into the bright sunshine where the temperature hovered somewhere between seventy-five and seventy-seven degrees. A cool breeze from the East River enveloped them as the water flowed past on its way to meet the Hudson. The walk to the diner was pleasant and the girls seemed to know what they liked in men because the six individuals just effortlessly morphed into three distinct couples on the way there. It seemed that June's girlfriends did in fact find the other two guys appealing.

At the diner, they shared a booth, girls sitting opposite the fighters. The fare was typical for that age - burgers, salads and beer. The conversation eventually turned to boxing and it was obvious that the girls were curious as to how the fighters planned their time. Sarah asked, "Do you have to come to the gym every day?"

"The short answer is yes," answered Henri, since the question had been directed toward him. "We have only three weeks to get in shape for this fight, so yeah, we'd better be there most every day until the day of the fight."

Gonzo chimed in, "We'll probably take the day before the fight off, but Henri's right. We only have three weeks to get in condition, so we can't afford to get lazy or sidetracked." The women's faces all fell a bit. Sarah had another question and once again looked to Henri to answer. "Couldn't you sneak away for a night?" she asked coyly, fluttering her lashes.

"No," Henri answered quickly and in a most matter-of-fact manner.

"You mean you can't take one night off to go out?" she pursued.

"No."

"Why not?"

Swifty took this question. "Look girls. It's not that we don't want to do other things. We do but we just *can't* and especially we can't do things with *women*. Okay now, don't take this wrong, but there's an old sayin' in the boxin' world that if a fighter has sex with a woman it weakens him, it weakens his legs, and that small difference could mean winnin' or losin'. Now, I am not sayin' that any one of you will be havin' sex with any one of us or with anyone else for that matter. I'm just explainin' what can happen to a boxer's determination and concentration and . . . physical strength. Each of us have fought for different reasons in the past - Henri to send his brother to a good school, Gonzo never really trained - he's just a street brawler, always looking to make some money and then there's me. I only fought when I needed somethin'. My new manager pegged me right. He said I had all the talent in the world, but that I was a lazy bum. I realize that now. He's givin' the three of us a chance to be great fighters, but we have to do what he says." He pointed at Henri. "I fought Henri three times to a draw. I was a cocky kid thinkin' I could beat anyone in my weight class, but I was wrong. Henri taught me that. He's the greatest fighter I ever fought and now we're fightin' on the same team. Even Gonzo has some ambition now. He's motivated to rise in the standings and make somethin' of his life, so in answer to your question - we can't break our trainin' regimen even though we really would like to."

The three girls looked sheepishly at each other. They were three little rich gals who were used to getting what they wanted. The guys they knew would pretty much drop everything to go on a date with any one of them. These three rather attractive men sitting before them were different from the others. It felt in a way like they were being rejected. Most of the men they knew had expectations of dinner and sex. It was almost as though the two were synonymous, yet here were these guys carefully avoiding the female race for fear of intimacy. What a reversal.

June had never met a man like Swifty. He was tough, yet tender, and handsome, with a body that looked as if Michelangelo carved it. June knew he wouldn't stand for the nonsense she usually doled out. Sarah, too, was attracted to one of the boxers - the Latino Henri. She couldn't wait to see him in the ring three weeks from now. The only fly in the ointment was her father. She wasn't quite sure how to explain to her father that she had a crush on a fighter. Her father envisioned her marrying a doctor or lawyer - a Puerto Rican fighter would be a hard sell. Loretta had sorta' liked Gonzo when she saw him with his head gear on that day, trading punches with a sparring partner, but what sealed the deal was when she saw how tall he was walking next to her. She didn't care if he wasn't handsome in the classical sense. His nose had been broken several times, but oddly, it seemed to add character to his face. She could never remember seeing a more perfectly formed body on a man. His face, even with the visible scar tissue around his eyes, seemed to light up when he smiled. Loretta loved his manly confidence. It made her feel safe. The next three weeks would be a long wait for the girls.

chapter twenty

The tall hedges hid the car that was parked near the entrance of the long driveway leading to the Morgenstein house. The three men had been watching the house for quite some time and had noticed two men come and go – men that didn't match any of the photos and descriptions they'd been given.

"Who are those two guys and why weren't we told about them?" one of the men in the car asked.

The other man replied, "I hear what you're saying, but orders are orders. We were told to grab the wife and kids so let's not question it. Do you wanna go back and tell the boss that two strange guys stopped us from doing our job? I know I don't."

"Yeah, I guess you're right. Well let's go and get this over with."

Two of the men left the car and hesitated by the gate for a moment, looking around to make sure they were alone. They walked quietly up the driveway until they were able to peek into a living room window while hiding behind a hedge. All they could see was a woman by the sink and a man sitting at the kitchen table. They couldn't see where the other guy was, and didn't know how many kids might be in the house. The men were told that Morgenstein had two daughters but they spotted only one – a young girl – another kink in the chain. Their job was to grab the wife for sure and the daughters, if possible. But these two guys were a problem. One of the men spoke up.

"Look Aby, if these two yokels give us a hard time, we just shoot 'em, grab the women, and get the hell out of there. We gotta do this fast – in and out quick like. Okay?"

"Right," the other answered. "Let's do it."

They moved toward the servants' entrance of the large house. Aby removed a lock pick set from his pocket and in a matter of seconds, had the door unlocked. The men eased themselves into an entrance which was nothing more than a small foyer. It led to another door that gave them entry into the main portion of the house. From there, the two intruders tiptoed along the hallway that led to the kitchen and crept past it to the large living room.

Aby whispered to Fred, "She was in the kitchen with one of the men a few minutes ago, so let's head to the kitchen and when we get there, let's just open up on him and grab the woman before the other guy realizes what happened."

"Okay," Fred answered. "Let's get the show on the road." The two men moved quietly along hall, staying close to the wall. They raised their guns high into the air and stormed the kitchen but . . . no one was there. As they turned to make a hasty retreat, they found Shooter standing, about six feet in front of them, his gun trained right on Aby's heart. At that moment, Piss Clam emerged from the other side of the wall and covered the man known as Fred. Lydia peered out from the living room. She had been hiding in a closet.

Shooter turned to Lydia and asked politely, "Would you escort us to your basement?"

"Why, yes of course," Lydia answered, her voice trembling and her face as white as a ghost.

"Do you have a plastic drop cloth somewhere in the house or maybe in the garage?" Shooter continued.

"Yes, there's one in the closet in the basement." Shooter thanked her and asked if she would be so kind as to spread it out over the basement floor. She seemed confused.

"Why do you need it spread out?"

"Well Ma'am," Shooter answered. "I wouldn't wanna get any blood on your nice new rug now, would I?"

"Blood? What blood? I don't understand?" Lydia stammered.

"Ma'am, just do it please," he said slightly annoyed with this conversation. "I'm kinda' busy right now and really don't have time for this." That jolted Lydia into action. "Of course. How silly of me," she said as she rushed down the stairs in search of the drop cloth. She found it and did as she was told.

"It's done," she said.

Shooter looked at the two men and said, "Ok, let's take a little walk downstairs and we'll see what you have to say. Boys, I hope and pray that you have some good news for me. I don't have a lot of patience and I'm just itchin' to have some target practice."

"Wait a minute," Aby said. "I saw you and the Mrs. in the kitchen. How did you know we were in the house?"

"Morgenstein has a camera system. Red got it for him after he seen it in the Starlight Club – not even on the market yet," Shooter stated. "He's got cameras all over the place. Can see everything that's happenin' on his property. I saw you two jerks lookin' straight into the camera talkin' to each another when you were snoopin' around the gate. Now would you rather tell me what I want to know up here or . . . down there?" he asked as he pointed to the stairs.

"What are you planning on?" Fred asked.

"Nothin' much," Shooter answered. "I'm gonna ask you a question and if you don't answer it, I'm gonna shoot one of your kneecaps off. Then, I'm gonna ask you another question and if you don't answer that one, or if I catch you lying to me, I'm gonna shoot off your other kneecap. And I'll just keep shootin' until there are no body parts left. Now what's it gonna be?" Lydia stood rooted in her position at the front of the refrigerator with her hand to her mouth. She couldn't believe what she was hearing and her mind was racing – these nice young men, were they capable of doing what he said he would do? Nah, she told herself – probably just a ploy to scare those guys. Lydia didn't move from that spot. She watched as Piss Clam, Shooter and the two uninvited guests made their way down the steps into the basement area. Once there, Shooter started up with his questioning.

"Okay, here are the rules," Shooter said. "I'm gonna ask each question one time and one time only. If you don't answer, my little trigger-happy finger will do its business. Now, who wants to talk first?" Aby looked at Fred and nodded slightly to indicate that they'd better cooperate.

Fred put up his hands and said. "Okay, ask and I'll tell you what I know."

"Who do you work for?" Shooter asked.

"Sal Migliore, capo in the John Magardi family out of Detroit."

Shooter sarcastically shot back, "Well, you don't work for Sal Migliore any longer . . . because we killed him this afternoon." The men's eyes widened as they looked at each other. Somehow, they believed him.

"But you're doing real good so answer this question," Shooter said. "Now why does Magardi want Mrs. Morgenstein?"

"For leverage," Fred responded. "He has documents and film that could destroy four of Columbia pictures top stars, but he doesn't want to use them if he doesn't have to. He wants Bernstein and Morgenstein to turn control of Columbia Pictures over to him. He figured that if he strong armed them, that eventually they would give in. We weren't going to hurt Mrs. Morgenstein. We were ordered to just snatch her and take her to our boss. We just figured that we'd get in fast, grab her, and you know . . . in and out fast."

"Yeah, I know," Shooter said as he nodded sarcastically. "In and out fast, with her as your hostage, and us dead on the floor. Wasn't that the plan?" The two men's eyes narrowed. They knew they'd been caught. They did not answer.

Shooter looked over at Mrs. Morgenstein and he asked, "Lydia do you have a pad and pen handy?" She left and returned a few seconds later.

"Here," she said as she handed the items to Shooter. Shooter then handed them to Fred. "Write down the address where you were supposed to take her." Fred hesitated a moment, but then picked up the pen and wrote on the pad. "How many guys are all of you total?" Shooter asked.

Fred replied, "If it's true that you killed Sal and the three that were with him, then there's just us and two others left."

"Is Bob Gray one of them?"

"No, he had to go to Detroit but he was coming back right away. He may be home now, but I'm not sure."

"Do you have his phone number?" Fred nodded yes.

"Okay," said Shooter. "I want you to call your two friends and tell them to get to the Morgenstein home right away. Tell them that you have everything under control. After you do that, call Gray and tell him the same thing."

"I can't do that," Fred said. "What kind of mug do you think I am?"

Shooter continued, "If you don't make the call, I'll show you what kind of mug you'll be - a crippled one, right after I put one right in the center of your knee." Shooter pulled the hammer back on his Colt 45 and laid it on top of Fred's kneecap. "I'm usually not this patient," Shooter said, "so I'll give you five seconds to make the call."

"Okay, okay I'll make the call," Fred relented. Piss Clam whispered to Lydia,

"Do you have a second line in the house?"

"Yes," she answered. "In my husband's office."

"I want you to take me there in a minute." He nudged Aby and told him to stand alongside his buddy Fred. Aby obeyed and inched closer to Fred.

"Is this where you want me?" Aby asked. He was a pitiful sight, acting like a little boy.

"Yeah," Piss Clam answered. "Stand next to him and don't move. Shooter can you handle both of these guys? I need to make a quick call to Red. I want to tell him what we found out."

"Don't worry about these two," Shooter replied.

Piss Clam dialed Bernstein's private line. Bernstein picked up right away thinking it was Red. "Larry, it's Jackie. Put Red on."

"Red's not here," Bernstein said. "He's gone to find Bob Gray."

Piss Clam spoke quickly. "If he calls you, tell him to drop everything and get over to John's house as soon as he can. Tell him I have good news and it's important."

chapter twenty-one

Red, Trenchie and Tarzan parked across the street from the Imperial 400 Motel. It was on Fifth Street in a seedy area of San Bernardino. Trenchie and Tarzan waited in the lobby as Red talked to the desk clerk.

"I'm supposed to meet Bob Gray, one of your guests, but I'm a little early. What room is he in?" The desk clerk looked offended.

"What kind of an establishment do you think we run here?" the clerk answered. "We never give out our guests' room numbers . . . never! You'll need to wait until he gets here." Red calmly reached his hand into his pocket and pulled out a hundred dollar bill. He placed the bill down on the counter in front of the clerk.

"I understand what you're saying," Red answered, "and I'm impressed with your dedication to the rules and regulations of your hotel and normally, I wouldn't think to ask you to do anything like this, but you see, this is very important to me." And with that, he tapped a c-note twice on the desk as if to make a statement. "It's very important to me," Red continued as he slid the money closer to him. "I can see that you're a reasonable man and I would hope that you would understand and make an exception this one time." The desk clerk stared at the bill lying on the counter in front of him. This fella only earned sixty-five dollars a week and he was now staring at a week and a half's pay. It didn't take much convincing. He scooped up the bill and put it into his pocket, trying very hard not to let anyone see him do it.

"Sir," he said. "I didn't understand the importance of this meeting. It is the policy of this establishment to assure the total satisfaction of our customers and we strive to follow our company's policy to make sure every customer leaves here happy. Mr. Gray is in room one twenty-five. Out the door and make a left. His room is on the ground floor facing the parking lot."

"Oh and one more thing," Red added. "Has he been ordering from room service?"

"Why yes," the clerk answered. "He has ordered a few times."

Red thanked him and motioned for his guys to follow him. They walked along the long cement sidewalk in front of the rooms facing the parking lot.

"Here it is, room one twenty-five," Trenchie said. There was a car parked outside the room. Tarzan checked the number on the bumper and it matched the room. There was no peephole on the door so Red knocked loudly.

"Who is it?" a voice asked from inside the room.

"Desk clerk sir. I forgot to get a signature for room service. It'll just take a minute, all I need is a signature and I'll be gone."

"Okay, hold on a minute while I grab my pants." The door opened and a surprised Robert Gray stood staring at armed men standing in his doorway, and while he didn't recognize any of them, he had a feeling that he was in a whole world of hurt.

"Who are you guys?"

Tarzan smiled and said, "We're your worst nightmare, that's who we are and if you don't tell us what we want to know in the next few seconds, we'll be your worst nightmare to the second power." Gray was visibly shaken.

"Whatta you wanna know?" Gray asked as he tried to remain calm.

"Who are you working for?" Red asked.

"Sal Migliore."

"We know Sal, but he's dead now and so are the three guys who were with him." Gray was shocked and he looked at Red with almost some sign of relief.

"How? Who killed him?"

"Sal and his three men kidnapped Trenchie here and worked him over," Red said pointing at Trenchie. It was as if Gray noticed him standing there for the first time. Trenchie's face was bruised and cut and looked like it had been hit with a sledge hammer, but in spite of the bruises, he was still an imposing presence. Gray knew just by looking at him. He was big, he was very angry, and his eyes bored into Gray's eyes, unflinchingly, forcing Gray to look away from him and back to Red who continued talking.

"As I was saying, your pal Sal and his boys were about to hurt my buddy here so he was forced to hurt them first." Gray was silent for a moment.

He then asked, "You mean . . . this man . . . he killed all four of them, by himself?"

"That's right," Red answered as he nodded his head.

Gray was now skeptical. "Those men were stone killers and you want me to believe he killed all four of 'em without any help?"

"Well, I don't want you to believe anything. You can think what you want, but this man here has some bruises to show for it and those other guys, well they're worse off than bruises. Now tell me how many of your men are still in California?"

Gray replied a little testily, "Hey wait a minute. What men? Those aren't my men. I only told Magardi that I had information on some of Bernstein's stars. He's the one that decided to use it against him to take control of the company."

"Why do they want control of Columbia pictures?" Red fired back.

"The Detroit mob is looking to expand. They want a foothold in either Vegas or Hollywood and with my information and their muscle, they decided it would be in Hollywood." Red seemed confused by this information.

"Wait a minute. Hold on there. John Magardi sends men to Queens and tries to take over some of my establishments. Then he sends men to intimidate John Morgenstein, then he sends other men to harass Larry Bernstein? I could see them going' after Bernstein and Morgenstein, but why me?"

"Magardi knows that Bernstein has a powerful friend in Queens. He watched your buddy Jimmy the Hat become a big Hollywood star. When Magardi ordered a union rep to have one of the Bernstein stars killed, you stepped in and put the fear of God into that big-mouthed union guy. So . . . he was forced to put his movie studio ambitions on the back burner until he dealt with you."

"Why didn't he just have me whacked and get it over with instead of takin' such an amateurish move by makin' it look as if he was tryin' to take over a few of my places?" Gray was more relaxed now as he answered Red's questions.

"He was testing you. He wanted to see how you reacted when you found out that a few of your places were being taken over." Red shook his head.

"Tryin' to take over Trenchie's business was a huge mistake. And goin' after the Zebra Club was another. I don't own that club – a friend of mine does, but he's under my protection. Maybe that move was also a test to see how I would or wouldn't react."

"That's exactly what it was," Gray agreed. "Detroit was about to make their move into Hollywood, but you were their big obstacle. He knew he had to get rid you."

"I'll ask the question again. Why didn't he just send a couple of men to Queens and have 'em take me out?"

"I don't think he really wanted you dead. That might be too risky. He just wanted to shove you around a bit, maybe invite you at some point, to come over to his side – I don't know, form an alliance or something."

"That don't make a bit of sense to me," Red said. "No Gray, you're wrong. There's somethin' else goin' on here that even you don't know about. Either that or you're hidin' somethin' from me. Which is it Gray? Are you keepin' somethin' from me?" Red scolded as he tilted his chin down a bit and squinted his eyes as if sending a message.

"I'm telling you the truth. I'm telling you what I know," Gray swiftly replied.

"The only thing that makes sense to me," Red said, "is that he knew I was Bernstein's protection so . . . he had to lure me into a trap, try to get rid of me. He tried doing that by havin' his men pretend to move in on me. Now that scenario is the only one that makes sense to me. How about you guys? Does what I just spelled out make sense or do you have another theory to offer me?" No one answered. "Then let's go with the supposition that Magardi had to get me out of the way so there would be no opposition to his takin' control of Columbia Pictures."

Gray shook his head and said to Red, "There's another reason why Magardi didn't want you killed."

"What would that be?" Red asked.

"He was afraid the council would find out he was the one who had you killed and they would take action against him. So he tried to take you out of the picture, but not by killing you."

Red thought about what Gray had just said. "Yeah. He couldn't start another gang war so soon right after the Gallo–Profaci war because the council wouldn't stand for it, and he certainly wouldn't want to answer to the council as to why he had me killed, so he's between a rock and a hard place. So the only thing he could do is lure me somewhere and take me out quietly, try to make it where no one would know he was the one behind my disappearance. Well that makes sense and it answers that question for me. Now here's another question for you. Where's the evidence you said you have? Did you give it to anyone to hold for you? Magardi maybe?"

Gray shook his head. "He doesn't have it. If I gave it to him, he wouldn't need me any longer and I wouldn't get a dime out of him, so I stored it someplace safe, somewhere only I know about." Red smiled.

"So you still have it?"

Gray nodded again, this time in the affirmative. "Yes I still have them."

Red clapped his hands. "Okay then, what are we waiting for? Let's go get it." Gray looked a bit disturbed by this. His one last shot at making a big payday was about to go up in a puff of smoke. Red picked up the telephone on the desk beside Gray's motel bed and dialed Bernstein. He wanted to check his messages before heading out.

"Red," Bernstein said immediately, "Piss Clam called and said to call him right away. He said he's got good news for you. Told me to tell you to get over to Morgentein's house right away."

"Ok, I'll call Shooter as soon as I hang up."

"Wait a minute Red. Did you find Bob Gray?"

"Yeah, we found him. He's been cooperative and we're just about ready to leave his motel to get that information that's so valuable. I don't wanna say too much over the phone. I'll fill you in when I get back. Just stay close to the phone and keep me posted in case one of the boys calls you." Bernstein gave a palpable sigh of relief. He was clearly happy to hear that the blackmail goods were about to be retrieved. "Don't worry Larry. Everything's under control," Red said as he placed down the phone.

On the way over to LAX airport, Bob Gray tried to bargain with Red. "Look Red, I want your word that when I turn over my information to you, you'll let me go. I thought I was safe with the Detroit mob backing me but I was wrong. When your friend James Roman broke my knee, I was sure my friends would deal with him, especially when Roman threatened me. When nothing happened to him, I knew Roman had been right when he told me emphatically that I didn't know who I was dealing with. I know that I made a terrible mistake. James Roman made me a cripple and all I could think about was getting back at him for doing this to me."

Red nodded and asked him, "And you didn't think you deserved what you got when you tried to blackmail Lana Thompson?"

"No, I didn't think I deserved what he did to me, not then. It was after Magardi got involved that I knew I was in way over my head, but by then I was trapped by my own stupidity. I couldn't get out. I had to go along with whatever they were planning. I just kept hoping that I could somehow get out of it all. Look, I'll give you what you want and I'll disappear. You'll never see or hear from me again. Deal?" Red was silent a moment. So was everyone else, meaning Tarzan and Trenchie.

"Look Gray," Red answered, "you've cooperated and did as we asked so I'll let you go, but not right away. I have to take care of a few loose ends but . . . if what you're tellin' me is true and leads us to the goods, then you have my word that you won't be harmed." Red then pointed his finger at him and added, "But if I ever see or hear from you again, then all bets are off. I'll see to it that you're cut you into little pieces and fed to the dogs. Understand?" Bob Gray's face matched his name - he was as ashen as day old embers in a fireplace. He was terrified of these men, yet Red had just said that he wouldn't be harmed. Gray had no idea what to believe.

The men arrived at the airport. Gray led them into a room that was part of some special Captain's lounge. As agreed, he emptied the contents of a secluded box, inside a locker, and handed them over to Red. Red then ordered everyone back into the car.

chapter twenty-two

Shooter met Red and the boys at the door and led them through the house, down into the basement. When the two hostages in the basement saw Bob Gray, they knew that if Red's guys didn't kill them that Magardi would surely order it. Red complimented his two men for the job they had done protecting Mrs. Morgenstein and rounding up the two Detroit gunmen. Shooter told Red what the two men had told them. Red, in turn, briefed the boys on the information that Bob Gray had relayed. With everything out in the open, Red began to form a plan.

"Call your friends," Red ordered as he handed Gray the phone. "Tell 'em you're at Morgenstein's home with Aby and Fred. Tell 'em to write down this address." Gray called the men as Red had instructed. Red nudged him and said, "Tell 'em that you'll fill 'em in when they get here."

"Take down this address," Gray said. "Yeah, I'll fill you in when you boys get here." Gray hung up the phone. He looked like a defeated man. "I'm a dead man," he said to Red. "The first moment they find out I talked, I'm a dead man."

"Nah," Red jumped in. "These two bums talked first. They spilled the beans and told us all about the move Magardi was makin' - tryin' to take over Columbia Pictures, so if he's gonna kill anyone, he'll kill those guys first."

Gray slowly exhaled. "I hope you're right, but you don't know John Magardi. The guy's a mad man, crazy for power. You should have seen the look on his face when he thought Columbia Pictures could be his for the taking - like a rabid dog, frothing at the mouth."

"Tell me somethin'," Red continued. "What are you in his organization? How come you can count on their support? You told Jimmy the Hat when you tried to shake down Lana Thomas that he didn't know who he was dealin' with. So, you had support even back then, didn't you? So why are they not backin' you?"

Gray was sitting at the kitchen table with his face in his hands, looking every bit the distressed man. "Well, I don't have that protection any longer," he said as his voice trailed off. Red was confused.

"Why not? You had it then, why don't you have it now?"

"My protection," Gray said slowly, "was my brother-in-law. He was a capo in the Detroit mob. He was Sal Migliore,"

"Holy shit!" Trenchie shouted out. Red's eyes shot from Gray to Trenchie back to Gray as his lips mouthed, "Ohhh."

"Yep, one of the guys your friend Trenchie here killed in the warehouse today. That's why I'm sure that Magardi will have me whacked . . . because I don't have Sal standing between him and me anymore. If he's lost his chance at Columbia, he'll be on a rampage. He'll come after you for sure - you can book on that." Just then the doorbell chimed. Someone was at the front door.

"Go, answer the door," Red told Gray. "If it's your buddies, invite 'em in and we'll take it from there." Gray opened the door and there stood two of Magardi's men. "Come on in," Gray said. Seconds later, Piss Clam and Shooter had their guns trained on them. The men, taken by surprise, offered no resistance. They, too, were herded down into the cellar. There, sitting in the middle of the room, they saw two chairs, with two men, bound with duct tape.

Red wasted no time. "Piss Clam, go get two more chairs from the kitchen for our new guests here. This little party is growin'." Shooter kept his gun aimed high while Piss Clam strapped the men to the chairs with thick rope and duct tape like the other two. Red gave his usual instructions - just answer the questions and not get hurt. Lie and be painfully crippled.

"Okay, let's start with your names," Red began. "You first," he said pointing to a smaller, older man sitting in the chair to the left of his partner.

"Teddy," the man said.

"And you?" he asked the younger guy sitting next to him.

"Dominic," the young man answered." And the line of questioning continued.

"Are there any more guys with you that we don't know

about?" Dominic shook his head. "No, this is all of us that are left."

"What were you supposed to do next?" Red asked.

The young man decided to cooperate. "John told us not to come back until you were dead. That was our assignment . . . to kill you. I didn't like it, especially when I heard what happened to the other men, but what were we supposed to do? We had our orders and we were trying to figure out a way to carry them out when Bob called. His call was like a little reprieve to us. We were hoping that they had captured you because that would have taken the pressure off us. What would you do if you were in our position? You expect your men to follow orders don't you?" Red was silent. He knew the answer to this. It was a good question.

"Well, so does John," the young guy continued. "What else do you want to know?" Red thought for a moment.

"Let's assume you had killed us, then what were you supposed to do with us?"

"We had orders to kill your men but hold you until John got down here. He didn't forget what you did to the men he sent to Queens. He wants to kill you personally. I told you he's crazy."

"Shooter," Red called. "Is there a phone down here?"

"Boss, on the end table over in the corner," Shooter answered. Red pulled Dominic over to the phone and told him to call his boss. "Tell him that you have us at the Morgenstein home. Tell him that the others were killed but you saved me for him. Do it!!" Red ordered. Dominic calmly held the phone and started dialing. Magardi actually giggled when he heard Dominic say that Big Red was captured.

"I'm taking the early flight out of here tomorrow," Magardi said excitedly. "I'll be in sometime late afternoon. Keep him on ice because I want to deal with him myself. I've been looking forward to meeting him. I couldn't take care of him before because of the council, but now I'll teach that bastard not to mess with John Magardi. Keep him safe and don't let him out of your sight." Click. The phone went dead.

chapter twenty-three

Red called Frankie at the club and told him in turn to call Joey Bones to let Joey know that he was to go to the Morgenstein home in Long Island right away. "Joey's going to stay in the house and protect the daughter June. Wherever she goes, he goes . . . no exceptions. He'll be her shadow and tell him to behave himself – this is business – nothing more."

Frankie called Joey and gave him the news. Joey loved his assignment. After all, how many guys were ordered to spend every minute of the day with a woman, and call it work? Joey had already found out – this gal was a beauty so how could anyone even call this a job? Joey was an up and coming hoodlum in Red's mob and Red relied on him more frequently as of late. He was slowly beginning to fill the slot vacated by Jimmy when he left for Hollywood. Joey, like Jimmy, had brains and he could think on his feet. Red would have normally used Shooter for this job but Shooter was with Red. Red wasn't concerned. He knew that Joey would do the job just as well. Red had grown to depend on these two boys more each day. Jackie Piss Clam was their backup but Piss Clam couldn't think on his feet like the other boys. He was street smart but had his limitations. Joey and Shooter were different – they were rising stars. These boys could assess a situation, make a quick decision, and follow through. Both showed courage under fire – didn't rattle easy, but then again, neither did Piss Clam. Red was the puppet master. He knew which strings to pull to get the best out of each of his men. Piss Clam had guts, followed orders, and in an instant, would kill anyone that Red ordered him to.

Before Joey left for the Morgenstein Long Island home, Frankie filled him in on what the Detroit mob was up to and explained to him that Joey's job for the next few days was to protect Morgenstein's older daughter June.

"Don't get carried away with her good looks," Frankie

warned. "Remember, beauty can get you killed if you're not careful. Don't forget to watch your back. We're in an undeclared war with Detroit and even though Red doesn't think it will last much longer, be careful. Remember, even though it's a long shot, these guys may try to grab the girl. They'll take you down if you're in their way. Think of her as just someone you have to protect"

"Okay, I understand," Joey said with a lop-sided grin. "Yeah, she's just somebody I have to protect . . . somebody that happens to be drop dead gorgeous." His smile faded and he suddenly became serious. "Understand this Frankie. The only way this girl will be taken by someone while I'm watching her is if I'm dead . . . and that won't happen."

John Morgenstein called his daughter that evening and told her that Red was sending a bodyguard of sorts to watch after her. June was silent for a moment and then asked, "What time is this man coming here?"

"You can expect him in the morning around ten," her father replied.

"Dad, can this man be trusted?"

"You think I would let anyone in my home to protect my daughter who wasn't trustworthy?"

"No, I guess not. It's just that I'm all alone here and I wish you and mom were with me." John knew what his daughter was feeling. He felt the same way. He wished he was there too. To his family, he was this fearless husband and father, but deep down inside, he was a frightened man. But, he reminded himself, he had Red and his boys for protection, and that gave him comfort. June had always been the independent type but she still depended on her family a good bit. He was her father. It was his job to provide security and peace of mind for her and it worried him that she was alone. Morgenstein even toyed with the idea of calling Swifty and asking him to look after her but this was Red's call and so far Red had been right on the money, like a general making decisions in combat. "Red assures me that this man is a professional. Look, I have to go now," he said. "But I'll call you tomorrow. I love you."

"Love you too dad."

June had been up since seven. She prepared a pot of coffee and placed it on the back burner. After the perking had stopped, she poured herself a large mug of the black liquid and took it to the small table by the window where she sipped it while browsing the newspaper. Carefully she turned each page, glancing at each of the ads and not concentrating on anything really until she came to an article on page four that caught her attention.

FOUR MEN FOUND DEAD IN WAREHOUSE

She read the article intently and for a moment wondered if this might be remotely connected to her father and Columbia Pictures. Nah, she thought – just her imagination getting the best of her. She placed the paper into the small magazine rack by the window and made a mental note to mention it to her father the next time they spoke.

Around ten o'clock the doorbell rang. June was a little nervous as she walked toward the door. She peeked through the blinds first and saw a man standing in the driveway. Cautious, she called out to him. He smiled and introduced himself as Joey.

"I believe that someone should have called you," he said, "either Red or your father to let you know I'd be knocking on your door this morning."

"Yes," June answered, "my father called me last night. Please, come in. I have some fresh coffee and danish in the kitchen."

Joey lit up. "That would hit the spot ma'am, thank you."

"Please call me June. I'd much prefer that than ma'am."

The two made small talk for a while, exchanging stories about where they'd grown up and talked a little about family. It was after his second cup of coffee that Joey said, "Ma'am . . . I mean June. You do understand that I'll be here in this house with you until your father returns or until Red calls me to say that there are no more concerns?"

"Yes," June answered, "he told me that you'd be staying here. We have several spare bedrooms, so you'll be comfortable. You'll have your own dressing room and bathroom and if you need anything, just ask – I'll see to it that you get it."

"If you have to go anywhere," Joey smiled and said," just think of me as your chauffeur. I'll be with you and sorry if this seems a nuisance, but I really can't let you out of my sight so if it seems like I'm a little puppy dog following you around, well, I guess I am - just following instructions. All it takes is one second for somebody who's up to no good to grab somebody. Don't mean to scare you, but that's the way it is. And now, if you don't mind, if you could show me to your room, I'll put my things down." Joey didn't know which looked bigger at the moment - June's mouth or her eyes. It had never occurred to her that having a bodyguard meant a having a sleeping buddy.

chapter twenty-four

Red had a restless sleep. Major decisions always did that to him. Finally, at four in the morning, he got up, showered and shaved. He walked to the window and looked out as though the answer would appear from outside somewhere. In a few hours, John Magardi would walk through the door and Red would have him. But then what? If he killed him, he'd have to kill the four others and probably Bob Gray as well. Red had given Gray his word that if he cooperated fully, Red would spare his life. Gray had complied. If Red 'disposed' of all these guys, he would now have to go to Detroit and kill everyone up there too? That would mean another gang war.

Red pensively gazed out the window, looking at nothing, just staring and thought of what Jimmy the Hat's dying words. 'The devil is whispering in my ear but God still loves me.' Suddenly, it was as if a door opened in a part of his brain that had long lain dormant - a little thought began to bubble up, a seed of an idea - rough at first, but Red recognized the significance of it. He mentally massaged that seed until it became more polished, refined, until it broke through the surface, sprouting through his subconscious and breaking into his conscious mind. There it was. Red knew what he had to do. He picked up the phone and dialed the one sacred number to which all the 'family' were privy, sort'a like the red phone in The White House, the one that goes right to the President - a number for emergencies only. A refined sort of voice answered.

"Who's calling?" the voice asked. Red checked his little black book for his code name.

"Ted Williams."

"Yes, Ted what can I do for you?"

"I have a party with one of our friends." Red checked his code book once more. "Roger Maris. After the party, I'm afraid he'll be takin' a long vacation to Australia, you know, down under. I thought I'd call you and ask you to perhaps talk him out of takin' that trip. His family needs him. It would be a shame for him to go and if he does, it will leave his family and the extended family in a mess. It just isn't worth it. I don't think he understands that. He'll be my guest startin' tomorrow so I thought I would talk to you and see if you might persuade him to stay around a little while longer."

"I see," the voice on the other end of the phone, said. "I guess it would be an inconvenience to have him come here, am I correct?"

"Yes you are very intuitive. It *would* be inconvenient for me to bring him to you. *But* . . . perhaps you can come to my party and I'll make sure he gets to say hello to you before he leaves. You could probably talk to him about old times, catch up a bit. I'm waitin' for him to arrive, but I already have five of his friends with me. I insisted that they remain as my guests until he gets here tomorrow mornin'. I'd really appreciate it if you could make the party - the sooner the better." The voice remained very calm.

"Yes, I see the urgency of attending. Thank you for the invitation. I'm sure I will be able to make it. I have your address Ted. It hasn't changed recently has it?"

"Yes, actually, it has. I'm at a friend's home. He's the head of a large movie studio and that's where the party is being held. Do you have pen and paper?"

"Sure do," the proper voice answered. Red recited the address slowly and carefully, enunciating his words and careful to repeat them for accuracy sake. He hung up the phone and allowed himself to relax for the moment. If things worked out the way he planned, he just might have averted killing six men – something he did not relish doing. In Red's line of work, sometimes killing was necessary, like what happened to Trenchie when he was trapped, or the guys he had to kill in the junkyard, but overall, it was not something he enjoyed.

Red knew John Magardi's flight number and its expected ETA. Red wanted all this nonsense over so he could get back to his three fighters waiting for him in Queens. The young boys were expecting him to be in their corners the night of the fights and although Red had never planned to make boxing a business, the thought of it now excited him a bit. He couldn't wait to just sit back, relax and watch . . . if you call watching two men beat each other's brains out, relaxing.

Magardi rang the doorbell of the luxurious Morgenstein home and as expected, he wasn't alone – two men accompanied him. He looked around as he waited at the door. Maybe, he thought, that when this was all over, he'd buy a home like this one. He could afford it. Hell, he chuckled, maybe he'd buy this one.

The door opened and Bob Gray greeted Magardi. Magardi was surprised but tried hard not to show it. He had expected one of his guys, either Aby or Fred, but instead there stood Gray. As Gray ushered Magardi and his men into the living room, Magardi calmly asked Bob about the rest of his men.

"They're in the basement making sure Red doesn't get any funny ideas . . . like escaping," Bob said. Magardi nodded as if to say 'good idea' as his eyes and lips visibly relaxed a little. Gray was watching the mobster's every move – his body language, his eyes – trying to determine if Magardi was buying into it.

"So what are we doing up here?" Magardi shot back. "Let's go . . . I wanna meet this tough guy from Queens, this 'Big Red Fortunato'," he said mockingly.

The entrance to the basement was open. There were wide steps with ornate, hand crafted metal railings on either side of the steps and unlike other homes, there was no door to open to gain access to the lower level. The basement was breathtaking. Thick, taupe-colored rugs covered the floor and red velvet chairs, accented in gold, were strategically placed in the corners. It looked like a long lost movie palace of yesteryear. As Magardi rounded the stair landing to enter the room, he found himself face-to-face with Angelo Torelli, the council's negotiator. Magardi was so fixated on Torelli that he failed to notice Big Red sitting at a large table, at the far end of the room. Magardi's eyes darted about and landed on his men – sitting against the wall near Red, their hands and feet bound.

"What the hell is going on here? Why are my men tied up

like that?" Magardi snarled.

Torelli answered in a quiet voice. "Sit down, John. We have to talk."

"Talk about what? You wanna talk? Then let's talk about why my men are on the floor tied up like cattle. Let's talk about that okay?" he yelled in anger.

Torelli used his calm voice tone again. "Sit down John. I'm not going to ask you again." This time he obeyed. It seemed like the reality of something serious began to settle in.

Red's phone call had elicited an immediate response. Torelli's only job was to answer that number, assess the situation, and determine if it necessitated a visit from him. He was bound by the rules of the council to fly, drive, or even swim to the problem and find a solution, peacefully, if possible, but by force, if necessary. Torelli was appointed by the council and entrusted with making tough decisions. His 'rulings' were final, irrefutable, even if that meant loss of life. John Magardi was as aware of this as anyone. In all the years that Yip and Red had been the heads of the Queens family, neither one had ever dialed this number but by doing so, Red needed to prevent a gang war. Repercussions like this could shake the mob's foundation, eliminate territorial boundaries and wreak havoc on their bottom lines, which meant money.

Magardi sat quietly and listened to Torelli explain the rules to both him and Red. Torelli listened to Red's story first, then to Magardi's, and again to Red's, while Torelli's assistant, a scrawny younger man, wrote everything down on a yellow pad, in shorthand. When each man had finished stating his case, Torelli looked at Magardi and said, "You had four of your men kidnap Trenchie, a 'made man', with the intent of killing him. Your men, under your instructions, attempted to take over a brokerage house owned by friends of Red here. You attempted to take over three establishments owned by Red and his associate. You tried to take over a legitimate major movie company using blackmail and force. You threatened to harm their families, which is against the council's rules. What do you have to say in your defense John?"

"Hey, I'm the boss of my family and if I want to expand into other territories, I have every right to do so."

Torelli nodded. "Yes, John, as long as you play by the rules. *Our* rules . . . which you chose to ignore."

This really wasn't what John had expected to hear. Well, this wasn't really what John had expected *period*. He had come to this location thinking that everything was under control, that he could make his move before any chance of reprisals. He knew at that moment that he had underestimated Big Red Fortunato.

Four hours of back and forth testimony ensued, lengthy discussions, elaborate explanations, rationalizations. Torelli had heard enough. The single juror trial had come to a close. He turned to Red.

"You will release these men. They are to return to Detroit and no harm will come to them," Torelli stated unemotionally, yet firmly. "If there is any blood by your hands, you will be held responsible. Is that understood?" Red's eyes didn't waver from Torelli's as he nodded at the negotiator's decision. Magardi smiled. It appeared that things were going his way after all.

"You men," Torelli said, pointing to the men being untied by Red's men, "You are free to leave. You will return to Detroit and are ordered never to return to California under penalty of death. Do you understand the consequences you face if you disobey this order?" He waited for acknowledgement from each of them. The men readily agreed. They were only too happy to leave the house. Torelli dismissed all five of Magardi's men and instructed them to leave . . . *without* Magardi.

Torelli continued, "Red, you and your men are free of any charges and can leave if you desire. I would prefer that you stay and we leave this house together." Red instructed his men to go upstairs and wait until further notice.

As the men headed for the stairs, Red asked Bob Gray to wait for a moment. Gray was clearly troubled by this.

"What is it Red?"

"I just want to remind you that I'm keeping my word to you, but if I ever see you again, I'll kill you myself, with my own hands." Gray looked into Red's eyes. He knew that Red meant business. At that moment, death was staring right back at him.

Gray answered, "You'll never see or hear from me again."

"Good," Red said. "Go on. Get out of here." Gray turned. His impulse was to sprint up the stairs and get out of there, but the best he could manage was a fast limp. It seemed an eternity before he finally stepped outside into the California sunshine - a free man.

"John, you are ordered to step down immediately as the head of your family," Torelli ordered. "A replacement will be chosen by the council. This decision is final. This meeting is closed." That was it. End of trial. Trial by mob or trial by wise guys, whatever you'd like to call it. Torelli was judge and jury. His decision was final. There would be no appeals, no retrials, no last minute reprieve by any Governor.

Magardi, stunned, sat for moment trying to process what he'd heard. Finally he spoke. "I won't do it. Who the hell do you guys think you are? I fought and scratched my way to get where I am and I don't intend to step down. I don't give a damn what your decision is. Got that?"

"Yes I got that," Torelli answered softly. "Is that your final decision John?"

"You bet your ass it is."

"And you're sure you won't reconsider?"

"No. I will not give up what took me so long to build." Magardi got up abruptly and began to storm up the stairs. He stopped halfway up to say, "You want a war? I'll give you a war that you'll never forget." He kept walking until he exited the front door, slamming it behind him, and marched toward his car. He was surprised to find that his two men hadn't waited for him. That just made him angrier. "Damnit," he said as he yanked at the car doors only to find they were locked. Magardi cupped his hands and looked at the ignition, hoping to see a key, but there was none. Not giving up, the mobster looked around and spotted a bus stop and began to walk toward it. As he did, two men stepped out, flanking him, one on each side. They spoke no words as they nudged the man back toward his car and ordered him into the driver's seat. One of the men jangled a set of keys in his hand, unlocked the door, and grabbing his upper arm, guided Magardi behind the wheel. The man with the keys sat in the passenger seat, put a key in the ignition, and told Magardi to start the car and drive.

"Where?" Magardi asked.

"Just drive. We'll tell you."

"Look, I know who you guys are," Magardi said as he looked at Trenchie. "I'm sorry my men grabbed you and roughed you up, but I ran out of options. Understand that it wasn't personal, just business."

Trenchie nodded sympathetically. "I understand."

"Look," Magardi said. "I'm a wealthy man. Whatever Red's paying you I'll double it, I'll triple it. I'll make you both very rich men." Tarzan, who was sitting in the back seat, patronizingly patted Magardi on the arm.

"You were given a way out John, but you chose not to take it," Tarzan said. "But don't worry, we promise that it'll be quick and painless."

Trenchie and Tarzan weren't familiar with Southern California so after a little discussion, they decided to do a little scouting. They drove for about twenty minutes until they found a quiet construction site. It appeared that work for the day was finished. They sat for a few minutes, observing, looking for anything in motion, workers or security guards, who might be on site watching over equipment or supplies but they saw nothing. The car passed through the makeshift fence and slowly drove deep into the site past cement trucks and bulldozers. The equipment engines emitted a ticking sound as they cooled off. They passed some half framed buildings and circled around them until they found an area behind the foreman's shack - an area that was nothing more than a trailer converted into a field office.

Trenchie reached over and shut off the engine. He got out of the car and waved his gun at Magardi, indicating that he should step out of the car, too. Magardi began to shake and placed his hands into the praying position.

"Please, don't do this," Magardi began to plead. "Look, I'll step down. I'll do what Angelo said. I'll do it, I promise - just don't kill me," he said as he started to cry. Tarzan shook his head.

"You're pathetic John. Don't you have any pride? You live by the gun, now you're gonna die by the gun, so take it like a man.

What's with this pansy shit?" Ignoring Trenchie, Magardi kept talking. Red's men led him into a copse of woods behind the trailer and before he had even stopped walking, Trenchie and Tarzan both riddled him with lead, emptying their weapons. It wasn't so much an assassination as it was a *statement* to others who might think of ignoring the commission's rulings. Magardi lay there on his stomach, his eyes open but not seeing, his face half visible and partially hidden in an ever-widening pool of blood. Seemed so simple - all he had to do was agree to Torelli's terms and step down. When Magardi had refused, the council's negotiator had tapped the table twice with the fingers of both hands. It was a pre-arranged signal giving Red permission to proceed. Red had then nodded, almost imperceptibly, to Trenchie and Tarzan. That was it. Red had secured the necessary approval to eliminate Magardi and his threat.

Back at the Morgenstein house, Red followed Torelli out of the basement and walked into the kitchen. Oblivious as to what has been taking place outside, Mrs. Morgenstein had prepared coffee waiting and laid out a lovely presentation of bagels and lox, cream cheese, capers, onions, and had made scrambled cheese eggs on the side. There was every color juice known to mankind. She was a classy lady - one with a style that matched her meticulously decorated home. Larry Morgenstein and his boss, Bernstein had arrived and seemed antsy, eager to know what had transpired down below, but each knew better to wait until there was complete privacy.

"You did right by calling me," Torelli said as he pulled Red aside. "The council would have frowned on trouble so soon after the Gallo - Profaci war." "Do you know," he continued, "that this is the first phone call I've received on that line since we decided to use it. I was surprised when it rang, but I knew it was serious. It's too bad about Magardi. Pride and ego got in the way of common sense. I will give my full report to the council after I have the typed transcript from the hearing. I'll take the next flight out and go straight to Detroit. We need to fill Magardi's position soon, but carefully with someone more reasonable."

Red nodded and said, "Angelo, I plan on opening an

independent movie studio. I'll work with Columbia Pictures and allow them to release a completed movie through their network. I don't want any misunderstandings with the council over this move. Do you have a problem with this?"

The negotiator mentally scanned through the council's laws and guidelines that dealt with one family encroaching on another's territory. "If you were moving in on another mob's territory," Torelli said after pondering for a few seconds, "or looking to take over their action for your own purposes, I would advise you not to proceed with this venture. However, you intend to open a legitimate business by investing your own money into a venture that may or may not succeed. Therefore, I see no problem with moving west. I will inform the council of your plans and tell them that you discussed it with me and that I approved the move." Red smiled and patted Angelo on the shoulder as he clasped his hand in a firm handshake. Mission accomplished. It was exactly according to Red's plans.

"I hope I never get this kind of call from you again," a smiling Torelli said. In a more serious tone he added, "But keep the number handy just in case." The mob's chief negotiator smiled again, said some pleasant goodbyes to the Morgensteins and thanked them for the use of their home.

Angelo Torelli had barely gotten out of the door when Bernstein, the studio head, with Morgenstein nearby, turned to Red and blurted, "Tell me what happened, my curiosity's killing me."

"Magardi won't bother you again," Red answered him. Your company is yours, your stars are yours, and no one will be threatened with blackmail from Bob Gray or any of Magardi's men."

"How can you be sure?" Bernstein asked.

"Because Magardi's dead, that's why," Red said in a whisper, concerned that the Missus might hear. Red turned to Morgenstein and added, "John, I'm calling your house and instructing my man to leave Long Island. The danger has passed. You folks can now go on with your life. Let's just say that these nasty little obstacles have all been eliminated." Morgenstein looked at Bernstein. Red noticed the silent interaction-taking place between them. He rarely misread signals or people.

"Is there something else?" Red asked.

Bernstein spoke up. "Well, there was something we wanted to know."

"What's that?" Red asked.

Morgenstein searched for the right words. After all, he didn't want to offend his benefactor so he simply said, "Red, you went beyond anything we expected but we're businessmen, and no one would do all this for nothing. We never discussed fees so we wondered what your help is going to cost us." Red smiled. He was enjoying this.

"I do want something from you boys and it's not money or part of your company." He waited, letting the tension build up a bit.

"Okay," Bernstein answered. "Tell us then."

Red began to elaborate. "I want the two of you to come to Queens as my guests. We'll celebrate the successful conclusion of this nasty little business at The Starlight Club. Then, I want both of you to accompany me to some matches to see my three fighters in action, especially Swifty. I'd like you to observe him and tell me if you think he has any potential for the movies."

"Is that all?" Bernstein asked.

"No," Red continued, "there's one more thing. I plan on opening a movie studio. I would like to have Columbia Pictures release the pictures I make, but only if the pictures meet your high standards. I have no plans to compete with you. I just want to get into a legitimate business and I intend to invest my own money to build the studio and to finance the pictures that I make. Another thing, gentlemen, I will need your help and advice in proceeding with this venture. I know as much about making a movie as I do about making an atomic bomb. So, will you help me?" Both men laughed. Each man nodded and verbalized their eagerness to assist - if that was all Red wanted, they were fine with showing him the ropes, fine with most anything he needed or wanted at this point.

Morgenstein had been to Red's club but Bernstein had not, although the movie head had certainly heard enough about it from his partner and others.

"You have our word, we both will be there, at The Starlight Club, at the fights, wherever you like," Bernstein reassured.

"Great!" Red said as he smiled. "Bring your families. I know they'll enjoy it. If he's not booked, I'll try to get Jerry Vale for the night and if not him, then Vic Damone and if he's booked, I'll get someone else just as good, maybe even Sinatra." And that was it. All in a day's work. A day in the life of Red.

chapter twenty-five

Spending three days with Joey Bones was not what June considered fun. He was a scary guy - nothing like the movie tough guys portrayed in the pictures that her father made. This guy was creepy. He seemed fearless, exuded 'danger'. June guessed it must have been the reason that Big Red had assigned him as her protector. She had never envisioned having a real life mobster as a bodyguard. While it was uncomfortable having him right up under her, she had to admit that she felt pretty safe with the guy. Joey had accompanied her everywhere - to the gym every day to watch Swifty train, to the supermarket, the gas station, everywhere. For the last several days, Joey Bones had been right at her side.

Joey was downstairs in the kitchen as June headed toward the pot of black gold to pour a cup of coffee. She put a slice of whole-wheat toast into the toaster and offered Joey one as well. He shook his head as if to say no. June took a few sips of her coffee, then excused herself to the powder room for some last minute touches to her makeup. She wanted to look her best for Swifty. As she and Joey were heading for the door, the phone rang. June answered it.

"It's for you, Joey" she said. "It's Red."

Joey held the phone to his ear. "Hi Red. What's up?" Joey asked. "A little early in the morning for you, isn't it?" Joe listened for a moment. "What? Okay, I'll do that. When will you be back? That soon, eh? Okay then. I'll see you at The Starlight Club." With that, Joey hung up.

June asked, "Are you ready to leave now?"

"No June. You're going by yourself from now on." She looked confused and frightened.

"Why? What happened?" June asked. "You're not going to be protecting me anymore?"

"No, my job is finished, it's over," Joey said. "No one will be bothering your family."

It took a moment for it to sink in. June's emotions were conflicted. She composed herself, took a deep breath, and smiled. She was free now. This nightmare was over. June walked over to Joey and kissed him sweetly on the cheek. That caught Joey off guard. "Thank you for watching over me," she said. "I will never forget what you've done." Secretly, he yearned to take her into his arms and kiss her properly, but he didn't dare. He could hear Frankie's words as he whispered into Joey's ear the warning of not being tempted by her beauty. Joey thanked her and right as he was getting into his car, he waved one last time. His heart was heavy. The guy was smitten. He thought about June all the way home on the drive to The Starlight Club. June was hung up on Swifty. Joey knew better than to pursue it. He had seen how she looked at Swifty while he trained. Sometimes Swifty wasn't even aware of it. Joey convinced himself that even if she wasn't attached, she was out of his league. Nevertheless, he continued to think about her all the way back. Joey sometimes memorized lines from poems - the ones that spoke to him and had meaning to him personally. He didn't discuss this with the boys. They probably wouldn't understand why a guy like Bones would do that. Anyway, the thought of June's warm lips kissing him on his cheek reminded him of a line from John Greenleaf Whittier's poem *Maude Muller*.

"For of all sad words of tongue or pen, the saddest are these:
It might have been!"

Tough guy mobster Joey Bones drove all the way back to Queens pining for the woman he had just left and could never have.

chapter twenty-six

Red had only been back for a week. It felt good being home, at The Starlight Club, sitting at his favorite table, by the window, enjoying his years long routine of sipping coffee and Sambuca while reading the news and watching the comings and goings of his guests. He opened his newspaper to the sports page. At that moment, Tarzan walked in. He appeared angry - seething was more like it.

"Did somethin' happen?" Red asked.

"Yeah," Tarzan answered. "My daughter. Some girls ganged up on her in school, beat her up. She came home bruised and terrified out of her mind. While she was explaining to me what happened, the girl, the one who beat her up, showed up outside our door with some of her girlfriends." "How'd you handle that?" Red asked.

"Simple," Tarzan said. "I walked outside with my arm around my daughter. The girls were all there and they didn't seem too scared, to be honest with you so I asked the girls, 'Did any of you girls come to fight with my daughter?' And one girl raised her hand."

"Good I said. Come over here. She walked tentatively toward me and stood right there looking at me defiantly. I asked her 'do you really want to fight my daughter?' The girl nodded that she did. I guess that this must have been some sort of required initiation or somethin' and that the girl couldn't back down in front of her girlfriends, so I told her. 'Alright, you have my permission to fight my daughter, but first I want you to do something for me." 'What's that?' she asked. 'Go home,' I said, 'go get your father and bring him back here with you. Cause I'm gonna kick the shit out of him until he begs for mercy. Then I'm gonna kill him and bury him right there in that grassy area in front of my house. Now go on and get him and tell him I'm on my stoop waiting for him."

"What happened after that?" Red asked.

"Nothing. I waited all day and nothing happened. None of the girls came back. I think I must have scared them a little." Red chuckled.

"Tarzan you would scare the buh-Jesus out of the devil himself . . . just by looking at him. Well, as a student of human nature," he laughed, "from what you just said, I don't think these gals will give her any more trouble at school. In fact, don't be surprised if they invite her into their little gang, their group, ask her to join them at their lunch table."

Tarzan ordered an espresso with his usual shot of Sambuca. His blood pressure seemed to lower with each sip he took. The conversation then turned to their recent adventure.

"You know," Red began, "I was at a logjam. I didn't know what to do and that rarely happens to me. If I had rubbed out those guys, I'd have had to whack Bob Gray too, and I gave him my word that I wouldn't harm him. If I didn't do anything to them, then that would be seen as weakness and I would have been lookin' over my shoulder for the rest of my days. Just as I was about to make a decision to kill the whole lot of them, I remembered the negotiator. That's all fairly new, you know, this negotiator business, but the council appointed him to that position to mediate situations just like that. In other words I passed the buck and whatever he decided, I would have to abide by. No matter what Torelli instructed me to do, I would have still been ahead of the game. If he had told me not to harm Magardi or his boys, that would have been fine because they would have been ordered to stay away from us. As it turned out, he judged pretty fairly. Torelli saw right through Magardi and how he was itchin' for a war that I wanted no part of. If the egomaniac had just listened to the negotiator and abided by his decision, he would still be alive, but, no, he had to go act tough. Look where that got him," Red said, shaking his head.

"When are Bernstein and Morgenstein flying in?" Tarzan asked, shifting the discussion.

"They'll be here Thursday. They want to have a day to rest before comin' with us to the fights. I want Larry to meet Swifty. I'm gonna ask him to give him a screen test. If he does okay, I want Larry to make a star out of him. We're expandin' into the movie business and Larry is the guy who can make that happen." Tarzan nodded in agreement.

"I figured you were going to do something like that," Tarzan replied. "By helping Bernstein and his buddy Morgenstein, you kind of neatly painted them into a corner. They have no choice but to help ya."

"Yeah," Red said, "but my way is painless. I'm not shakin' 'em down for money and I don't want to take over their business so I think what I'm askin'for is reasonable and far less expensive than they thought it would be. They knew they'd have to give me somethin'. They figured it wouldn't be money. No, they thought I was gonna ask for a piece of Columbia Pictures. They seemed relieved when I told them I was going into the movie business on my own. I told 'em that all I wanted was their expertise and their partnership with my movies, *plus* . . . I wanted him to look at Swifty. He knows I sent him a winner with Jimmy the Hat, so I think he's probably pretty curious about Swifty. Hopefully, he likes what he sees, even though I really don't care what he thinks of the idea. I want Swifty in pictures so Swifty is gonna be in the movies. That's what I want . . . period."

Shooter and Piss Clam walked in. Shooter approached Red.

"Hey boss. I hear you're havin' a blast next Saturday night. Are we invited?"

"You kiddin'?" Red said. "Sure you're invited – you and Piss Clam over there, sulkin' at the bar." Piss Clam had been preparing for the big "No" but when he heard Red's remark, he perked up.

"Thanks boss. We were talking about the bashes you throw and we never been to one and we were kinda hopin' we'd be invited."

"Well, now it's official," Red said. "You're both formally invited. You guys did a great job." Trenchie walked in and joined Red at the table. He heard the tail end of the conversation.

"Red, did you call your regular customers to tell them about the party we're havin here?" Trenchie asked.

"Yeah, I made all the calls. Everybody I spoke to said they'd be here. Especially when I mentioned that we're havin' a surprise guest entertainer and a few Hollywood mogul - types attendin' the party.

chapter twenty-seven

On a Wednesday morning, a black stretch limo was waiting outside LaGuardia Airport where Moose met Bernstein, Morgenstein and their families and took them straight to The Starlight Club. Shortly after his return from California, Red had instructed Moose to hire an interior decorator and completely revamp a vacant house in Corona Heights. His California guests would stay there. Moose called a contact in Manhattan who specialized in the rental of fine furniture and working with the decorator, each piece was hand selected and matched to the décor as designed by the interior specialist. This area of Queens appeared to be questionable, far from upscale, but the two families entered to find an elegant home, resplendent with its golden walls, silk drapes and tulle-crowned canopy beds. Red assured them that they would all be perfectly safe there. This was mob territory - Red's country. There was no such thing as "unsafe" here.

News spread fast in the neighborhood and word was that some Hollywood mogul would be staying in the area for a few days. Neighbors were advised to be on their best behavior. But to ensure their privacy, Red had Shooter remain with the Bernstein and Morgenstein families, on a sofa bed in the finished basement.

On Thursday, Red had his club chef prepare an eight-course feast for his dinner guests - oysters rockefeller, pasta fagiole, antipasto, caesar salad, intermezzo, prime rib, tiramisu, and all the champagne, wine and other spirits that his guests could hold. Red wanted to show The Starlight Club in all its glory - lights on, band playing, guests dancing - "Starlight Fever", he liked to call it. The Morgensteins, Bernsteins and Red's other invited guests were served in the formal dining room. Red invited Marco, the famous clothing designer that he had met long ago and he had introduced him to Trenchie. Marco in turn introduced Trenchie's wife, Mary, to the high fashion world of couture. Red invited

Marco and his wife, Karen, to join them for dinner, which they gladly accepted. Trenchie and Tarzan brought their wives as well.

"Absolutely delicious," Larry Bernstein raved with each bite he took. Conversation at the main table split, as it always tended to do, into separate discussions with men talking about the fights and the women talking about all things children and shopping. Lydia was excited to meet the one and only Marco of fashion fame and she found his wife Karen to be most enjoyable. Morgenstein and Bernstein, even though clearly out of their element, were surprisingly at ease among these 'rough' men.

The evening began to wind down and Shooter got the signal from Red that it was time to bring around the car. Shooter crossed the street to the limo parked in the lot and drove it around to the front of the club where he gathered the California guests, and headed back to the hotel - the beautifully redecorated home in Corona Heights. Shooter parked the car in an alley beside the house and settled himself comfortably into the basement.

The following day was fight day. Red, Bernstein, and Morgenstein spent the day at The Starlight Club relaxing and talking business. Shooter drove the women to Karen and Marco's home in Rye, New York. It was palatial - once owned by the Bloomingdale family. Shooter waited while the ladies lunched and drove them back in time to join the men for early evening coffee and cordials at the club.

Red checked his watch and alerted everyone that it was time to leave for the fights. When everyone was comfortably seated in the limo, Shooter pointed the car toward Sunnyside Gardens. The stretch limo slowly made its way to the arena entrance where he let his passengers off. There was a double spot by the curb only a block away, perfect for the long car. Shooter parked there and hastily began his walk. He didn't want to miss a single fight. These were Red's fighters. This was a special night.

Trenchie, Tarzan, and Piss Clam took their seats at ringside saving Joey Bones a seat while Red, Larry, and John Morgenstein walked down the long hall toward the area reserved for the fighters. They passed a few doors before entering the second one immediately before the end of the hall. The last room was reserved for their opponents. Red wasn't a superstitious man, but he did have one request and it was that all of his fighters occupy the same room before a fight. Maybe he thought the fighters would motivate each other, or engage in conversation to briefly take their minds off the coming bouts, but whatever it was, it was an instruction, more like an order, and the fighters obliged.

Red walked into the room with his two guests as their trainer, Gil Clancy, was giving the fighters their last minute pointers. When Clancy saw the men, he smiled and walked toward them. Red introduced the legendary trainer to the movie moguls and then requested a few moments in private with his three fighters.

"Sure," said Clancy and he promptly departed.

Swifty was the first to speak. "It's good to see you Red. We thought that maybe you wouldn't make the fight."

"I told you boys that I would be in your corner come hell or high water when the fight started. Now are you boys in shape?" Red asked.

"Yeah, don't worry about us," Henri chimed. "We talked it over and decided that if we have to fight on a steady basis, we might as well be wearing championship belts." Red looked at Gonzo.

"And what about you big guy? Are you ready for a championship belt?" Gonzo smiled as if he didn't have a care in the world.

"I'm with them," he said pointing at Swifty and Henri. "We think it would be great for you to have three champions in your stable and we made up our minds that we're gonna do it. We're all gonna become champions. The only problem we have is with Swifty and Henri." Red looked at the two men with concern showing on his face.

"Do these two have a problem?"

"Well, they fight at the same weight and they both can't hold the same title, so one of them is going to have to move up or down a weight class. Swifty volunteered to work toward putting on a few pounds on and move up in class." Red looked relieved.

"Well now, you had me worried there for a second, but I

think that's a good move if it doesn't weaken you, Swifty, or pit you against much bigger men. What do you think about moving up a class Swifty?"

"Well, I'm fighting at one sixty now. If I gained a pound or two, I'd automatically be put in a different class so . . . yeah, I think I can handle it. In fact, the way I'm bulking up, I think it would be natural to move up a weight class."

"Good. Then it's settled - eventually, I'll have three champs in three different weight classes." Red summoned his two guests to join them and introduced his fighters. He pulled Swifty aside and said, "Mr. Bernstein would like a few words with you." Bernstein didn't say anything to him at first. He just looked him up and down as if he were buying a horse. Swifty was waiting for him to check his teeth. Bernstein mentally measured his height and pictured one of his leading ladies standing beside him.

"How tall are you Swifty?" Bernstein asked.

"Five eleven," he replied.

"That works," Bernstein mused. Then he asked Swifty some rather mundane questions, more to hear him speak than to gain information from him. He liked what he heard - clean, clear enunciation. Swifty's voice didn't have that John Barrymore timber to it - his voice was softer, more like Marlon Brando, and Larry was sure it would work on film. Satisfied with what he saw, Bernstein shifted his attention to his facial features. He was an expert in choosing a star. He hand plucked them using his own little battery of tests before granting a screen test and most every one of them had gone on to enjoy tremendous success - success that translated into dollars for the studio. When Red had sent James Roman to him, he knew immediately that he had a winner.

Bernstein examined Swifty's face as if he were a surgeon. Swifty had blond hair. Most of his stars had black hair, including Roman. His nose wasn't broken, but you could tell that it was a fighter's nose because of the flesh that was built up on either side of it. Bernstein noticed the scar tissue around his eyes. It wasn't much, but just enough to add some character. His skin was smooth and Bernstein had to admit that this fighter standing before him had an easy manner, was a handsome kid, and reminded him of a blond John Garfield. The only question mark was sex appeal - that unspoken something that makes the women swoon. Roman and Garfield each had it. Roman had animal appeal. It oozed from his pores. Larry wasn't quite sure yet if Swifty would have this effect on women. But as long as Swifty could bring a little of the essence that Bernstein first sensed, that might follow.

"Thank you Swifty. I'd like to chat with you some more before I leave so put aside some time for me over the next few days." Swifty smiled, exposing a perfect set of pearly whites. The smile, Bernstein thought. That was his gift, his smile. It filled the room and that wasn't lost on Bernstein. Bernstein's instinct was kicking in more with each passing second. This boy just might be his next star.

"Sure," Swifty answered. "After my fight tonight, I'll have plenty of time on my hands so whenever you want, I'll be available."

As Swifty walked away to join his pals, Red asked, "What do you think?"

"I like him," Bernstein answered. "He has a good speaking voice. He is certainly a good-looking lad but it's his smile that gives him that star quality. Now we have to check out the acting. Can you fly him out for a screen test?"

"Sure. When?"

"Could you arrange for him to be at the studio next week?"

"Sure can. We'll settle on a day and time later and I'll confirm it with you before you leave."

"Good," Bernstein said. "Now that that's settled, let's go watch us some fights."

When the four, six and eight - round bouts were finished, it was time for Henri to step into the ring. Henri had an aura about him - a quiet confidence that impressed Bernstein. Most fighters showed nervousness before a bout, but not Henri. He looked so relaxed he could have been in church. But he wasn't in church, he was about to do battle with a man looking to beat in his brains and yet he didn't seem the least bit concerned. His opponent was a rough looking black boy with finely cut muscles threading through his body. This would be the first ten- round fight on the card. Swifty's bout was next and the last ten rounder of the night was Gonzo's heavyweight fight.

The bell rang for the start of the fight and right from the beginning, Henri's class and poise made a statement. He danced around the ring like a larger version of Willie Pep, the legendary featherweight champion of the forties and fifties, the man with the lightning quick jab and devastating left hook. In the ninth round, the fight eventually was halted because the other fighter could no longer continue. Henri had beaten him down. Bernstein, ever the eagle-eyed observer, was taking it all in.

It was now Swifty's turn. Swifty, in his scarlet robe and towel draped around his neck to keep his body and muscles warm, sauntered through the door, threw a few jabs for show, and made his way down the aisle to the ring. Bernstein took a moment to soak up the reaction of the crowd, paying careful attention to the women. He jumped nimbly up the steps, swung himself through the ropes and danced around a bit, warming up. A glossy sheen of sweat coated his body indicating that he must have been doing the same in his dressing room. Red pointed out to Larry that most fighters come into the ring sweating to prevent being knocked out quickly. He explained that by working up a sweat in the locker room a fighter doesn't come into the ring cold. If a fighter comes in cold he's at a disadvantage and stands a chance of being knocked out quickly.

The women in the audience didn't escape Bernstein's notice either. His mind was racing with thoughts of this boxing world as a potential market for a good fight film. He would mention it to his team upon his return to California. A cheering section in the crowd suddenly interrupted his creative ideas.

Larry looked around to see find the source. To his surprise, it was June, Morgenstein's daughter, screaming in delight at everything Swifty did. She carried on like that the whole time, beginning with his walk down the long corridor leading to the ring. This had merit. If Larry's partner's notoriously picky daughter was attracted to Swifty, screaming like a teenager when he climbed into the ring, then most likely the women of America would have the same reaction seeing him on the big screen. This excited the studio head. Yep, he had a good feeling about this young fighter. This heightened his curiosity as to Swifty's prowess in the ring.

Johnny Addie announced the fighters. Unlike the droning, modulating tones of other announcers who caused audiences to cringe, while taking forever to announce the names of each fighter, Johnny's high pitched, staccato voice was perfect for this venue. Addie was all business and perfect for his time.

Swifty removed his robe and Bernstein noted the sculpted musculature of the young athlete - perfect for the big screen. The bell rang to start the first round and June, sitting with her girlfriends in the row behind Bernstein, bounced in her seat like a giddy school girl. Bernstein watched other women, sitting near ringside, as they looked admiringly at the young fighter. His attention returned to Swifty who had visibly changed from the docile likable lad he was introduced to in the dressing room, to a ferocious gladiator, stalking his opponent. Swifty didn't have Henri's finesse. Henri's style was finesse, hitting but not being hit. When an advantage presented itself, Henri attacked like a tiger but not a second before. Swifty, on the other hand, moved relentlessly forward, daring the fighter to swap punches with him. Swifty's advantage, as Red had said, was that he could knock an opponent out with either hand. Swifty fought toe-to-toe with his opponent in the first and second round. In the third round, his opponent threw a roundhouse right hand. Swifty ducked and the blow passed over him. But he then responded with a perfectly timed right uppercut to the jaw. Bam! That was it. His opponent was down for the count. Game over. Swifty had easily won the match.

Red's last fighter was up. It was now Gonzo's turn. Red was more interested in this fight than the other two. He had seen his other boxers fight, knew what to expect. Big Red had never seen Gonzo fight. Gonzo seemed in good condition for a big guy. Henri, Swifty and Gonzo were all on the same training regimen. Gil Clancy, the hard taskmaster, had made sure of that. His training methods produced champions. Red knew Gil wouldn't take on a fighter without talent and he also knew that Clancy cared about his fighters. If they didn't have the crucial skills needed for the sport, he would point them elsewhere, on to other dreams and goals. Gil had assured Red that each of these boys had champion potential. Clancy had worked hard with Gonzo to reshape his bar room brawling, bull-in-the-china-shop style, into something akin to a professional prizefighter, fighting with mind and skill. Boxing, Clancy always said, is 90% mental and 10% physical. What Clancy devised for Gonzo was a Marciano type style. He trained him to use his jab. In his previous fights, Gonzo had just come at his opponent wildly throwing lefts and rights, with abandon, looking for just a single punch to land. Now, he used his jab and followed it with a left hook or a right hand. Clancy would yell out, "Jab, jab, jab! Let it make an opening for your right hand. Again now - jab, jab, jab, now the right hand. Good! Now let's do it again." And so it went until Gonzo's style was developed into something that resembled a more professional style.

The first round began and Gonzo took short steps shuffling, inching toward his opponent. The two men had a 'feeling each other out round', stalking each other, looking for weakness, getting to know the style of the other. It was only the first round but Gonzo hadn't shown anything yet. Red wondered if he could punch. The round ended. The fighters returned to their corners. Clancy leaned into his boxer's ear and said," I spotted a flaw, a big one. I want you to look at his eyes, Gonz. Don't look at anything but his eyes. Whenever he's about to throw a punch, he raises his eyebrows. Now, when he does that, I want you to immediately throw a right to his gut and follow that up with a right hand to his head. Remember, first to his gut to drop his guard, then the head. Do you understand?" Gonzo nodded in the affirmative.

The bell rang for the second round to begin and Gonzo steadied his eyes on his opponent's, looking for the telltale sign. They jabbed a bit, teased each other a bit and each got in a few punches, then, there it was. His opponent raised his eyebrows. Instantly, Gonzo fired a hard right to his midsection. This brought the man's guard down. Now was the time. Gonzo hit him again, this time with a hard right to his unprotected jaw. His opponent was dazed. Gonzo seized the moment and followed up with a right, left, right, left, right, right, left, right until the man went down, literally for the count. The fight was called. Gonzo was left feeling a little disappointed. He didn't know what to make of it all.

"I want you to schedule another fight for me as soon as you can," Gonzo said to Red back in the dressing room.

Red was surprised by the request. "Why so soon Gonzo?"

"Because this fight was bullshit. I knew exactly when the guy was gonna throw a punch. That's no fight. That's no way to really test skill. Get me a real opponent . . . and soon." Gonzo was clearly miffed about the whole thing. He had something to prove. Red assured him that he'd check with the matchmaker before leaving the arena tonight.

Meanwhile, Red addressed all of his fighters in their dressing room. "I was proud of you boys. You did real good tonight. Clancy says you have talent and someday you'll be champs." Red then left to find Benny Spinoza, the match maker. He found him in his office, getting ready to leave, and he told him about Gonzo and his request.

"I'll check my schedule and give you a call tomorrow afternoon, but I believe I have a cancellation coming up for next Saturday night. I'll check on it and let you know."

Red walked back to the dressing room. "I have the limo outside waiting to take us back to the Starlight Club. Do you boys want a lift?"

"No," Swifty answered. "We're going back with the girls. Now that our fight's over and we're not in training, I plan on enjoying some sack time with a pretty woman." Red smiled a little.

"Go on," Red said, "You boys deserve to relax and have a little fun. Look, I'm throwing a party Saturday night at The Starlight Club and the three of you are invited. Why don't you bring the girls? Let me know and I'll reserve a table for you."

"Thanks Red," Swifty replied. "Go ahead. Reserve us a table. We'll be there."

chapter twenty-eight

The two movie moguls and their families were dressed in their finest. They had been to The Starlight Club the previous Thursday evening and had been duly impressed by Red's food. The formal dining room itself had been nothing special but the food was good. As movie moguls, evenings out were routine and neither Larry Morgenstein nor John Bernstein relished the idea of another evening out, but they owed it to Red.

Red met his guests at the door and escorted them to the bar and explained that the ballroom would open soon, but in the interim, to please enjoy drinks while waiting. Marco and Karen joined the movie men and Bernstein watched as Red greeted a few recognizable politicians at the door. Red motioned to a tuxedoed waiter who led the politicians to another area of the club. In the background, amidst the chatter of patrons enjoying cocktails, there was the sound of instruments being tuned. Approximately ten minutes later, the walls from the ballroom pulled back revealing in slow motion the splendor of the room until they rested like accordions on each side of the wall and those background noises morphed into the symphony sounds of a foxtrot, luring customers from the bar into the ball room. The room was magnificent. Larry Bernstein was in awe.

"Where the hell have you been hiding this room?" he asked Red.

"We just portion off enough for the dinner crowd," Red answered, "and we open the room when we have a big party, you know, a wedding or a special occasion like tonight." Bernstein, a man not easily impressed, was now.

"This is like the Stork Club or the Copa, but . . . even grander. It's beautiful. Why have I never heard of it before?" Bernstein asked as he gazed at the walls and ceiling.

Red was happy that Bernstein liked the club. "I have a select mailing list – friends, politicians, some actors and a few other

Hollywood types. The list is limited and exclusive. The Starlight Club is my hobby," Red answered. "I serve the best food money can buy and I keep the prices moderate so people can afford it, but . . . I don't advertise. That's why you don't hear so much about it. This big ole ballroom is a secret. It's not so much for revenue purposes as it is for my sanctuary," Red laughed as he patted Bernstein on the shoulder. Then he continued, "That 'list' gets invited to my special parties and events like the one I'm havin' right now."

"When we had dinner the other night," Bernstein said, "I never dreamed this part of the club existed. I love it."

"Well, then, my friend, you'll love it more as the night goes on." Just then an older gray-haired gentleman entered the club with two men walking behind him. He walked right over to Red's table and politely excused himself.

"Red, I hope you don't mind my coming here unannounced," the man said, "but I heard that Jerry Vale is singing tonight and I like the way that boy sings, and besides," he said as he leaned into Red's ear and whispered, "I wanted to tell you personally that the mediator told me what happened in California. You did a good job with the way you handled that situation. Now, would you please have someone show me to my regular table if it's not taken?" Bernstein's tried to contain his composure. "Is that who I think it is?" he asked Red.

"Yes," Red replied. "That's Carlo Gambino, the boss of bosses himself."

Red looked up to see his three fighters entering - each one with a girl on his arm, one of whom was June, Morgenstein's oldest daughter. Morgenstein leaned over to Red and said, "It looks like you were right. I let my guard down and Swifty stepped right in with my daughter."

"Don't say I didn't warn you," Red laughed.

Dinner was a feast to behold. Oysters Rockefeller, Potato Leek Soup, tableside Caesar Salad, Angel Hair lightly tossed in olive oil and herbs, fresh Maine Lobster Tails and New York Prime, and for dessert, miniature chocolate pianos adorned with the Starlight Club logo and filled with a combination of decadent milk chocolate and white chocolate mousse, almost too beautiful to destroy by tasting. Irish coffees, flaming brandies and cordials were served from specialty carts.

After dinner, the guests migrated to the dance floor, and embraced the tunes of the big band. There the guests remained dancing until the music began to slow to a lull – a signal for Red to approach. The bandleader handed off the microphone to Red.

"Excuse me ladies and gentlemen," Red began. "As is the custom of The Starlight Club, every so often you have to put up with me while I say a few words. The last time I picked up the mic I told you about my friend Trenchie and his wife Mary's pregnancy. Before that, I announced their engagement and if you remember, it was James Roman who brought up the engagement ring that Trenchie presented to his future wife. That night, James Roman visited each table and chatted briefly with everyone in the room. That was the kind of guy he was. Bear with me, this is all goin' somewhere. Well, I'm pleased to announce that Larry Bernstein, the President of Columbia Pictures is sittin' right there." He pointed to the table. "Stand up Larry and let everyone take a look at you." Larry stood and gave a short wave then sat back down. "And yesterday, we had three young men who were recently discharged from the army, who fought their first fights under my management and trained under the watchful eye of none other than Gil Clancy. Stand up fellas." The three men stood and acknowledged the applause and sat back down.

"Swifty, would you mind standin' again?" Red asked. Swifty was hesitant, not sure why he was being singled out, but did as he was told. "James Roman," Red continued, "worked for me before he became a movie star, thanks to Larry Bernstein. Now I'm pleased to announce that Swifty, that young man standin' there, will be leavin' for Hollywood for a screen test next week." The room thundered with applause. June whispered, "You never told me anything about a screen test, Swifty." "That's because I didn't know anything about it till just now," Swifty replied with a surprised look on his face.

June's father, John Morgenstein, was sitting at the table behind his daughter. June reached over and tugged his arm. "Dad, is it true that Swifty never w**as** told about a screen test?"

"That's right," her father answered. "Larry decided at the

fight, after talking to him, that he had the potential and he asked Red to fly him out next week." Red was still talking.

"And Ladies and Gentlemen, I have one more announcement. I am proud to announce that we have a special treat for you tonight. For those of you who were not present when he last sang for us, you're in luck because he has agreed to do an encore performance at The Starlight Club so . . . without further ado, I'm proud to present for your entertainment Mr. . . . Jerry . . . Vale." The guests went wild. Everyone knew the name Jerry Vale. What a surprise it was to have this superstar singer performing live! Bernstein and his wife, completely impressed, were captivated by the singer. Larry was enjoying himself this night more than any he could remember in recent years. He turned to John Morgenstein and asked, "Having fun John?"

"Can't remember when I've had a better time," Morgenstein replied as he sat smiling and tapping his feet to the sounds of the band.

"This has been one special night," the President of Columbia Pictures added. "Do you know what I think?" he asked Morgenstein. Without waiting for an answer he continued, "We need to make a movie right here in The Starlight Club. This will be the backdrop. As soon as we return to California, I want you to get right on it. I want you to assign a team, research story lines and when we have what we're looking for; I want our top writers to start on the screenplay."

"I will, but don't you think you're being a little premature Larry? I mean, what story could we possibly tell? Gangsters? Hoodlums?" Bernstein shook his head. Morgenstein didn't get it.

"The story doesn't have to be about gangsters or hoodlums. You're missing the point here. This place is magical. Don't you feel it? This is the place where James Roman walked out from behind that curtain. Why couldn't we change the players and make Trenchie's character a shy, likable boxer? We can keep the storyline showing how this fighter met a girl and how he saved her from an abusive husband. We can make it a family film, a romantic comedy even, and we can film the story on location right here in Queens and center the story around The Starlight Club. I think I just found the right vehicle for our new, unknown star named Swifty," he said as he nodded his head and smiled, pleased with himself.

Bernstein loved the movie business. He felt the same way today about it as he did the first day he had started in the business. He always got the same feeling - that adrenaline pumping excitation laced with some happy factor - the thrill of taking a seed of an idea and watching it transform into something larger than life, something that would make its mark in history. It was challenging, it was money, it was ego, and he loved it. The thought of his next colossal success excited him. What had begun as a favor to Red, was turning into something that might just become a moneymaker. One never knew. Larry spent the remainder of the evening listening to Jerry Vale sing and watching the faces of the guests as they danced and laughed. They seemed like a family. He was inspired. The next day, Moose drove the families to LaGuardia airport. Bernstein settled himself into the plush comfort of the Lincoln limo, his mind abuzz with ideas for his next major movie.

chapter twenty-nine

Red instructed Swifty to head over to Valentino Maximus on Spring Street in Manhattan to get fitted for a wardrobe. He wanted Swifty looking like the movie star he was about to become when he walked into Bernstein's office. Red walked to his desk, took out his checkbook and tore off a check, signed it, and handed it to Swifty. "He has a nice selection of expensive Italian shoes," Red said, "so just tell him you'll need about six pair. Let him pick 'em out for you and just tell him to fill in the amount. Get a receipt and bring it back to me for my books."

Valentino was fully prepared as Moose and Swifty arrived in the limousine. Maximus had coordinated an assortment of clothing that included five suits, ten silk shirts and three sports jackets. Swifty promptly returned to the club where he delivered the receipt to Red. Red took it with one hand and handed Swifty an envelope with his other.

"What's this?" Swifty asked.

"It's a one way ticket to LAX. I have you booked at the Best Western Hollywood Hills Hotel. I included Shorty Davis's phone number. Have you ever met Shorty?" Red asked.

"No. Who is he?"

"He used to work for me. Now, he's a big Hollywood cameraman. Won a few awards for his work on films. One was for Jimmy the Hat's first film, *Mob Hit Man*. Give him a call when you get out there. He's a good guy. If he likes ya, he'll be a good friend to you. I already called him and told him you'd be in California this week and to expect a call from you. Call him the first chance you get. Ask Shorty to find you a gym. You'll need to keep in shape because I'm setting up more fights for you and the boys. I'll talk to Bernstein and tell him what day the fight is scheduled and I'll let him know that you'll have to return a week before for prep training. I know it's an inconvenience, but I want you to be set - to have two careers - movie star and boxin' champion." Red then handed Swifty another package, one that was thicker than the other and bulky.

"What's this?"

"There's ten thousand dollars in cash in that envelope. Be careful with it."

"What's it for?" Swifty asked.

"It's for you. You can't go to Hollywood with no money in your pocket." Swifty looked at the envelope and then back at Red.

"Gee thanks Red. I don't know what to say."

"Don't say anything. Just remember that no matter what job you're doin', you're still one of my boys - you represent me. Capiche?"

Thursday morning Swifty was on an American Airline's jet, on his way to Hollywood. Everything, besides the place, was moving at breakneck speed. Before Red had bought out his contract, he had been just another kid fighting for chump change. Now, here he was on his way to Hollywood to test for a movie. Unreal. Swifty didn't know if he'd be successful in films and like Jimmy, it was fine if he made it, fine if he didn't. Also, like Jimmy, he was a product of the streets. Swifty knew he was a good fighter and he knew that, with Gil Clancy handling him, he could be a champ someday. Clancy had a reputation for working slowly, methodically in developing his talent. He turned out boxing greats. Yep, he was the champion maker. Swifty's hopes had always been set on that kind of success, not really the movie star gig, but if Red thought it was the right move for him, he'd follow through. Red was boss and that was that. Swifty would meet with Bernstein and he would do as he was told.

The flight was close to five hours long. Jimmy waited patiently as a mother and her children slowly made their way into the plane's aisle. He headed out the exit into the jet bridge and toward the baggage areas. Near the luggage carousel, he spotted a man holding a sign flashing a grin and the name "Swifty". Swifty approached the man. "I'm Swifty. I know you must mean me 'cuz ain't too many Swifty's around." The man put out his hand and broke into a broad grin.

"I'm Shorty Davis and I'm here to take you to my place."

Swifty smiled and said, "I'm already booked at the Best Western Hollywood Hotel."

Shorty shook his head. "Not anymore," he answered. "I cancelled your reservation. You're staying at my place with me. Tomorrow I'll drive you to Larry's office." Swifty grabbed his luggage off of the carousel. Shorty nudged his arm and said, "Come on. Let's get going. My wife has dinner waiting."

The following morning it was time for the Larry Bernstein test. Part one of the process was to leave Swifty, all handsomely outfitted like movie royalty, sitting, for a while, in a chair across from Bernstein's receptionist. The women were the greatest gauge for measuring a new actor's sex appeal and potential popularity. Funny how his assistants never caught on after all this time. It was his secret and sure enough, an empty lobby suddenly turned into quite the center of activity. Ladies buzzed around and around, like bees to honey, one after another, each one having an excuse to walk into the lobby to catch a glimpse of the rugged hunk waiting to see their boss.

Swifty was impeccably dressed. He sported a soft pin-striped, navy blue Valentino Maximus suit, a pale blue silk shirt and a coordinating blue and white silk tie. He looked like a GQ ad. Bernstein could see Swifty from the monitor in his office. Larry noticed Swifty's poise and control - he didn't seem the least bit ruffled by this meeting. Next, Bernstein's gaze went to the women in his office. He watched as they chatted and giggled like school girls, each vying for attention from the handsome young man still waiting. After twenty minutes of waiting, a young lady appeared. "Would you come with me please?" Swifty rose and followed along behind her.

Bernstein's office was grand. The walls were lined with movie stars, each singing their praises and signing their thank yous to the studio head - the one who had single-handedly catapulted their careers into the stratosphere. Swifty's eyes went straight to the photo of Jimmy, all smiles, with his leading lady, Lana.

Bernstein casually looked up. "Sorry for keeping you waiting, Swifty, but I couldn't get off the phone. Please, have a seat." Swifty positioned himself close to Bernstein's desk - a sign of confidence, Larry thought - a good thing. Larry leaned over and pressed the intercom. "Marla, please come to my office." A brief moment passed and Marla entered the room.

"Marla, this is Swifty. I'm giving him a screen test for a fight movie I've scheduled for production. I'd like your opinion of this young man."

"A fight picture you say?" Marla questioned. "What kind of fight picture? Is it Kung Fu or karate or what?"

"No, no - a boxing film," Bernstein answered.

"Well, in that case," Marla said, "you'll need to take off your shirt."

Man, Swifty thought, he knew what it must have felt like standing on that trade block, waiting to be sold as a slave. He acquiesced but was none too happy about it, mind you. Marla circled him like a piranha and studied him from all angles.

"Yes," she said finally. "I believe I can do something with him." Unbeknownst to Swifty, she had just told Bernstein to sign this boy . . . *in a hurry*. Swifty turned and reached for his shirt and was surprised to see a gaggle of girls, peering into the doorway, ogling. That was it - if the guy could act, that was it - the deal would be sealed, sealed according to Larry Bernstein, Columbia Pictures studio magnate. He had the gals, he had Marla, and that was good enough for the star maker. The studio had a winner if and only if he could act. Bernstein felt it in his bones and his instinct had never failed him.

Swifty was no name for a movie star and Bernstein blurted aloud, clearly out of nowhere. "We have to come up with something better than that." Swifty had no idea what he meant. "Tell be about yourself, how you first became a boxer," Larry said while pretending to look for missing paperwork. By now, Swifty was putting on his tie and a little embarrassed that the girls were still hanging around, staring at him like he was naked or something.

Swifty answered, "I come from a pretty rough neighborhood and was always being picked on so I told my junior high school gym teacher, Mr. Cassidy, about the trouble I was havin' with bullies. He told me to come see him after school. He walked me over to the gym, had me put on some boxin' gloves, and showed me some basics of how to defend myself. I liked it immediately so

I began trainin' and I grew to love boxin'. I found that I had a talent for fightin'. One day at Stillman's gym, I met Rocky Marciano and when he went to the mountains to train for a fight, he asked me if I'd like to tag along with him. That was just too good to turn down so I did and I trained with him. We became friends but over time, lost touch. Three years ago, he called Red and asked him if I could fight for him, but Red refused him."

"Why did Red refuse him?"

"I owed Red a lot of money." Bernstein face expressed surprise.

"You mean Red prevented you from fighting for Rocky Marciano because of money? I just can't believe Red would do that."

"Oh no," Swifty continued. "You see, it wasn't the money that worried him. It was the principle. I wasn't doin' anything with my life and I wasn't really makin' an effort to pay him back so soon, so Red had to teach me a lesson. It wasn't the money - it was the respect. He had to teach me to respect my obligations to others. It was never about money with Red." Bernstein smiled because now he had a perfect name for Swifty - "Rock" - but he couldn't use it. Hollywood already had Rock Hudson. He would find another one.

"Tell me your real name," Bernstein said.

Swifty looked uncomfortable. "Donald Cardelli," he answered.

"I have it," Bernstein blurted out. "Your new name will be Swifty Card. Since you fight under the name of Swifty, we'll leave it as it is, but we'll shorten your last name from Cardelli to Card." Swifty just nodded in agreement. It really didn't matter to Swifty what they called him as long as they didn't mess with Swifty, the name everyone knew him by.

Swifty called Red that night and told him everything that had transpired that day including his new name. "Swifty Card," Red said. "Not bad. It'll take a little getting' used to but not bad. When's your screen test?"

"Tomorrow mornin' at eight. Red, did Larry talk to you about makin' a movie at The Starlight Club?"

"Yeah, he called me last night and ran it by me. He's havin' his writers do somethin' about a boxer, loosely based on how Trench met Mary and he wants to use you and he wants The Starlight Club in the picture as eye candy."

"Are you gonna let him?"

"Sure, why not. So long as it's above board and doesn't infer anything shady about the place."

Swifty added, "You know . . . he was really impressed with The Starlight Club. I don't think he expected to find a place as elegant as the Stork Club since it closed. I'll give you a call tomorrow and let ya know how I make out with the test. I'll probably fail the damn thing. What the hell do I know about actin'?" he laughed.

"Just do what they want you to do," Red advised. "Look, Jimmy the Hat wasn't an actor either and he won an Academy award, so just go in there relaxed and do what they ask you to do. Remember – be yourself and you'll do fine."

"Got it. Okay, Red, I'll call ya tomorrow night."

chapter thirty

Bernstein had assigned Lana Thompson to play opposite James Roman for his screen test. After it was completed and viewed on the large screen, Larry Bernstein and the studio executives all agreed - he'd found a future star. Lana had worked so well with a novice like Jimmy that he decided to use her talents once more. Swifty, with Red's words echoing in his ears, showed up dressed like he was already a star, but that didn't last long as the director pulled Swifty aside as soon as he entered the room and handed him a pair of boxing trunks. He pointed toward the dressing room so he could change. Shorty Davis, who was in charge of the cameras, then accompanied Swifty onto the set. The setting was supposed to be a boxer in his dressing room, just before entering the arena. The storyline went like this: the mob had a great deal of money riding on the fact that this boxer would lose. They threatened to kill him if he didn't throw the fight. The boxer refused. Lana, his leading lady, is in the boxer's dressing room, pleading for him to let the other guy win.

Lana had never met Swifty. She knew nothing about him, including the fact that he was a real fighter. All she knew was that Larry Bernstein had insisted that she do a test with this unknown actor. When Swifty walked onto the set bare chested, Lana perked up. Swifty had studied his lines and felt confident that he had them committed to memory but he was uncertain about his delivery. If he couldn't remember a line, he had planned on just winging it. How hard could it be to play himself? That's what he kept telling himself.

The scene began with Lana begging her boyfriend not to put up a fight, to simply get battered or fall down and not get up. Swifty listened intently but, after hearing her voice, his mind went somewhere else - to a place where he asked himself how would he *really* feel if somebody was leaning on him, threatening him if he didn't throw a fight. With that emotion in mind, he blurted out angrily, "I don't throw a fight for nobody!" And so it went from there with such conviction that everyone in the room got into it. Swifty acted just like the street guy that he was, a tough fighter who didn't let anyone push him around. This went on, line after line, until the director called, "Cut!" Swifty knew enough to know that 'cut' meant to stop. He stopped talking and was beginning to walk away. But with every screen test, the studio head and the director need to see the chemistry, the male/female dynamic and how that manifests itself on screen. The best test - the screen kiss. Bernstein instructed Lana to jump ahead to the last. Lana was only too happy to oblige. She spoke her last line, then rushed toward Swifty, into his arms and began to kiss him passionately. Swifty reciprocated and both seemed to forget that this was a screen test. "Cut," "Cut," "Cut," the director called out, but the kiss lingered.

"Done!" said Bernstein. "That's it. That's the magic," he said as he turned to his director.

The director asked Swifty to stick around while the studio heads reviewed and studied his performance. Swifty changed from his boxing trunks back into his suit and rather than stay on set, Swifty and Shorty headed toward the studio cafeteria for coffee. Lana asked if she could tag along. As the conversation progressed, Lana asked Swifty if he knew James Roman.

"Jimmy the Hat?" Swifty repeated. "Of course I knew him. We were from the same neighborhood. He was a little older than me, and we didn't hang out together, but we both worked for the same guy, even back then. Why do you ask?"

"I don't know," Lana answered. "It's just that I did the screen test with him and you have similarities - both of you seem to have that same kind of attitude, sorta' laid back, 'I don't care' attitude. Most people would be devastated if they didn't pass their screen test, but you don't really care, do you?"

"This test?" Swifty laughed. "This is bullshit. This don't mean nothin' to me. What I care about is becoming the welterweight champion of the world, that's what I care about." Lana looked surprised.

"You really are a fighter?"

"Sure," he said. "Twenty-nine fights. Undefeated."

The three of them sat in the commissary, killing time, waiting to be summoned back to the set and to Larry. Two cups of coffee later, Swifty heard his name over the studio intercom. He was asked to report to Larry Bernstein's office. Swifty made his way back across the various studio lots and into the building that housed the executive and his team. Before he could settle completely into his seat, Bernstein slid a pile of paperwork - a contract - with pen resting on top, across the table to the boxer.

"Read it, if you like," Bernstein said, "but sign the last page in the two places where the X's are marked in red. Swifty glanced at the contract but his eyes fixated on his salary - eight hundred fifty dollars a week beginning the first of the month. Swifty tried to act unfazed but Bernstein noticed him studying it and added, "Your salary for this month will be prorated from the date this contract is signed. It will increase to fifteen hundred dollars a week after your fourth picture."

Swifty wasn't worried about the words in the contract. It didn't take a rocket scientist to know that Bernstein wouldn't cheat Big Red. Nobody cheated Red. It was just understood so without hesitation, Swifty signed. He was now an official employee of Larry Bernstein and Columbia Pictures. Bernstein gathered the papers, pressed his intercom button and asked his secretary to have Marla bring in a script for Swifty.

"This is a rough copy of your script for your first movie as it stands now. As an actor, you'll learn that a script is never finished until the scene's been shot and sometimes not until we've called a full wrap, so just like in the boxing ring, you have to adapt. Shooting starts Monday morning seven am, sharp. Study your lines and don't be late. Marla will ..." his sentence was cut short midsentence as Marla entered with a script marked *The Prize Fighter.* "Ah, we were just talking about you," Bernstein said and then turned his attention back to Swifty. "Marla is our drama coach. She will assist you if there is anything that you don't understand about the script. That's her job. She's the best in the business." Bernstein's compliments were normally reserved for the director. Marla, hearing praise from the man who rarely gave it, stood a little taller and expanded her chest a little fuller in response.

"Swifty, pay close attention to what I'm about to say," Bernstein said. "A few years ago I thought I was doing Big Red a favor by giving one of his men a screen test. Little did I know at the time that it was he who was doing me the favor. James Roman turned out to be a superstar who died well before his time. I'm giving you that same opportunity - to become the studio's next superstar. This script was written specifically to match your profile as a prizefighter. I hope to capitalize on that talent by having you essentially play yourself. I saw what you did during your screen test."

"What was that?" Swifty asked.

"You lost it when the script called for you to throw the fight."

"Yeah, I guess I did get a little carried away. Sorry about that."

Bernstein smiled. "No, don't be sorry. That's exactly the reaction the script called for. That's what convinced my staff that you would be good in the part. Continue to think of the character you're playing as a real life character and think and feel what you would do if you were him and if all this was really happening. Do that and we'll have a hit. We'll start by shooting some on-location exterior scenes on Monday in Queens. Your very first acting job, you're starring in. I'm taking a chance by putting you in the lead. When we finish the interior shots at the studio, we'll move on to The Starlight Club's interior. I'm sparing no expense and I'm backing you up by putting some of our more popular stars in supporting roles and by giving the female lead to Lana. She starred opposite James Roman in two of his pictures and I think she'll be perfect in this part. She's your age and after seeing the screen test, I know the chemistry between the two of you will scorch the screen, so good luck and remember . . . if you need coaching, see Marla. I'm assigning her to this picture. She'll be there at all times watching you at whatever location. If she sees anything that needs correcting, she'll show you how to fix it for the next take. Your director is Sam Peckinpah who is as exciting a director as you'll find anywhere. Listen to him. Do you have any questions?"

"None at all," Swifty replied.

The script was finished. It looked pretty good to Swifty, but he didn't know a good script from a bad one so he placed his trust in his director who he liked. Peckinpah, the director, was a hard drinker, a rough kind of guy who was never one to back away from a fight, whether it was a debate or a bar drunk who was misbehaving. Peckinpah instantly took a liking to Swifty. Swifty was respectful to his director. The results of that relationship showed as the director took extra special care to retake scenes that weren't flattering to Swifty. He collaborated closely with Shorty Davis for the maximum camera angles to secure the best dramatic effect. In preparation for one scene, Shorty recounted a brief shot in *Body and Soul.* In that scene, John Garfield had been knocked down and rested on the ropes, totally exasperated, just breathing heavily. It became the publicity clip that echoed around the world. James Wong Howe, the cinematographer, had won an award for that picture and Shorty wanted to recreate the same drama for this shot. Shorty shared his idea with Peckinpah and the director readily agreed.

As for Swifty, he took direction easily and got along well with the cast and crewmembers.

The interior studio shots were completed within a week. It was now time to move on to Queens where the rest of the picture was about to be filmed. Shorty Davis was quite happy to be going back to the old neighborhood to see Red and all his buddies.

chapter thirty-one

The second unit director shot exterior scenes of The Starlight Club and collected some community B–roll. He had his stagehands set up the boxing rails in preparation for the scenes of the club. Meanwhile, over at Stillman's gym, Swifty made sure that his buddies, Henri and Gonzo, were included in some of the movie's shots.

Shooting for the third day was scheduled to be shot on the west side of the El (the above ground train) on Roosevelt Avenue. It was a beautiful June day in nineteen sixty–four and shooting was moving along, keeping pace with the schedule. Swifty and Lana had finished shooting their scene and were waiting to be called for the next one. Peckinpah went to his trailer while the two actors stood relaxing with their backs resting against the brick wall of a private home, chatting about nothing in particular. The peace of the moment was disrupted by a loud disturbance. The actors turned to see that a fight of some sort had broken out. Shorty, stationed about thirty feet away, was fiddling with his camera. Suddenly, out of the crowd, a big black man wearing a fez stormed over to Swifty. The man was too caught up in the moment to notice that Shorty had lightly swung around his jib and trained his camera toward the source of the noise and the site of the action.

"You don't belong here, you white piece of shit. Get your white ass out of this neighborhood, our neighborhood," the man barked at Swifty.

Shorty, filming it all, muttered under his breath, "Damn! It's dejá vu all over again," quoting Yogi Berra, and alluding to the similarities reminiscent of that day with Jimmy the Hat and Lana's blackmailer. Shorty kept rolling. He had no idea where this was all headed but he had a hunch that it was gonna be good.

The man wasn't finished with Swifty. Taunting Swifty further, he turned toward Lana and said, "You can stay right here, with a real man honey, and get away from this honky loser." Lana began to tremble and pressed herself closer to Swifty. The big guy tugged at Lana and tried to pull her away from Swifty while attempting to shove Swifty out of the way. That did it! Swifty yanked the guy's arm off of Lana, gave Lana a slight shove to get her out of the way, slammed the guy with a hard right hand to his gut, grabbed him by his jacket collar and hit him again, and again, and yet again, until the bloodied man fell to the ground, unconscious. Swifty pulled Lana close to him, his arms cradled around her. Her face was pale with fear and she was scared, but not so scared that couldn't spot from the corner of her eye, two men running full speed toward Swifty, yelling at him for hurting their friend. The guys looked to be bodyguards or something. They tag teamed Swifty, boxing him in - one behind him and the other in front. When he tried to defend himself from the guy in front, the guy behind hammered away at him, but . . . . Swifty was in fighting shape . . . and these guys *weren't*. These were big guys, with big guts - they had more brawn than brains. Swifty knew he had to think fast. He slowly backed up a few feet toward the brick wall of the house until his back was flush against it. Now, he had the men in front of him, but he had to be careful because they were strong, and if one of them landed a lucky punch that staggered him, that would give both of the guys the opening they needed to come at him from both sides - Swifty wouldn't be able to defend himself from the punches. One of the men immediately rushed Swifty but Swifty blocked his punch and landing a one -two combination. The man doubled over, but Swifty couldn't follow up because, bam, the other slammed him with a sucker punch - he never saw it coming. Swifty took that pretty well but now thug number one was back on his feet. Apparently, he had seen an opening. That was a big mistake. Swifty bobbed and weaved, rolling with the punches. He came back with a left-right combo to the gut and chin that knocked the man, once again, off his feet. The guy jumped right back up and joined his buddy. Together, the men came at Swifty - two against one. Swifty bent down into a crouch. He looked for the one big lug that he knew he had to go after first and once that guy got into range, Swifty hit him with a left hook on his chin, followed by another left. He then surprised the other guy with a roundhouse right that landed right on the sweet spot on his chin. He laid out both of his attackers, right there in front of him, bringing it to a grand total of three unconscious men on the ground, in full view of Swifty, Shorty, Lana, and the rest of the crew. He took a deep breath and looked around, searching for others that might be a threat but there were no more takers. He rubbed his hand gently against his eye to see if there was blood but there was none. The message was clear – Swifty was a force *not* to be reckoned with.

Swifty immediately walked over and took a hysterical Lana into his arms trying his best to soothe her. Tears streamed down her face, leaving trails of white, as it washed away her movie star make–up. She buried her face deep into his shoulder. Swifty just kept stroking her hair, trying to console her. She looked up at him and said, "I was so scared Swifty. I thought they were going to kill you and then do something horrible to me like rape me or something."

"Now, now," Swifty said. "Ain't nobody gonna hurt you while I'm here. It's all over now." Just then, she withdrew from him and tried to collect herself, doing her best to get her emotions under control.

"Sorry," she apologized. "I didn't mean to get hysterical like that. I'm all right now."

"You sure?" Swifty asked.

"Yes, I'm sure. I'm feeling much better now. Thanks."

Shorty just kept thinking over and over again – who said lightening doesn't strike twice in the same place? He could almost envision another Oscar sitting on his shelf come award time. Shorty's camera had captured that entire fight scene on film and oh how he hoped it could be edited into the picture just like they had done with Jimmy's first movie. "Man," he said right out loud to everybody, "you can't make this stuff up, nobody would believe it." The police arrived on the scene and Swifty asked, "What's goin' on here? What's with this crowd?" "Two threats were made against Malcolm X," the cop answered. "Court ruling – the court agreed with the Nation of Islam that the house that X lives in belongs to the Nation. But Malcolm wouldn't leave, so they came here with a gang, to forcibly take over 'their' house. The fight you witnessed was between the Nation of Islam and Malcolm X's men. Those three guys you fought were bodyguards for the Nation of Islam. I guess after seeing their men like this, they'll be looking to interview some newer, tougher men to replace them," the cop laughed. Shorty had been standing within earshot of this conversation. That's all he needed to hear. Shorty ran over to his camera, removed the film, and began looking for Peckinpah. Once he located him, Shorty handed the film to the director and told him to take a look at it.

"What's this?" Sam asked.

"You have to look at this," Shorty insisted. "This is gift footage, that's what this is. It's a gift."

"Gift footage? What the hell is that supposed to mean?" Peckinpah huffed.

"Just look at it," Shorty answered. "I told you it's something special I shot and I think you're gonna like it." When shooting ended for the day, Peckinpah headed to the film lab and gave the 'gift footage' to his projectionist. "Put this up for me," he said and the footage began to roll on the big screen that was used to view the dailies, the unedited raw footage collected for that day.

Peckinpah watched in fascinated, stunned silence as the color footage flashed onto the screen. "This is fantastic," Peckinpah shouted. "Get the chief editor in here quickly," he called to his assistant. A few minutes later a small man with glasses and thinning hair appeared.

"You wanted to see me Sam?"

"Yeah, take a look at this. Okay. Show it again," he yelled to the projectionist." The film flashed once again onto the screen and the editor matter of factly responded, "Oh, I see. You wanna know if this footage can be inserted into the picture?"

"That's exactly what I want to know. Can we use it?" asked Peckinpah.

"Well," the editor said, "we can if you're willing to rewrite a scene or two. Then, I can fit this right into the picture as though it's a part of it. Good for Shorty. He used a boom mike and recorded the dialogue cleanly. We'll have to edit a few words but it'll work."

Marla, the acting coach, had been assigned to Swifty and she never left his side. She had watched, helplessly, while Swifty was being attacked and tough Marla was frightened. She feared for his safety and also worried about her own. This could have caused the film to be shelved, costing Bernstein and the studio millions. She was amazed at how calmly Swifty had taken care of matters.

Meanwhile, Peckinpah asked Lana for her version of what happened.

"My leading man was fantastic," she boasted and went on to tell Peckinpah that if Swifty hadn't protected her, she might have been kidnapped or harmed. Peckinpah, who liked to pull a cork once in a while, asked his assistant to bring him a drink - his usual - scotch on the rocks with a splash of soda.

"Make it a double," Peckinpah added. He needed one after hearing what had gone down on his set. The director now had another reason to like Swifty - he had a newfound respect for the guy. It seems that the director was unaware that the leading man was a prizefighter. Peckinpah, himself, was known to get into an occasional brawl or two after a few drinks and he was the type of director that normally didn't alert the studio heads about on set activities. He did his job, called the shots, and asked that no one interfere with his work. This was no different. So it was Shorty who called Bernstein. Bernstein asked Shorty to overnight a copy of the film to him immediately. Shorty used a courier to take the footage to the airport and send it express mail. It arrived later that same day. Bernstein watched in fascination as he envisioned 'Academy Award.'

Lana was Mary, Trenchie's wife, in the film. Swifty convinced the director, his buddy now, to have Gonzo play Julius, Mary's ex-husband. Once Gonzo was on set, Swifty lightened up and even began to enjoy his work, making this film. Because Gonzo had now moved into a lead role, his Stillman gym shots had to be deleted. After the first day's shooting finished, the three fighters along with Shorty Davis, Sam Peckinpah, and Lana Thomas headed to The Starlight Club. Swifty could now see Red and the boys. Once at the club, the actors and crew dined and loaded up on house specials, 'alcoholic refreshments.' Sam asked Red if he would open up the ballroom for a little peek - Peckinpah wanted to see what all the fuss was about according to Larry Bernstein. The room at first was pitch black. Everyone waited for Moose to flip some switches. Suddenly, light flooded the room and The Starlight Club awakened from its slumber and sprang to life, illuminated by the myriad of colors reflecting off of the crystal chandelier.

"Well, what do we have here?" Peckinpah asked, obviously pleased with what he was seeing. "This place is exceptional. Now I understand what Larry meant," he said to Red. "This typically isn't the type of picture I normally direct," the director continued, "but Larry was insistent, telling me The Starlight Club would be the primary setting. Said it had great possibilities for a big, showy film. Okay," the director continued, "I'll bring in a twenty-five piece orchestra, dancing girls, some high powered entertainers like Frank Sinatra for a cameo or two," he spewed, "and we'll make The Starlight Club the talk of the country. It'll be the focal point of everything that goes on in the picture. I know exactly how I'll use this beautiful setting. Great, I've seen enough - back to the bar," he said as he turned to walk away. "I need another drink."

The following day, the script was rewritten to include the footage that Shorty had captured. Weeks passed and much of the filming was held inside the magnificent walls of The Starlight Club grand ballroom. The movie wrapped on schedule and the film came in on budget, a testimonial to Peckinpah and the justification for hiring the high-powered director. It was now up to postproduction. Bernstein's talented bevvy of visual, music and sound editors would now lend their hands to clip, snip, splice, and piece together what everyone anticipated to be the studio's next great film.

chapter thirty-two

Larry Bernstein had once again done it. The footage of Swifty fighting three hoodlums from the Nation of Islam was dramatic and 'realistic'. The film was in the can. What made the film more relevant was that shortly thereafter, there was the real life burning, to the ground, of Malcolm X's house. The fight scene written into the picture clearly alerted the audience that it was the Nation of Islam's bodyguards that Swifty had fought. What they didn't know was the fight scene they thought was staged, was real. The audience had no clue that the thugs were real. The total effect of the added scene was stark realistic brutality that appeared unstaged.

The Prize Fighter opened to rave reviews. The critics were universal in their praise of the picture. One critic stated, "Swifty Card burst onto the big screen much like James Roman did a few years ago, complete with fight scene reminiscent of Roman's famous 'knee and a wrench' scene. The Starlight Club with its high profile clientele and its grand lady ballroom will be a secret no more."

The New York Times wrote, "Card is a prize fighter playing a prize fighter, so it is no surprise that he looks good throwing a punch, however his three-on-one fight scene was so realistic I could almost feel the blows he received. I smell an Oscar."

Time Magazine said, "Talk about good acting. Look closely at Card's facial expressions as he's getting hit in that tremendous fight scene. I winced with each punch. Now that's real acting! Kudos to this new actor for his realistic performance."

While all the hoopla was going on in the press, Swifty was back East, training for his next round of fights. He won his first fight with a second round knockout and was surprised to find himself ranked fifteenth in the top twenty-five fighters. There was talk of a fight with the champ. Trainer Gil Clancy was pleased with Swifty and his performance, but felt he wasn't quite ready for a title bout, so Red stepped back, passed on a few fights, waiting for the signal from the trainer of champions.

"When do you think he'll be ready, Gil?" Red asked.

Clancy didn't hesitate. "I'd like to see him have three more fights with a few more contenders. It could be six months or even a year, but he's close. I just don't want to see him get hurt, that's all."

"I agree," Red said. "The main thing is not to overmatch him. I don't want him to get hurt either."

Clancy added, "Let's not rush him then. We'll have him fight three more fights, see how it goes, and then talk about taking on the champ."

Swifty's hit picture and escalation to movie star status stifled his championship plans for a while. Due to his many required appearances and the promotion of the movie, his timetable was constantly being adjusted. The plan was for Swifty to fight in between pictures. Hopefully, that would be enough to keep him in shape.

Swifty had moved out of Shorty Davis's home with the first movie check he received. He was renting an unpretentious, yet spacious apartment, on Elm and Wilshire in Beverly Hills. His intention was to eventually buy a house. Swifty had gone from movie straight to training, and now he needed a vacation. He booked himself a flight to back to his roots, New York. He was anxious to get back to Queens and The Starlight Club and he knew that he could stay in the room upstairs if no one was using it.

The cab picked up Swifty, curbside, from the front of his apartment and headed for LAX. The cap driver recognized Swifty instantly but said nothing. As a professional, the diver knew to honor his privacy. Swifty noticed the driver staring at him and finally, put two and two together - must be the movie. Swifty was still getting used to his newfound celebrity. Swifty gave the cab driver a large tip - a story the driver would tell time and time again - and stepped out of the cab looking every bit the movie star heartthrob. He was wearing one of his Valentino Maximus suits. He looked good and knew it. What a journey, what a long way from street kid to boxer to soldier to . . . move star? While waiting in the first class line, he noticed people nudging their spouses and even brazenly pointing at him. Swifty noticed it all but somehow remained oblivious to what it all meant. Before he knew it, he was surrounded by autograph seekers and fans who just wanted to say hello or to have a few words with him. Swifty wasn't anything like Jimmy the Hat who relished the attention. The Hat knew how to work the crowd. Poor Swifty was a bit uncomfortable. Being in the ring was one thing - the ropes separated you from the fans. You fought, you ran around a bit and then you retreated to your dressing room, but here there was nowhere to retreat. He wasn't sure if he liked this play acting stuff. The crowd loved his natural shyness and his down to earth demeanor and Swifty, to his credit, handled it with class, shaking hands with the men and signing autographs for the ladies.

The call for first class passengers seemed to rescue him. Normally, he was a coach flyer, but he wanted the extra room this time to spread out and nap but with his now steady, impressive salary, he could afford the upgrade. One thought kept him from drifting off to sleep. He was anticipating having a problem getting his luggage. He would have to wait until he landed and find a phone away from the crowd and then call Red and ask him to have Moose meet him at the luggage carousel.

The plane landed at LaGuardia but Swifty didn't move from his seat. When every passenger had deplaned, a pretty stewardess approached and asked if everything was all right.

"I just wanted to wait until everyone else got their luggage. If I go get mine, I'll never get out of the airport."

"I'm sorry to hear that, but I'm afraid that you'll have to leave now. How about this? I'll take you to security where you can wait without being disturbed." She looked at him and said in an understanding voice. "I guess it's pretty rough not being able to travel without being recognized and annoyed by the public. Forgive me for bringing it up, but I saw your movie and I thought you were wonderful in it." Swifty smiled and answered, "Thanks but I'm still not very comfortable acting. It's new to me you know. I'm a prizefighter and all I ever wanted to be was world champion. I thought I would have some measure of fame in the ring . . . not as an actor." She liked this guy. He had a down-to-earth, unaffected manner about him. Secretly, she hoped that he would ask her for her telephone number. He had just appeared in a picture with Lana Thomas, one of the most beautiful women in the world, so realistically, the stewardess knew her chances were slim.

Swifty hadn't really talked to June since his last fight. June had tried to make contact but shooting the film gave Swifty the excuse he needed. Swifty felt that the novelty of June dating a fighter would wear off and she'd realize that he wouldn't, couldn't, fit into her social strata.

The stewardess accompanied Swifty to a security office where he made his phone call to Red. She felt a twinge of empathy for this big star who now sat so patiently while waiting for his friend to get his luggage. Without thinking she blurted, "Would you like to come home with me?" She realized how her words must have sounded to him and added, "Sorry, I didn't mean it the way it sounded. I meant - would you like to come with me to avoid your fans? And once we're out of the airport, I can drop you off and you can go on your way." Swifty looked at her as if seeing her for the first time. She was young, right around his age, with dark hair, vivid blue eyes and a great body.

"Oh, thanks but I don't know," Swifty answered. "I have my friend meeting me here and picking up my luggage. Do you have your car parked nearby?"

"Yes, in long term parking."

"That's very nice," Swifty said. "Well maybe I'll take you up on that offer. Do you have a pen and paper handy?"

"One second," the stewardess said and she walked to the security desk. She tore off a sheet of paper from a pad on the desk, took a pen from her purse and handed them to Swifty. Swifty jotted a note to Moose that read, "Moose, I'm going for breakfast with a young lady. Please take my luggage to The Starlight Club and tell Red that I'll see him later today or tomorrow morning." He handed her the note.

"Could you please take this out to the carousel and give it to my friend Moose? He'll be the man with the luggage with large orange stickers on the sides. Those'll be mine." The pretty stewardess, note in hand, found Moose easily. Most everyone else from that flight had already left the airport and were on their way home. Moose was the only one standing by the now silent baggage carousel.

"Are you Moose?" He nodded and she handed him the note. Moose grunted something which sounded like *thanks* and turned and walked away, pulling the luggage behind him. When she returned to the security room, she said to Swifty, "Come on. It's all clear now. We'll go out through the security exit and take the shuttle bus to my car."

"Great," said Swifty. "Take Northern Boulevard instead of the parkway. You know, I don't even know your name."

"It's Sue, but everyone calls me Susie."

"Nice to meet you Sue. I'm Swifty."

She laughed, "I know who you are silly, you didn't have to tell me."

"Let's get some breakfast," Swifty suggested.

"Where?" she asked.

"Make a U-turn up above and take the side road. We'll go to the Airport Diner. It's up a little way right before the Steinway Street exit." Swifty was recognized the moment he entered the diner. They chose a booth by the window. At first there were murmurs, then whispers, then people began to stare at him. One brave soul came to their table and said he had seen *The Prize Fighter* and loved it and of course asked for an autograph.

"Sure," Swifty sweetly replied. "How do you want me to sign it?"

"Could you sign it, 'To my friend Frank' from Swifty?" Swifty added a little something extra and ended it with *Keep Punching, Swifty*." Before he knew it, his booth was surrounded by autograph–seekers. Feeling a bit overwhelmed, he finally put up his hands and said, "Hold on a minute," and then asked Sue to order take out from the waitress. "Get anything you want," he said as he slipped her a twenty-dollar bill. "Tell the lady at the counter to keep the change."

As they walked through the parking lot back to Sue's car she asked, "Is it always like this?"

"Well, I guess," he replied. "Kinda happens a lot now since the picture came out. Jimmy could handle it a lot better I think.

I'm not cut out for this bullshit, I don't think," he said in a slightly frustrated voice. "Sorry ... didn't mean to say that." Sue smiled.

"Jimmy who?" she asked.

Jimmy the Hat."

"Jimmy who?" Sue asked, still confused.

"Jimmy . . . James Roman," Swifty explained.

James Roman!" she exclaimed. "I loved him! You knew him?"

"Sure did. We had the same boss. Like I said, he could handle bein' famous better than me. I'm not good at this stuff and I may just pack it all in. I'm that close to doin' it right now," he said as he used his thumb and index finger of his right hand to show what he meant. Swifty then realized that he might have said too much.

"Hey," he said, "you're not gonna talk to any newspapers or magazines about what I just told you, are you?"

"Nah," Sue replied. "You don't have to worry about me. I don't repeat things. So, where do you want to go now?" she asked, changing the subject.

"Let's go to The Starlight Club. That's the one place where I can be myself and not have to worry too much about the public." Sue nodded in agreement. Swifty guided her through some back roads and motioned her toward the lot across the street from the club, assuring her that her car would be safe. Inside, Red was stationed in the corner, at his favorite table, and waved as soon as he saw the two of them and motioned for them to come over.

"Susie, this is Red. He's the guy responsible for all my success. If it wasn't for him, I'd probably be a bum." While Red was pleased with the compliment, he didn't care for Swifty's self–deprecating tone.

"How long will you be in town?" Red asked.

"Bernstein wants me to do a light comedy for my next picture and he wants The Starlight Club to be used again in the picture. It's supposed to start shootin' in a month."

"That's great," Red said. "That means that I'll have you to myself for a while. Maybe I'll schedule a fight for you at Sunnyside, or maybe even Madison Square Garden. You know you're ranked number fifteen by ring magazine?"

"No, I had no idea I was ranked that high. But I can't take a fight. It's in my contract - can't take a fight up to one month before we start shootin'. They're afraid the bruises will show during filming and my face will be all messed up."

"Well," Red added, "maybe we'll schedule you for a fight two months before then. We'll honor your contract."

"Well, I guess it's okay but honestly, I'll bet that Bernstein won't be too happy. I'd hate to see his face when he finds out." They both laughed and Red said, "Well then, let's not tell him." Red got serious for a moment. "You know Swifty, this whole scene . . . you makin' a hit movie and then comin' back to The Starlight Club - it's exactly what Jimmy did. It's like history repeating itself, only we don't have a jealous husband to worry about this time." Red looked at Susie. "You don't have a jealous husband we should be worryin' about do you?"

"No," she said smiling. "I don't."

"Good, then that's settled. We're havin' a party here this Saturday night and you, Gonzo, and Henri are gonna be The Starlight Club's special guests that night, so don't make any plans okay?"

Swifty excused himself for a moment. Moose was tending bar and caught Swifty on his way to the men's room. "You can sure pick 'em kid. This one's a knockout."

"Yeah," Swifty answered. "She seems nice, not affected by who I am. I like that. She kind'a rescued me," he said as he laughed.

Swifty returned to the table, looked at his watch and said, "We still have time. Red, we'll see you later." He took Susie by the arm and led her back to her car. "Come on," he said. "I'm takin' you to meet a friend of ours." He guided her through the labyrinth of streets and highways of New York City. Exhausting all possibilities of a parking space, Swifty told Sue to park in one of the hourly parking garages. Swifty asked for the receipt which he placed into his pocket as he and Sue set afoot. At eleven hundred Broadway, they took the elevator to Suite 600, naturally on the sixth floor. When the elevator door opened, they faced a large sign that said 'Rene Dumas'. Swifty asked the receptionist, who recognized him instantly, to get Marco. The front desk girl invited the couple to have a seat as she rushed off. A few minutes passed before Marco walked in. When he saw Swifty, he headed straight toward him with open arms. They embraced.

"It's good to see you Swifty. What can I do for you today?"

"Red's havin' a party Saturday night."

"Yes I know. I'm looking forward to being there myself. His parties are always unforgettable experiences. So what is it that you need?" he said, eyeing Susie.

"I want something special for Sue. She's comin' with me Saturday night." Swifty had grown up around all these guys. He had learned from the best. Whenever they met a lady they liked and invited her somewhere special, it was just something the guys did out of courtesy - they took their little lady to be outfitted. That way, it eliminated the burden and expense of her having to shop for something appropriate for this magical venue. Sue was a little embarrassed.

"Look Swifty, I have clothes. I don't need you to buy me anything," Sue said.

"I know," Swifty said, "but I want you to have somethin' special. I'm sorry to break it to you but you will be in the company of a, ah hum, screen star, and uh, well, I want my lady to look good, if you don't mind."

"Well, okay, I understand," Sue said as she smiled sweetly.

In a matter of moments, a number of women paraded past Sue wearing magnificent, one-of-a-kind creations. Marco asked her to write down the numbers of the dresses she liked. It was the first dress she tried. There were several but it was the shimmering emerald green dress that stood out. Sue exited the plush dressing and headed toward the mirror in the center of the room. Swifty almost lost his breath. Damn, he thought - I've lost my breath from being punched in the gut but not quite from a gal modeling a dress for me.

"It's just beautiful," Sue said as she twirled lightly around. "I've never seen anything so beautiful. And you were right, Swifty. I said I have clothes but not like this. This dress is special."

"Yes it is," Swifty said as he admired the dress and

everything about Sue. "Wrap it up Marco. Oh, but first, let's find the shoes and accessories to go with it." Sue smiled. Wow, what a treat. First a dress, and now the accouterments. Marco reappeared with a host of necklaces and earrings and had Sue try each and every one, along with an assortment of varying colored shoes in order to achieve the perfect look.

"Voila!" Marco finally proclaimed, satisfied that his work was complete. "I'll see you and your beautiful lady there this weekend."

Once in the car, they headed back to The Starlight Club. Susie asked, "Swifty, I just met you. Why would you buy such an expensive dress when you hardly know me?"

"Cause I like you," Swifty answered candidly. "And besides, you're my date. In that dress, you'll be the most beautiful girl in the room." He became quiet for a moment and looked back at her. "You've never been to The Starlight Club for dinner, have you?"

"No, I haven't. With you today was the first time going there at all."

Swifty smiled. "Well, you're in for a treat. You'll see on Saturday. I'd like to pick you up at five, if you don't mind. We'll make our way back here, have some cocktails, and join Red and his guests for dinner around seven thirty. Marco and his wife and some other friends of mine will be there. I know you're gonna enjoy the evening." Swifty passed her a piece of paper. "Please write down your address for me." Sue obeyed. "Now," he continued, "I have some things I have to do. See you Saturday night . . . in your beautiful green dress." He smiled, his eyes smiled, and he walked back toward the street. And off Sue drove, she too, smiling, all the way home. Once home, Sue phoned her mother, her friends, and anyone who listen, to tell them the story of the hottest movie star around, Swifty Card, and where she was having dinner with him on Saturday evening.

Susie knew the problem Swifty had when he went out in public so she was surprised that he offered to pick her up at her apartment. How unselfish, she thought, sacrificing his own privacy for her. That spoke volumes.

It was Saturday night. When Swifty and Sue arrived, Red pointed them to a table by the window where Karen and Marco, and Trenchie and Mary were conversing. Sue looked stunning and Karen jokingly punched her designer husband, Marco, on his arm. "How come you never bring me home a dress like that?"

Swifty said, "Sue, you met Marco earlier and this is his wife Karen. Karen, I'd like you to meet Sue."

Karen looked her up and down and then said to Swifty. "Well I must say that you do have good taste in women. Have a seat Sue and join the party." After she was comfortably seated, Swifty introduced her to Mary and Trenchie. A short while later a waiter walked over to inform them that their dining room table was ready. The couples slowly made their way toward their table, shuffling in and out, between arriving guests. The Starlight Club was filling up quickly. It was typical when Red sent invitations to his 'exclusives' list. The invitation always had triple meaning - an exclusive event, at an exclusive venue, for exclusive guests only. Let's just say that the 'not attending' list was always miniscule. The club was filled to capacity, both at the bar and in the ballroom, and the party hadn't even started.

Swifty pulled Red aside and told him, "Look Red. Don't pull that shit that you pulled on Jimmy the Hat. I don't feel comfortable goin' to every table like he did. Promise me, you won't do it." Red patted him on the shoulder.

"You're gonna do it, Swifty . . . for me . . . and for yourself. You're gonna go to every table and say hello. Shake the guys' hands and compliment the ladies. Make everyone feel special. Some are fans so you're gonna treat them nice. Give a smile, say something nice, and excuse yourself and go to the next table. Capiche?" Swifty reluctantly answered, "Capiche."

"Oh my, Swifty," Sue said as she entered the ballroom. "I never knew a place like this existed in Queens. I've never even heard of the place."

"Yeah I know." Swifty said. "Red built this palace just for hisself I think. He don't really advertise it. He's been renovatin' different parts of the place ever since he became the owner. And little by little, he turned ordinary into extraordinary."

"It's . . . special," Sue said. "Absolutely captivating. It's truly beautiful." Swifty laughed. Her eyes were darting everywhere.

"It gets better after a few drinks," he added.

The band played favorite familiar tunes. Swifty extended his hand toward Susie inviting her to join him on the dance floor. Susie gazed softly up at Swifty as they danced to the music of a slow foxtrot and said, "What a wonderful evening," and she placed her head on his shoulder and snuggled closer to him. She could feel his heart as it beat sensually to the rhythm of the music. She wanted him. The dance ended and as they were returning to their table, Sue excused herself to the powder room. There, she took a moment to collect her thoughts, freshen her make-up and assess the emotions welling up inside of her. When she returned to the table, Swifty noticed a face of slight concern.

"You feelin' all right?" he asked.

"Yes, yes I'm fine but thanks for asking."

The band took a short recess and Red picked up the mike and took to the podium. "Ladies and Gentlemen. Welcome to The Starlight Club. I would like to inform you that Columbia Pictures is plannin' a second movie to be made featurin' The Starlight Club. Most of you were here when James Roman, who was a local boy who used to work for me, was our guest of honor for the night. Well, tonight I have another young man. He is a prize fighter and I just happen to be his manager. He went off to Hollywood a few months ago and like Roman, made it big with his very first movie. I'm talkin' about none other than Queen's own Swifty Card who starred in *The Prize Fighter*. Let's hear it for Swifty." Red pointed to Swifty and said, "Stand up Swifty." Swifty stood, took a slight bow and cringed, just waiting for Red to announce that Swifty would be making the rounds to say hello to Red's guests. What he heard instead was, "Thanks Swifty, you can sit down now."

epilogue

Present

Bobby reached for the coffee pot and poured himself another cup of his favorite drink, espresso with a healthy shot of Sambuca. He took the little cup, sat back in the comfortable leather recliner, extended the seat and put up his feet, careful not to spill the coffee on the rug.

His daughter Lynn had sat almost motionless for two hours listening to her father's stories about The Starlight Club, Red, Swifty and the rest of the gang.

"Wait a minute, Dad. There has to be more to the story. What happened to Swifty? Did he make any more pictures? And what about June and Susie? Did he get involved with either of them? Why didn't he get serious with June? Or did he? And Susie. She seemed like a real nice girl. Did they ever have a relationship? And what about Big Red? Did he ever go to Hollywood and open up a studio and if he did, did he ever make any pictures?" Bobby chuckled at her questions.

"Hell, Lynn, that's a whole lot of questions that would take me a week on a quiet beach in the Bahamas to tell." Lynn laughed. Bobby continued, "When you took me to where The Starlight Club used to be, I'll be honest with you, it made me sad. It brought back memories of my friends, most of 'em dead now, passed on. Lookin' at that store was like lookin' at a mirage, like seein' something that another person might have said was never there. The beautiful Starlight Club, now a little grocery store, is hard for me to accept."

Lynn still had questions. "Dad, you never explained what happened to The Starlight Club. And whatever happened to Big Red, Tarzan and Trenchie and all the other colorful men you told me about?"

Bobby rested his head on the back of the recliner and looked up at the ceiling. He saw nothing but memories.

Then he looked at his daughter and smiled and said,

"Another day, dear daughter. Another day."

Thank you for reading my book. I hope you enjoyed reading it as much as I enjoyed writing it. If you liked this story, please leave a review on amazon. Then visit my website www.corsobooks.com and leave your email address. I email my friends to notify them about discounted or free book promotions as well as any new book releases.

An Invitation to Book Clubs

I would like to extend an invitation to book club members across the country. Invite me to your book club and I will be happy to join in your discussion. I am available to join via phone (speaker), online (via discussion board, Skype or FaceTime), in person, or by any other means. You may arrange a day or time by contacting me at corsobooks@yahoo.com. I look forward to hearing from you.

Made in the USA
Middletown, DE
10 November 2015